LET ME PIMP

OR

LET ME DIE 2

=The Hoe Chronicle$=

CAUJUAN AKIM MAYO

This is a work of fiction. Names, characters, places and incidents are either the product of the authors imagination or are used fictitiously. Any resemblance to actual events or locales or persons, living or dead is entirely coincidental. From The Mind Of Caujuan Akim Mayo

Copyright © 2014 Caujuan Mayo

All rights reserved.

ISBN-13: 9781500120207
ISBN-10: 1500120200

DEDICATED TO MY LOVING MOTHER

= My Original Black Queen =

Your Mother is always with you. She's the whisper of the leaves as you walk down the street, she's the smell of certain foods you remember, flowers you pick, the fragrance of life itself. She's the cool hand on your brow when you're not feeling well, she's your breath in the air on a cold winter's day. She is the sound of the rain that lulls you to sleep, the colors of a rainbow, she is Christmas morning. Your Mother lives inside your laughter. She's the place you came from, your first home, and she's the map you follow with every step you take. She's your first love, your first friend, even your first enemy, But nothing on earth can separate you. Not time, not space...Not Even Death.

=UNKNOWN=

May You Forever Rest In Peace

CHAPTER 1 THE CHRONICLES OF CHERRY

1974...

I woke up today like any other day. Focused and ready to go make my Daddy some money. My name is Sabrina, but they call me Cherry because I have the sweetest pussy that money could buy. At least that's what my Daddy tells me. I've been with my Folks for two years now. I guess you can say I'm the "Bottom."

My Folks is "Trust Tha Pimp." I met him when I was eighteen. I'd just ran away from home for good. I'd finally had enough of my drunken mother and no good child molesting step father. He'd been raping me since I was six. I remember the first time as well as the last like it was yesterday. The last time was on my 18th birthday, and the final straw. "Happy Birthday!" My stepdad said, waking me up while climbing into bed with me. "My little girl is not a baby anymore," My stepdad whispered in my ear while massaging my breast. The bastard disgusted me and my

Mother disgusted me even more for turning the other way for all these years, acting like she didn't know and allowing the shit to happen.

"Fuck you, get your nasty ass off me!" I screamed. He smacked me and told me to shut up before he gave me something to scream about. Momma was in the other room, passed out like always, from a drunker the night before. This was a daily ritual since I was six. Sometimes I felt like my mom just pretended she was asleep and passed out to avoid the realization and confrontation of what was taken place under her roof, next door to her bedroom.

How could she "not" know? Shit, I told her myself one day finally working up enough courage when I was ten, only to have her not believe me and call me a filthy little liar. That was the worst day of my life. Even worst than the first day I was raped four years prior. This was also the day I lost respect for my Mother.

"Now play nice and let Daddy get a piece of that sweet pussy. Let me be the first to fuck you into adulthood," my stepdad said, more like a statement than a question. That's when I pulled out the straight razor from underneath the pillow I'd been concealing, grabbed his dick, and..."AHH!"

"Bitch, you fuckin cunt! You cut my shit off!"

"Take that, you dirty mutha fucka! I bet you won't be stickin this in anymore women or children now. You sick bastard!" I screamed while holding his detached, blood dripping dick in one hand, and the straight razor in the other. And so the bastard couldn't get it sewed back on like that John Bobbit mutha fucka, I went and flushed it down the toilet.

"OH MY GOD! What the fuck did you do?" Momma said busting in the room looking at the aftermath of her husband dickless, screaming like a bitch in a pool of his own blood.

"Oh now you're woke huh?" "What happened to all them times I was crying and screaming for help Momma? Where was you all the years I was being rapped by this asshole? Where was you when I needed you the most? My Guardian, My Protector, MY Mother!"

"Fuck you, you selfish whore. You never wanted to see me happy." Those words cut through my heart like a butcher knife in a Friday the 13th movie as I watched her run to my stepdad to comfort him in her arms.

"Call 911!"

"I ain't callin shit, Momma! You love him, you call 'em. I'm packing my shit and leaving this place for good."

"Then get out bitch. You're no longer my daughter. You're dead to me!"

"And you've been dead to me since the day you took that sick bastard's word over mines." I packed my shit and left my Mother with her dickless bleeding husband to rot happily ever after, together. They deserved each other, and I deserved better. I slammed the front door with the intentions to never return again.

I met Trust in a small diner Downtown in San Diego. I had no place to go and $200 dollars to my name, which I stole from my Mother's purse as I was leaving the house. It was a cold winter morning and I was leaving the diner to escape the weather.

Although San Diego is usually pretty hot all year round, today was unusually cold, so I stepped inside and ordered a hot chocolate with whip cream to warm me up. That's when a handsome light skinned brother with a long perm walked in and sat on the stool next to me.

He was dressed nice in a suit and had on some expensive boots. I could tell they cost a lot because they were made from snake or alligator skin. I'd never seen boots like that before in person. His suit wasn't too flashy nor was it conservative like the ones you'd see people wear to church. It looked to be tailor made by the way it perfectly clung to his body, like the frame on a Corvette.

When I glanced down at his perfectly manicured hands, on his pinky finger sat a large gold ring with a Princess Square Cut diamond in the middle. When I looked up at his handsome young face, I figured he couldn't have been a day over twenty-two.

"Hey pretty lady," he said to me as he stuck out his hand to shake mines in a gentle greeting like way. "My names Trust, as in you can trust and believe that today can be the start of something beautiful for us both."

"Oh is that so?"

"Trust!" He smiled and flashed his pearly whites. He had a sexy goatee and long thick side burns like Shaft! I never dated a black man before but had always fantasized about them. In my era, it was still sorta taboo and frowned upon to be in an interracial relationship. Even though this was California and not nearly as bad as the South, some people would still look down upon, talk about, and treat interracial couples a lot differently than everyone else. Whites would call you a "race traitor" and blacks would call you a "sell out." Nevertheless, I was intrigued.

"Well, I have a hard time trusting people, especially men."

"Well, I promise you can trust me."

"Well, you know promises are meant to be broken. How do I know you won't break yours?"

"You don't, but you'll never know or find out if you don't at least take a chance, keep a little faith, and even more so 'trust' in me and this situation."

"I can respect that. I like your honesty. You seem genuine to me."

"As genuine as it gets. So what's your name?"

"Sabrina!"

"Nice to meet you Sabrina."

"Like wise."

And that's how I met Trust. At the time I was square and green to the game. I had no idea he was a pimp. Shit, I didn't even know what a pimp looked like. All I knew was, here's a nice, handsome, well dressed man who looks like he has his stuff together, interested in and attracted to me. We talked for over an hour that day at the diner. Something about his aurora made me feel comfortable enough to open up to him. I told him that I had ran away from home, just turned eighteen, and was now on my own. I left out the reason why and gory details. I wasn't "that" comfortable yet, so I just gave him the basic, to the point, scaled down version. Most important, I told him I had no place to go, and that's when he offered to take me in and help me get back on my feet. I was so naive that at the time I thought Trust was a Godsend. Like God sent this man to help me out, no strings attached.

I would soon learn that that was not the case and everything came with a price. Nothing in life is free except love. Shit, and even that can "cost" you. Trust lived in the Chula Vista area of San Diego, in some apartments off Third and H Street. At the time, I was his only girl so it was easy for me to feel like his girlfriend and not his hoe, but all that would soon change. I had been with Trust for a little over a month when he propositioned me to become his hoe. A proposition and decision that would ultimately change my life forever. At first I was shocked and couldn't believe what he was asking of me. Why would my man want and be comfortable with me sleeping with other men, especially for money? I asked myself a thousand times, dumb founded as he continued to run game and prep me.

"Sabrina, you know I care about you right, and truly only want what's best for you?"

"Yeah, I know. A least I thought I knew."

"No, you said it right the first time. Why would you second guess yourself?"

"I don't know. I'm just confused."

"Haven't I made you happy this past month? Haven't I been there for you? Mentally, physically, as well as financially?"

"Yes."

"Didn't I tell you over a month ago back in that diner downtown that you could always trust in me?"

"Yes."

"So what make you think anything has changed? All I'm tryna do is continue and maintain the lifestyle you've come accustomed to. It cost to be the boss and I'm just tryna make you a boss bitch. I feel you have a lot of potential to become something great. I see big and even greater things in your future and I just wanna help you get there. Money makes the world go round and life stands still for no one."

I just sat back on the love seat size sofa in Trust's two bedroom apartment and listened to him talk.

"You see, up until now life has continually dealt you a bad hand, but just like poker and black jack, eventually the cards will turn in your favor. At that point, its up to you to raise the stakes or throw in your hand. Right now its time to raise the stakes Baby Girl, because you're holding a royal flush!"

Trust went on for three hours straight in this manner. Runnin more game than NFL Sunday. At the time I couldn't see it for what it was, "Game." As time went on and countless bitches got pulled, prepped, and turned out in the same manner, I soaked up game like a sponge and recognized it for exactly what it was. Needless to say, Trust turned me out that day. From that day forward I was no longer considered his girlfriend, but his hoe. Sabrina, aka "Cherry."

At first I was scared to walk the stroll because everything was so fast paced. You could tell I was new to the game. I felt like a fish out of water. The "Track" was what they called the stroll, and hookers lined the block like a welfare cheese line on the first and fifteenth. Trust bought me a short mini skirt to show off my long firm legs and four inch heels which boosted my calves and had me "looking like a Stallion," as my Folks would say. I had on fishnet stockings and a garter belt. Daddy told me it was to play into the tricks' fantasies. I was a natural blonde, which I would come to find out later, that the tricks loved.

My hair was well pass my shoulders, skin naturally toned, slight freckles and long eyelashes. With my natural 34D firm tits and ass to finish the package. It wasn't long before I realized I was the shit! My Daddy prepped me on how to deal with a trick as well as all the ends and outs and rules and regulations of the game. Like never looking another pimp directly in the eyes, never date black guys, how to watch out for vice, and shit like that. At the time it seemed like a lot of information and data to process and take in, but as time went on, all that would become second nature to me, like waking up in the morning and brushing my teeth.

The first date was the hardest but the money was easy. So as time went on, this too, became second nature. The more money I made, the easier it got, and I was making a lot of money. My first night out I made $350. Daddy told me that was good for a start, and mind you this was the 70's, but I had to step it up to $500. Eventually that became my nightly quota and I prided myself on making it every night. The first night I made my quota I was instantly hooked and addicted to the money. There was no turning back now and Trust knew it.

"Good job bitch. You been coming in wit yo quota for the past few weeks faithfully." This was part of the game I didn't understand. Why I had ta be a "bitch?" But in time it was something I got used to.

"Now its time to take this shit to the next level you dig. I need you to bring another bitch home to join the family." Now I didn't see that shit coming for a mile. If things was so good and I was making my quota everyday, then why did I have to find another bitch to bring home? I never had to share my man before and didn't know how I'd do in this situation. I guess Daddy could tell I wasn't happy with it by my emotions and said, "bitch, I know you know by now the game we play and that shit ain't football, baseball or NBA.

It's Pimpin and Hoe'n, the best thang going. We don't work with feelings and emotions like squares, tricks and suckas. You're no longer Sabrina the square bitch I met in the diner. You've been in the game for about three months now and know what it's about, better yet what we're about. This here is Mackaroni not Matrimony and bitch, you're married to the game. You should wanna bring another bitch home because that just makes your job that much easier, but even more importantly, helps our family grow. When the family grows, so does the dough! Bitch you took in thirty-two thousand dollars since you been with me. Now times that by two hoes, we're at sixty, three hoes is ninety, etc, etc. The sky's the fuckin limit. We out ta get rich bitch by any means necessary and right now the means is Pimpin and Hoe'n. Now either you're with me or against me Baby Girl. Either we're on the same page or two different books entirely."

"I'm wit you Daddy." Yeah, I told him what he wanted to hear but I still wasn't feelin bringing another bitch home, but I knew to argue would be pointless. One thing I learned in this short time being with Daddy was once his mind's made up, his thoughts is final and ain't no changing it. It's either hop along for the ride or get off at the next stop. Getting off wasn't an option in my book, I had already come too far. Like my Daddy said, I made thirty-two thousand in three months. Now what kinda bitch would turn away from money like that?

"Hey girl."

"Hey Cherry." I had just hit the track and saw Tina. Tina was an eighteen year old white hoe that worked for a pimp named Diamond. Diamond was abusive and very strict with his hoes. If a bitch talked back when spoken to, she got beat. If a hoe didn't make her quota by the end of the night, she got beat. Hell if a hoe put too much syrup on a mutha fucka's pancakes for breakfast, she got beat. Diamond was a Gorilla Pimp, a hoes worst nightmare, and Tina was just about tired of his shit!

"How you been girl?"

"Same old bullshit, different toilet."

"Really, wuss wrong?"

"Diamond! That's wuss wrong. It seems like no matter how hard I work or try, it's never enough. I could bring a million dollars home tonight and he'd still find a reason to beat my ass. I'm beyond sick of his shit. I wanna leave but I'm scared he'll kill me before letting me go. I thought about running away but without another home to run to, I'd just be a sitting duck waiting to get plucked. Most of the pimps out here are on some bullshit just like him, so me leaving may just go from bad to worse. Like jumping out the frying pan into the fire. How much sense would that make? You know these pimps a never let a hoe eat alone so renegading is out the question."

Wow, today may just be my lucky day. I think I can pull this bitch. Actually, I know I can. Work that magic girl like your Daddy taught you.
"Yea you right about that girl. Ain't no way you can work without proper representation and Diamond is as crazy as they come."

"Girl who you tellin? You know I know, I gotta live with his crazy ass."

"Well, what if you didn't?"

"Didn't what?"

Damn this hoe is slow. "Didn't have to live wit 'em?"

"I'd be outta there quicker than you could say get."

"Well, it just so happens me and my Folks is looking for a wife-n-law to bring home that would fit in with us. Until now I couldn't find anyone ta fit the bill, but I know you'd fit in just fine. You're exactly the type a hoe my folks like. Like he would say, 'About her money and white.'" We both started laughing, which was a good sign. Then she said, "Yeah, I been checkin yawl out for a minute. You seem happy. He keeps you jazzy and he seems to have his game tight and shit together."

"Girl you already know and most important of all, he doesn't put his 'hands' on me!" I knew that was all she really cared about and wanted to hear so I did as my folks had taught me and capitalized off her weakness. The yearn to be taken care of by a man that didn't beat her.

"So, what you say girl?"

"Shit, what I gotta lose? Other than a crazy ass pimp that maybe the death of me if I stick around. But what about my clothes and stuff?"

"Oh don't worry about that girl. I'm sure Daddy a get you some new shit." That night I surprised my folks and brought Tina home to join our family.

"Daddy, I got a surprise for you." I said as I walked into our apartment with Tina in tow following close behind. I could see and tell my Daddy was very pleased with my hoe selection. I introduced Tina to my folks, who really needed no introduction. They both knew of each other through the game. The Pimp-N- Hoe world was like a secret society. Like a money getting cult if you will, and everybody who was somebody either knew or heard of one another. I had already let Tina know the deal prior to bringing her home, that one was gonna have to bring Daddy some money, her "Choosers fee," before he officially accepted her. Tina didn't have a problem with it. She knew the game and how it worked. She was only eighteen but had been hoe'n since she was fourteen, so as the game go, she was damn near a vet. She had been stashing money from Diamond for the past month in her pussy. Since Diamond never slept with his hoes, she knew it a be the last place he'd look. She knew she wasn't gonna be with Diamond too much longer and was saving up for the day she made her great escape. Now today was that day, and she had fifteen hundred plus saved, plus the five hundred she made today to choose up with Trust. Tina and Trust hit it off right away.

Daddy served Diamond news and let him know that Tina no longer belonged to him and she was now under the instructions of "Trust tha Pimp," and we became one big happy family. Money was rollin in like an armored truck to a bank. Six months later, Daddy bought a nice three bedroom house in Mira Mesa. This was a step up from Chula Vista and I loved it. Things between me and Tina was great. She played her position well and made a good wife-in-law. I was actually surprised at the fact that I wasn't jealous and even found myself growing very close to her.

We were like sisters. The sister that neither of us ever had growing up but always wanted. Life was good, spirits was up, and money was great. Even though I broke myself every night for all my money to Daddy, I secretly kept track of how much I made. Not to be scandalous, believe it or not, "ALL" hoes keep track, and if she tell you other wise, she's lying. No, I was just keeping track out of curiosity and to see how far we came. Once I realized that Daddy took in over a hundred thousand in the past six months between me and Tina, I knew we were doing it big.

"Where my two pretty bitches at?" Daddy said as he walked into the house and closed the door behind him, sat his keys down on the coffee table, and headed towards our bedroom.

"In here Daddy."

"Wake up, or should I say, get up and get dressed. I have a surprise for yawl. Where's your wife-n-law at?"

"I think in the room sleep or taking a bath."

"Hey Daddy." Tina came out the bathroom down the hall in her bathrobe fresh out the tub and greeted Daddy with a hug and a kiss on the cheek.

"Hey Tina, get dressed, Baby Girl. I got a surprise for you and Cherry."

"Ok Daddy, give me fifteen minutes."

"Make it ten." By this time, I was already up and half way dressed. You know I loved surprises.

"Damn Cherry, you dressed already?"

"Hell yea Daddy, you said the magic word. You know you ain't gotta tell me twice." We both laughed. He was right though, It only took me five minutes to get ready. Lucky I had just taken my shower before he came home. Five minutes later, Tina was ready and we were out the door.

"Alright bitches, let me hip you both to something. Money been real good and you both have been performing like the stars you are. Today is the day you reap the rewards for your hard work. As you both know, I'm about elevation and the service elevator in the empire state building itself couldn't take you higher than this game." We got into Daddy's 72 Cadillac, white on white with the mink interior, and continued talking. We drove to Midway and Rosecrans by the track. My first instinct was Daddy tricked us and just wanted us to get ready quick so he could drop us off to work. That idea and thought went out the back side window when I realized we were pulling into the Ford Dealership. I was happy as a preacher with a collection plate full of cash.

"Ok hoes, you know I like to set myself apart from the rest which is why I'm the best. I talk slick, dress clean, and ride mean. I have two of the baddest bitches the game's ever seen. I'm a hoe's fantasy and another pimp's worst dream. That's because I take care of my bitches. From this day forward, I'll no longer be droppin you bitches off to work, nor will I be driving yawl around to run errands." Daddy honked his horn two times and a sales man rolled up in a cherry red 64 Mustang with the convertible top.

"This is the reward for fuckin wit pimpin, better yet, fuckin wit Trust. I told you hoes if yawl put yawls trust in me, you could trust that life would get better and everything would be alright. Well bitches, thangs is more than alright and the game has blessed us all. Take a look at yawl new hoe mobiles." Daddy honked again and another dealer pulled up in a matching 64 Mustang convertible, only difference was this one was Tina's favorite color, pink! I knew right away that the other one was mines because it fit me to a tee, "cherry red"!

"Oh my God!" Thank you Daddy!" We both screamed in unison. We got out of Daddy's Caddi and rushed straight towards our new cars. The dealer's sales people got out smiling and handed us both our keys.

"Alright now bitches, yawl be cool because neither one of you hoes have your license yet so I don't need yawl getting pulled over. I know yawl excited to test your new rides though so Im a let yawl drive to the house. First thing Monday morning we'll take care of yawls licenses and get cha legal."

That was one of the happiest days of my life. I'd never owned my own car before. I use to steal and joy ride in my Mother's car back when I was sixteen when she would fall into one of her drunken comas. Yea life was getting better by the minute. I had been with Trust for a year and a half now and on the nineteenth month, he brought home two new bitches. Of course they were both white and extremely gorgeous, Nicky and Candy. Nicky was tall, about 5'9, slim, blonde, double D titties, cat shape face, eyes and a sweet innocent sounding voice like Marilyn Monroe. When I saw her for the first time, even I had dollar signs in my eyes. Candy was a little thicker and real curvy in all the right places. She had long curly brunette hair and "dick sucking plump lips," as Daddy would say. She resembled the exotic Brazilian type. I knew she'd get money as well. Daddy was at the top of his game. He had four of the prettiest hoes money could buy and doing it real big. We were living large. It got to the point I stopped keeping track of how much money we were making because it was coming in so fast I could no longer keep count. Six months later and two years into the game, I was still happy, treated like the bottom, and 100% game related. The game had replaced every square bone in my body. I looked forward to going to work and making Daddy money. I enjoyed the lifestyle and was addicted to the cash.

$$$$$

1976…

I woke up today like any other day, focused and ready to go make my Daddy some money.

"Candy, you ready to go to the track girl?"

"Yea, just let me finish up my make-up. I'm just about done." Nicky and Tina was already gone. They got an early start to make up for coming in short the night before. I prided myself in never coming in short. I had to lead by example. If I didn't have my quota, then I wasn't coming home until I did. No if ands or buts about it.

"Ok, I'm ready," Candy said as she finished her make-up, turned the bathroom light off, and headed towards the door where I was standing, waiting patiently ready to leave.

$$$$$

"Hey sweet Daddy, you wanna date?" I said in my most seductive voice, bent over the car window with my tits strategically placed above the window in eye view of my mark.

"How much for full service?"

"Are you a cop or vice?"

"No."

"Well, prove it to me then honey and pull out your dick for Mommy." The trick did as I instructed and pulled his dick out, which was all I needed to see ta get down to business. "That'll be a hundred dollars." He agreed to my price, like he really had a choice in the matter. I prided myself in charging these tricks what I knew I was worth. Fuck that twenty dollar date shit. Daddy always taught me to never settle for less and as long as I was coming in with my quota every night, he didn't question how I did it or how much money I charged. In his eyes, whatever I was doing was obviously working so if it ain't broke, don't fix it.

"Pull around the corner honey." I instructed him to pull around the corner in an alley behind this huge warehouse that I've used hundreds of times before. It was semi secluded and pretty private, cut off from immediate traffic and the outside world. The trick had a Brady Bunch station wagon which made the date easy to conduct. He pulled down the back seat. Then we climbed in the back and started our date.

"Oh yea, fuck me baby! Harder! Fuck me with that big dick! Ooh, It feels good." I seductively told him everything I knew he wanted to hear so that he would get overly excited and cum quick. I was a master at seduction. I could get a trick to cum in sixty seconds flat. 58.2 seconds later…

"Ah, Ah, FUCK! I'm coming Ahhhhh!" As I felt his five inch dick throb inside me and bust into the condom I thought, *mission accomplished. Just another quick date, and easy money. Putting me that much closer to my quota for the day.*

Six Years Later...

A lot has happened throughout the past eight years since I first broke luck and started hoe'n. I have been through everything a hoe could possibly have gone through in the game, except drugs. Daddy wasn't having that. Drugs wouldn't have been shit compared to a lot of the stuff, I "did" experience. In six short years I had been raped, beat up, kidnapped, and lost a lot of friends to drugs. Even worse, a sadistic serial killer was on the loose that had yet to be captured. Countless gorilla pimps breakin me for my money and tryna catch me outta pocket. I've had over a hundred wife-n-laws come and go. Tina and Candy was still around holding it down. Nicky got pregnant by a trick and squared up with a Sugar Daddy. The rest of us was still holding it down to the fullest. Then one day, Daddy came home and said something that shocked us all like a bolt of lightning while standing in a puddle of water with one finger in a light socket.

"Today is my last day pimpin."

"What? I know I didn't hear you right Daddy." Candy took the words right out my mouth because I damn sure was about to say the same thing.

"Listen up. Let me rap a taste wit yawl. This lifestyle we live has been great to us and I wouldn't change a thing that we've been through because the game has got us where we are today. I love the game like I love myself. We all know that, all games must come to an end and the best players end while they're still on top, before they're washed up and hung out to dry. Right now I'm at the top of my game. Throughout the past six years I've banked over a million dollars. That was always my goal, to hit a million, then go legit. Well, today is that day and that time has come. I was good to the game and in return, the game was good to me."

"So where does that leave us Daddy?" Tina asked curious as to where she fit into the situation.

"You know I ain't gonna leave yawl out. I always told you, if you hold me down, then Im a hold you down. No if ands or buts about it. I'm leaving the game but I ain't leaving you. I'm opening up a car stereo, tint, and detailing shop in Chula Vista, a one stop shop for all your car needs." That's when the name came to him for his business, 'One Stop Auto.'

"As for you guys, I'm giving all of you a hundred fifty-thousand dollars to start a business and do what you like. If you choose to leave me or stay in the game, I respect that, too. I know once a hoe always a hoe, just like I'll always be a pimp. But also keep in mind that pimpin and hoe'n is a state of mind, not just a way of life. All I'm doing now is steppin my game up and pimpin Uncle Sam. Candy, I know it was always business wit you and you told me when I first knocked you, that one day you wanted to move back to Atlanta where you're originally from and open up a beauty shop. Well, now you have more than enough start up money to do so and I wish you well, if that's what you still choose to do." Damn, I didn't even know Candy wanted to open a shop. Hell I didn't even know she was from Atlanta, all these years we been together. It's funny how you can know someone and not really know 'em at the same time.

"Thank you Daddy. I can't believe you're doing this for me. You know that's always been my dream."

"I know Baby Girl and I told you the day you chose up that I was gonna make all your dreams come true."

"Well Daddy, you know I'm a hoe through and through," Tina said. "It's all I know. I've been hoe'n since I was fourteen years old. I don't have a clue or know the first thing about starting a business let alone running one, nor do I have the desire to."

"I respect that Tina and I understand where you're coming from a hundred percent, but don't sell yourself short. You can do anything you put your mind to. I always taught you that."

"Yea Daddy but you also told me pimpin and hoe'n was the best thing going, and I believed you."

"And it is. I told you Baby Girl, ain't nothing like the game. I love everything about it, but I'm also smart enough to know that it's a young hoe's game and a young pimp's passion. I refuse to die with a bunch of old hoes and no dough with a bunch of memories, pictures and pimp stories. Unfortunately, that's the end game for pimpin and hoe'n. Unless, you're smart enough to stack enough chips to retire early while continuing to live the American Dream."

"I understand where you're coming from Daddy, but I still feel it's not for me."

"Well, all I can do is respect that. Truth be told, the attitude you have now is what made you such a good hoe while you've been with me throughout the years. Your work ethic and dedication to the game has been superb and I wish you the best in life as well."

Tina was saddened by the news. She had been with Daddy almost as long as me and had grown to love him as I. With her it wasn't just all business, but being the die hard hoe she was, she always put her feelings to the side knowing that love had nothing to do with this game. I wish she wasn't so stubborn and could see where Daddy was coming from and trying to do for her. I loved her like a sister and didn't want her to make a bad decision or leave the family.

Ultimately, that's exactly what she did. Two weeks after the conversation with Daddy, she got up one morning and went to work just like any other day, only this time she didn't return. Daddy figured she blew up and decided she didn't wanna be apart of the family anymore. A part of me felt otherwise. Call it hoe'n intuition. A month later, Tina was found behind a warehouse in a dumpster strangled to death. The same warehouse I use to take my dates too. The family took the news hard and was the breaking point for us all. Candy took Daddy up on his offer and moved back to Atlanta to start her business and be closer to her family. Daddy opened up his car audio, rim and tint shop and was a huge success. All the local ballers and pimps got their cars hooked up there. I decided to stay with Daddy and help him run his business. Of course the money he gave me to start my new life I gave back to him. What can I say, old habits die hard. Once a hoe, always a hoe.

CHAPTER 2 THE CHRONICLES OF YUKI

I moved to the US from Japan when I was three. My Father was killed in a terrible car accident when I was five. One day on his way home from work, a drunk driver ran a red light and hit my father's car dead on, ejecting him out the driver's side window and killing him instantly on impact. That was the first turning point in my life. Prior to, we were living the American Dream.

The rest of my family still lives in Japan, whom I have no recollection of. Things got hard for me and my mother after dad died. He was the bread winner of the family and with him gone, mother had to find work to take care of us. With mother's limited work skills, she resulted to working in the local massage parlors in Downtown San Diego. Needless to say, massages wasn't the only thing taking place there, nor was it their specialty. During the mid 80's, San Diego began cleaning up the downtown area to welcome a high end outside shopping mall called

Horton Plaza. They closed the parlors down and most of the adult book stores with the exception of "F-Street." When they did this, mother began working and taking trips to Atlanta. Atlanta was known as "Hotlanta" and not because of the weather or sunny skies. They still had many strip clubs and massages parlors around. Mother would go to Atlanta on the weekends, work and be back home at the beginning of the week to see me off to school.

I remember having a nanny named Mrs. Mayo that took care of me! She was a nice black woman that loved cooking macaroni and cheese for dinner. Everyone called her "Queen." She would take care of and watch me when my Mother was out of town or at work. I loved her like my own Mother. She taught me a lot.

When I was sixteen she moved back to New York to take care of her aunt who was old and could no longer take care of herself. I missed Queen. By now I was able to watch and take care of myself when my mother went to work. Nothing was a secret. My mother never hid the fact of what she did for a living, nor did she try to. In our culture, sex and prostitution wasn't frowned upon like it was in the United States. For that reason, mother kept her job private to the rest of the outside world, but with me, she was an open book. I learned a lot about the game through my mother. But not as much as I would learn later in life from my first and only pimp.

When I was fourteen my 9th grade teacher, "Mr. Johnson," came on to me in a sexual manner. Believe it or not though, I didn't panic or freak out. I used the opportunity to my advantage. I lead him on throughout the school year and used him to get straight A's for the semester. Most girls would have told their parents and turned him into the cops, but not me. Guess you could say I'm my mother's daughter because thinking back to that day, time period and situation. I could see that I was born to be a hoe. I might not have known it then, but I damn sure realized it later. I could still remember like it was yesterday...

$$$$$

"Yuki, may I see you after class?"

"Yes Mr. Johnson,"

Riiiiiiing!!!

"Ok class, that's the bell. Don't forget to study chapters 29 and 30 in your books. We have a test Monday on what you've learned. Have a great weekend."

"You wanted to see me Mr. Johnson?" I asked as the last remaining student left the class.

"Yes, please close the door Yuki." I went and closed the door then walked back to his desk. Mr. Johnson was a skinny old middle aged white man that resembled the host of "Mister Rogers Neighborhood." He looked like a stereotypical class "A" pedophile. "Well, Yuki I just wanted to let you know that you're doing great and I've been 'watching' you very closely." He put emphasis on the word "watching" as he eyed me in a creepy seductive manner.

My mother always taught me that most men are freaky, tricks and perverted by nature. She told and showed me the signs to look for. When we'd go out in public she'd point out the lust in men that broke their necks to look at my mother as we walked by. Even sicker was when they would bypass my mother and look at me in that same way. I learned to recognize the look. The look I saw in countless mens eyes. The look that Mr. Johnson had in his eyes right now. I played along to see where he was going with this.

"Oh is that so? So what about me have you been watching?"

"Everything."

"And do you like what you see?"

"Absolutely!" This was starting to sound like a scene from "Debbie Does Dallas." I couldn't help but laugh to myself at the thought.

"Ok Mr. Johnson, so what do you want from me?" As if I didn't already know.

"Everything that you're willing to give."

"And what are you gonna do for me?"

"Anything that you want." Well, I knew that I had no intentions on sleeping or doing anything sexual with this old man. My mother taught me that you could get anything that you want out of a man as long as you string him along and mentally play into his desires. The minute you give in to his wants and throw in your hand the game is over. "The Art of Seduction."

As long as I made him feel like there was a possibility that one day he'd have the opportunity to sleep with me, he'd do whatever I ask of him. This was my first lesson on how to manipulate, play and get over on men. At the time, all I wanted was to pass the class with straight A's without having to lift another finger, and that's what I got. When I look back on it, I kick myself realizing I could've gotten so much more. Two years later Mr. Johnson was arrested and caught in a scandal for molesting and sleeping with one of his students. Hey, once a pedophile, always a pedophile, and that life's bound to catch up with you eventually.

When I was seventeen my mother was diagnosed with breast cancer. She died six months later. That was the hardest time and part of my life since the death of my father. First him, now her. I just felt like crawling up under a rock and dying. After my mother passed, I moved in with my high school best friend Kiesha, who graduated early and had her own apartment on Adams Ave in East Daygo. Her Mother got it for her as a graduation present under the agreement and understanding that she gets a job and maintains the rent. Her Mother agreed to pay the first and last month's rent as well as the security deposit. When I was eighteen I got introduced to the life of Pimpin and Hoe'n. My first and only pimp was 'Jackpot.' They called him 'JP' for short. This was the part of my life where things changed dramatically. "Bitch you outta pocket hoe. Who's your folks?"

"JP."

"Who the fuck is JP?"

"He is I and I am him," my Daddy said, arriving just in time to rescue me from this pimp that called himself California Mike."

"Go ahead back to work Baby Girl. I got this."

"Okay Daddy." I walked up the block and wondered what my Folks was saying to him. This was my first day on the track and my first experience with another pimp tryna shake me down and push up on me. I did exactly as my Daddy told me to do in that situation, put my head down, avoid eye contact, and walk the other way, but then he put his hands on me swinging me around by my arm to face him, forcing me outta pocket. That's when my Daddy stepped in, thank God. I wonder what would have happened if he hadn't of shown up.@ One thing I learned in the game is that a bitch could keep it 100% hoe'n, in pocket like a wallet, and still have these broke ass, no hoe having, pimp and wannabe players on her heels fuckin wit a bitch all night, tryna get her to choose while she's tryna work.

Damn, get a clue, didn't I put my head down and turn away from your ass? Yeah, them rules sound good, but truth be told they don't mean shit, because when the lion is out for prey, he's gonna pounce on the first meat he sees. After my first day working the track I was hooked, like so many hoes before me. Prostitution is addictive, just like dope. Once you're committed to the game it's hard as hell to get out. I was a natural on the track. My first day out I made over five hundred dollars. My only competition was a black and white pretty mixed hoe named Stacy that belonged to a pimp named 'Boo-J.'

"Hey girl, I see you out here gettin yo money. You new huh? I haven't seen you out here before."

"Yeah, today's my first day."

"My name's Stacy."

"Yuki, nice to meet you." We shook hands.

"This track is pretty cool, you just have to know what to look out for."

"Like pimps tryna shake you down and break a hoe every five minutes?" We both laughed

"Exactly! Nah girl but really, that's some shit you're gonna have to get use to. It's all apart of the life and comes with the game. You know actually you can use it to your advantage. The next time a pimp gets ta chasin you down and ridin your heels, flag down a trick and tell him you need a quick ride to get away from this crazy guy that won't leave you alone. Once you're in the car you can work your magic and turn the situation into a possible date. I do it all the time."

"That's smart." I could tell this girl had game about herself, was no wonder she made a thousand dollars every night and out hoe'd every other bitch on the track.

"The other thing you have to watch out for is them shady National City police officers and vice squad. They'll pull out their dick, fuck you, then still arrest you. Now the cool thing is right around that corner on Roosevelt is not considered National City, and is actually San Diego. Which means, when you're working on that side, the National City PD and vice can't fuck with you because it's out of their jurisdiction. So basically, when you see the police and vice rollin, just walk on over there and work San Diego. The San Diego Police don't trip too tough on us working, but on Tuesdays and Thursdays the vice be out kinda thick, taken down names, questioning, and harassing bitches. They really be fuckin wit the hoes they know have folks because they be tryna arrest and scare 'em into rollin over. So make sure when you're on that side you never let 'em see you with your pimp." Shit, Stacy was like an open book and you can best believe I was taking down chapters.

"See, I'm a tell you the shit that your folks conveniently left out, or don't know about. One thing I can and will say though is, there's a lot of money on this track. When they shut down Midway and Rosecrans, this became the place to be, 8th and National City."

"Good looking out on the run down."

"No problem girl. We hoes gotta look out for one another. If we don't, then who will?" With that being said, Stacy made one last comment, "Well that's enough hoe-cializin for one day. Time is money," and got in a trick's car to pull a date. I was grateful for meeting Stacy. Her wisdom was something I never forgot, took to heart and used throughout my hoe career. I wanted to be that bad bitch that made a thousand dollars "every" night, and other hoes envied. Within a short amount of time that's exactly what I became.

The first time I made a thousand dollars was in Hollywood. Hollywood was nothing like San Diego. Hollywood was ten times faster. This place looked like the Mecca for hoe'n. I knew five minutes after my arrival that there was no way I wasn't gonna clock a thousand dollars or more. That night I took in two thousand dollars and Daddy knocked a new bitch. Her name was Green Eyes. Daddy knocked her from a pimp named 'Payday.' Payday was a pimp slash Compton Crip, who was very hands on with his game. He use to beat the shit out of his bottom hoe Shasha and Green Eyes knew that it wouldn't be long before she suffered the same fate. So the first opportunity she got to choose up with someone else she did. Green Eyes was a young, pretty snow bunny with long blonde hair and beautiful green eyes. She had a very slim waist with a cat shape face. She was a money maker, I knew we'd do good together right off the bat. After work that night we went back to the hotel to talk and get to know each other better.

"So how long you been with Jackpot?"

"About two months."

"Oh so you're still new too huh?"

"Yeah, he turned me out to the game." We talked as Daddy ran down to Carls Jr to get us something to eat.

"Yeah, I been in the game about six months now. I met Payday, my ex folks, at the Greyhound bus station downtown. I had just ran away from home to get away from my drug addicted mother. I had twenty dollars to my name and had just arrived in Hollywood by way of Flagstaff, Arizona. I always wanted to be an actress and thought I could get discovered. Well, the only person that discovered me was Payday, who told me he could make me a star. Guess I just didn't realize what kinda star he was talking about, cause three weeks later, I was hoe' n."

Wow, hearing Green Eyes story made me realize that not every female chose to be a prostitute. Some were tricked, manipulated, and forced. Some had no other choice. I appreciated the fact that Daddy made me feel like it was my decision whether or not I wanted to hoe for him. The more I met and talked to females like Green Eyes, I began to wonder if he manipulated me into the game as well, getting into my head and playing on my emotions. By the time I knew the answer to the question it was too late and didn't matter. I was already hooked. This was the story for a lot of hoes and I was no exception. Funny thing is, in time, I would still grow to love my Daddy and work all night to get his money, if that's what it took ta make him happy. As warped as that may sound, it's the truth. I'm sure a million other hoes would tell you the same. Daddy came back with burgers and fries for us both as he talked to us about our new arrangement, and what he expected of us.

"Alright hoes, let me first start off by officially welcoming Green Eyes to the family. I see big thangs in our future. There's gonna be many obstacles in our path to cross and many mountains in our way to climb, but that should never stand in our way or hold us back. We playing for big stakes out here and settling for less ain't an option. You two are wife-n-laws now and sisters to the game. Yawl have to watch each other's back like she had a clock on her spine. It's us against the world. If a mutha fucka ain't wit us, then they're against us. Never let another bitch or hoe outshine yawl on the track. Shit, on or off that mutha fucka for that matter. Make sure yawl stick together like a fat bitch ass in daisy dukes. I don't ever wanna here about yawl hatin on each other or fighting wit one another you got that?"

"Yes Daddy," we both said in unison.

"Never lose focus on what this is all about. Never lose sight of our agenda and common interest which is ultimately our common goal. To get rich or die hoe'n. Nothinn better get in the way of yawl gettin that money. Rain, hail, sleet, or snow, twenty below you bitches hoe." We both just sat back at attention and listened.

"You cool wit dat Green Eyes, I mean can you dig it?"

"Yes Daddy. I understand and know what I gotta do."

"Alright then bitches finish up yawls dinner, get in the shower, then get in the bed so we can relax. Tomorrow's a long day and we have a lot of shit to handle and take care of. I'm proud of you both for the amount of money yawl made, and how quick you both got up yawls choosers fee. Good job and keep up the good work."

"Thank you Daddy," we both said proud of ourselves as well, with big Kool-Aid smiles happy to receive praise from Daddy. Things were great and going good until the next day when Payday cornered Green Eyes in a back alley off the track and jammed her up. He was still upset about her leaving him and was tryna force her to come back home through intimidation. Lucky for Green Eyes, Daddy found her just in time as she was tryna make a break for it and came to her rescue. Unfortunately, this created a feud between Jackpot and Payday that would ultimately end deadly. Money was coming in quicker than we could spend it and my Daddy was a master at stackin chips.

I remember one month we took a trip to New York and Washington, D.C. The track was right around the corner from the white house. You would have never thought or believed that this type of activity was taking place right in the nation's capital, not even ten minutes away from where the President of the United States rested his head every night. The cold thang about it is, the track was booming. I made just as much money there, if not more, as I made in Hollywood. I couldn't believe it. I fucked so many politicians I should have been a Diplomat. From there we drove down to New York and worked Hunts Point in the Bronx. We didn't stay long because H.B.O was filming a documentary about pimpin and hoe'n and we weren't trying to put ourselves on blast. My folks didn't want no parts of that.

The producer offered him a nice amount of money too, but my Daddy said no amount of money was worth your freedom, dignity and exposing game. So we took the opportunity to get some much needed shopping done. "Hey, I'm a take yawl down to Fordham Road to go shopping." Me and Green Eyes, eyes lit up like christmas lights ta Daddy's announcement. Fordham Road was located in the Bronx, and was one of the many places in New York where you could shop and purchase anything from jewelry to the latest fashions. From bootleg labels to designer bags, and everything else you could imagine. Those were good times, but things weren't always so great. Right after the incident that took place in Hollywood between Payday, Green Eyes and Daddy, we left Hollywood and headed for San Francisco where the drama unfolded.

"Hey wifey."

"Hey Yuki."

"I'm just about done. I just got this trick for three hundred so that puts me, just about at my quota for the night, if I add what I made earlier. One more call should put me over the top."

"Okay, I got a little ways to go, so let me pull a couple more dates so I can finish up and meet you back at the hotel."

"Alright then wifey. Handle your business. I'll see you back at the hotel."

"Ok girl, love you."

"Love you, too." I pulled one more date before heading back to the hotel. I had made my quota and knew that my folks would be pleased. I couldn't wait to walk in with his money. Just as I arrived at the front door of our hotel room, I heard a commotion inside. It sounded like someone yelling or arguing. It was a males voice, but not Daddy's. I opened the door and was shocked to see Daddy on the floor bleeding from a gash in his head with Payday standing over him with a gun.

Somehow Payday had found out where we were and followed us to San Francisco. I jumped on Payday's back to help my Daddy, but to no avail. He did something to knock me off of him. All I remember from that point was hitting the ground and blacking out. When I first entered the room, I screamed at the sight of Daddy bleeding on the floor at gun point, and for a split second it diverted Payday's attention towards me. That's when my folks leaped for Payday's gun. My folks wrestled with him holding the barrel, as I jumped on Payday's back.

POW! The sound of gun fire shocks the hotel manager.

"Hello? Hello?!"

"911, what's your emergency?"

"Yes, there seems ta be a problem. I think someone's been shot or hurt."

"Where are you calling from sir?"

"The Days Inn, 1322 Filmore St. Please hurry up and send Police. I just heard another shot."

"Calm down sir, I already have a unit in route. They should be there shortly. Stay on the line with me until they arrive." The Police arrived and found Daddy and Payday wrestling with the gun. When they yelled freeze, Payday turned towards them, gun in hand, ready to shoot. He never got off a shot, as the Police fired and gunned him down. Lucky for Green Eyes, she missed the tragic events of that night. By the time she got back to the hotel, the room was taped off and Daddy and me were downtown giving our statements to the Police. Even luckier for us, they ruled the situation as a botched robbery, break in, and assault, due to the door being kicked in as well as the gash on Daddy's head. I don't remember much else about that night, but I do remember that after the Police let us go, we hooked up with Green Eyes and got the fuck out of San Francisco. From time to time I still get nightmares and wake up in cold sweats about that night. Picturing Daddy on the floor of that hotel room, bleeding from the wound on his head. As I walk in and the gun goes off...**BLAM!**

"Ahhhhhh!"

"It's okay, It's okay Baby Girl. You were just having a nightmare. You okay?" Daddy held me in his arms comforting me like he'd done so many nights before.

"I can't shake that horrible nightmare Daddy. It felt so real. Daddy I don't know what I would ever do if I lost you."

"You're not gonna lose me Baby Girl. See, I'm fine. Pimpin's right here in the flesh." He kissed me on the forehead and rocked me back to sleep, like a real "Daddy" comforting his baby girl. Times like these is when I felt special and truly loved. Although Daddy would never admit that he loved me verbally, his actions would say other wise. Pimps always swore up and down that they didn't love their hoes, they only loved the money. In some cases I believe that to be true, but in other cases, not so much. I feel like if you build a foundation of any amount of significance with someone and stick by each other's side through thick and thin, then your bound to start having feelings for one another on some type of level.

Now maybe I'm just lying to myself, or wishful thinking, but that's the type of thinking that kept me around and holding it down. I was with my Folks for seven long years before shit hit the fan and life as I knew it was snatched from underneath me like a rug. I had been all around the United States, cross country and back. My folks had become one of the biggest pimps in San Diego, and I'm proud to say, I had a hand in help making that happen.

One day early in the morning, I was awoken by the front door of my Folk's house being kicked in by the Police and San Diego Vice Unit. That was the beginning of the end to the life I had grown ta love and was accustom to. Jackpot was arrested and charged with Pimping and Pandering. I was arrested for prostitution as well as my wife-n-law Green Eyes, who too was in the house at the time. Our charges weren't that serious seeing how it was just a misdemeanor, but Daddy's were. To make matters worse, a couple of his ex hoes that use to work for him, was now testifying against him. I couldn't believe this shit was happening. Once Daddy got locked up, Green Eyes slowly fell off. That's when I really felt alone. Money was slow, life was hard, and Daddy was gone. I still stuck by him and held it down the best I could, but by no means was it easy. We lost everything we worked so hard to accumulate, in an instant. I felt like I was back at square one. The Police seized our money, house, cars, and anything else that wasn't nailed down to the floor.

My Daddy fought his case for about six months before he was forced to plead out and take a deal. When he called and told me he signed for six years, I passed out and hit the back of my head on the living room coffee table which put me in a coma for eight weeks. When I woke up, the doctor said I'd developed slight brain damage from internal bleeding and would never walk or use the left side of my body again. Needless to say, I've been highly depressed and suicidal ever since. "Which is what brings me here Doc."

"Wow, that was an interesting story Yuki. I truly sympathize with you, and I'm especially concerned about these suicidal thoughts and tendencies that have occurred and taken place. Have you ever tried to act on any of them," the psychiatrist asked, while jotting down notes on his pad, as I laid comfortably on the long couch to his side. Arms folded, relaxed, telling my story.

"No, but I came close a few times. One day I had to use the restroom and couldn't make it on my own. I got extremely frustrated and embarrassed at the fact that I needed help. At that moment, I thought about slitting my wrist with the razor blade that only sat inches on my dresser. The only thing that kept me from going through with it was, I thought it might hurt too much and was afraid of the pain."

"Well, that's not good. I'm gonna prescribe you something to help balance your emotions. I'm also gonna write down and show you some mental exercises you can do when you're alone and feeling hopeless, or suicidal."

The doctor prescribed me some anti-depression pills and showed me some breathing, counting to ten, and yoga type exercises I could do on my own when I got upset, felt helpless, or suicidal. Truth be told, I felt like it was bullshit. I never took the medicine. Nor did I go back to see the doctor after that session. That night I thought about my life. The good, the bad and the ugly. I thought about dad, my life in the game, Jackpot and momma. I felt alone. I felt like everyone I ever loved or cared about eventually died or left me.

I didn't wanna live no more. I was tired of being tired. A single tear ran down the side of my face and dropped as I reminisced. As I sat in my bed depressed thinking, I looked on my dresser and saw the bottle of sleeping pills I used to go to sleep at night. Without them I couldn't sleep. I had a doctor prescribe me a heavy dose for my insomnia. That night I decided to take the whole bottle and wash it down with a bottle of Hennessy for good measure.

As I started to drift off in eternal darkness, I was awoken by a bright light and long tunnel, with my Mother and Father standing at the end, arms reached out for me to come, smiling. For the first time in a long time I felt free. I wasn't afraid, I didn't feel alone. This was my destiny...this was meant to be.

CHAPTER 3 THE CHRONICLES OF SWEETS

I knew I wasn't like other females when I was in high school. When all the other girls was chasing guys and looking for boyfriends, I was checking out the females. For some reason I was attracted to them. When I was a kid, I wasn't into Barbie dolls and playing house. I hung with the boys. Through the years, I began to dress and act like them as well. I grew up in Marietta Georgia, Atlanta. The gay capital of the United States.

Yeah, believe it or not, we have San Francisco beat by a mile. Their Gay Pride doesn't have shit on ours. Just go to Lenox Mall and watch how many fags, lesbian and homo thugs you see and run into. My name is Latricia Brown, but everyone calls me "Sweets." I picked up the name when I was young, because I always had a sweet tooth for candy. They'd call me sweets, or would say, "Here comes sweet Latrice." I graduated from high school in 96, the same year I met my female lover Lez. I met her at the Freaknic. Back in the day, that was the hottest event in Atlanta.

Every year people from all over the United States and Atlanta would flock to this event to see, party and pick up the hottest males and females Atlanta had to offer. Shit would get so wild that in later years they would shut down the Freaknic for good. Leaving it a distant memory of the past.

"Hello, may I take your order?" I had just walked into the Waffle House and sat down. The Freaknic was active and live as ever. I had been out all day and had finally worked up an appetite.

"Yes, I'll have some cheese eggs, raisin cinnamon toast, and a steak patty with a side of grits."

"Would you like butter and cheese on your grits?"

"Yes please, oh and can I also have a glass of orange juice?"

"Sure thing, coming right up." The waitress took my menu and went to go place my order. As I sat back sipping on orange juice the waitress had poured after taking my order. A nice looking female walked in looking fly as hell. She was light skin, had long natural braids with a Godfather on. Thugged out attire, baggy jeans, and butter Timbs. She resembled Da Brat from So So Def. At first glance, I actually thought it was Da Brat.

When she walked in we made eye contact. Right away I felt an instant attraction. I believe she noticed and felt the same because she smiled and sat down at the counter in the stool next to mines. She ordered a Texas cheese steak sandwich, then walked over to the jukebox, placed her money in the slot and selected "Nothin But A 'G' Thang" by Snoop Dogg and Doctor Dre, as well as a song by Outkast.

"Hey ma, how you doing?" She spoke to me, as she sat back down at the counter.

"Good and yourself?"

"Lovely now," she responded back in a seductive way and slight smirk on her face.

"Oh really, and what about 'now' that makes it so lovely?" As if I didn't already know the answer. "Meeting and speaking to a beautiful shawty like yourself. By the way, my name's Lez."

"Nice ta meet you Lez." We shook hands as the waitress came back with our orders and sat them down in front of us.

"So you got a name Ma?"

"Oh my bad, it's Latricia, but everyone calls me Sweets."

"And how sweet it is." I blushed. I never had another female come on to me before, and look at me in a way I usually looked at them. It was actually refreshing, and I welcomed the attention. At eighteen, I stood 5'7, weighed 135 lbs, thick thighs, slim waist, 34-C titties, caramel complexion and pretty face. Guys would always hit and come on to me, but I wasn't interested in them. We talked a little more and finished up our meals before heading back to the outside party that Atlanta and America had grown to love.

"So Ma, you come down here by yourself?"

"Yeah, pretty much. I don't have too many girlfriends," I responded.

"Well, you do now. That is, if you want one." I loved her confidence and take charge attitude. It was like she was a man in a woman's body. We kicked it for the rest of the day and well into the night. From that day fourth, we were inseparable. We began dating and I noticed right away that Lez seemed to have a lot of other females she dealt with as well. Not in a relationship type way because she spent most of her time with me. At the same time I couldn't understand what role these other women played in her life.

For instance, one day me and Lez was chillin at her pad watching movies. She lived in Atlanta Zone 3. The hood, but the inside of her house was plushed. She had some of the flyest shit money could buy. Like the dining room table that was also a see-through fish tank. Or the wrap around burgundy leather sectional in the living room with the matching fish tank coffee table. Not to mention her ten thousand dollar bedroom set and canopy queen size with Egyptian silk hanging from the top. All of this and I never saw her work a day since I been with her. Then came the women. While we were sitting back relaxing watching a movie we had just rented from Hollywood Video, the door bell rang. Lez answered it and opened the door. There standing, was a beautiful thick female in high heels that resembled a stripper. Lez introduced us, then told me she'll be back as they walked into her bedroom.

Five minutes later they came out. The girl said bye and left. At the time I didn't think nothing of it until three more girls came and went throughout the course of the day in the same fashion. Now I was curious and somewhat suspicious of what was going on. Lez must of picked up how I felt because that's when she explained and put my thoughts to rest. We had been dating little over a month when she finally came clean and told me her secret. "Hey ma, I know you're probably wondering wuss up wit all the bitches that been coming through."

"Yeah, actually I was. Not to be nosey or anything, but just out of curiosity."

"I can understand that. I would wanna know wuss up too." By this point, she had my full attention.

"Ma, I'm sure you noticed that I live a lavish lifestyle but you never see me actually go to work. That's because I'm a Pimptress."

"What's a Pimptress?"

"Same thing as a Pimp, but the female version." I was shocked. I never even knew that there was such a thing.

"So you're a female pimp? I didn't even know that existed. So all them girls that been coming over…work for you?"

"Yeah, and they were coming over to drop off my money." I was speechless.

"So is that what this is about, you fuckin wit me because you want me to hoe for you?"

"Nah shawty, it ain't even like that ma. I fucks wit you because I like you, whether you fuck wit me on that level or not."

"Well I ain't no hoe, nor do I have any desire to be one."

"I got choo Ma, and most of my bitches don't hoe either."

"How is that possible? From my understanding, you can't be a pimp if you ain't got a hoe."

"Yeah that's that male thinking and definition of a pimp, not mines. My bitches sell fantasies. They pimp a trick's mind and get him for every dime. I'm not gonna lie to you and say none of them ever turn dates, shit if the price is right who wouldn't."

"Me, I wouldn't."

"So you're telling me that if a mutha fucka offered you five thousand ta spend the weekend wit 'em you'd say no and turn it down?"

Even I had to keep it real with myself and think about that one for a minute. "Well, probably for five G's, but ain't nobody paying that much for no pussy, especially when you can get a bitch Downtown or Zone 6 for a hundred dollars tops right off the corner."

"That's just it Ma, my bitches don't work on no street corners, and they damn sure don't fuck wit Downtown, unless it's Magic City."

"Then where do they work?"

"In the strip clubs. All my girls is strippers Ma. Professional showgirls. Like I told you, they're selling fantasies. Leaving their tricks wit hard dicks and broke, back to their girlfriends or wives." That made me ease up a bit, I didn't really see nothing wrong with stripping. Shit, this was Atlanta, the fuckin strip club capital, just like Portland and Miami. More people went to the strip clubs out here than the regular club. On any given Sunday you could catch your favorite rapper, movie star or celebrity at the club.

"You see, I don't follow the same code as the fellas, and a lot of them hate on me because so. I could give a fuck about what the next nigga think. Most of them just hate me because they ain't me. When a bitch get wit me, she ain't gotta worry about all that drama that she would if she had a male pimp. Like me forcing you to work all night, or fuck and suck a trick off for twenty dollars. She ain't gotta worry about me going upside her head, verbally abusing and treating her like less than a woman.

"I'm a woman, so I know how a woman wants ta be treated, and I make it my business ta satisfy her every desire. A pimp says 'he don't love them hoes,' but I love all my bitches and they love me too. We're one big happy family with two big common goals, get rich and die happy. So far so good, because if I was to die tomorrow, I'd have a big smile on my face and G's in the casket. Unlike most pimps, I actually care about my girls. I done bent damn near every rule in the game except one, that a bitch gotta pay me all her money. But at the end of the day there's not a bitch alive that's been wit me that can say I haven't took care of her. All my bitches have nice cars and homes. I moved them from Bankhead to Buckhead. From the project streets, to condo suites. From the Metro to the Limo, Honda Civics to european whips that's vicious. I don't have my bitches looking like cheap hookers. My bitches wear top of the line name brand labels. Eight hunnet dolla Manolos and Gucci flats. Fuck JC Penny's. My bitches shop at Saks."

"Alright alright, I get the point. So once again, where do I fit in all of this?"

"Wherever you want Ma. I'm not gonna lie and say I don't want you, but I also know that the life's not for everybody. So if you don't wanna get down and be apart of this situation, I understand and respect your decision."

"So if I say no, is that the end of our relationship?"

"No, we could still be friends and kick it, but I couldn't see us being more than that because of the lifestyle I'm in. We'd be in two different worlds apart. That's why I'm being honest wit you. That's why I told you the truth about me before we got too close or slept together. So you can make a conscious decision, with a clear mind and level head. I don't trick girls into being with me, they're wit me cause they wanna be."

"I can respect that, and I know we haven't been dating long, but I 'do' have feelings for you. Don't know if I could say its love, because I've never been in love before. Maybe its lust. Shit, truth be told, I'm still a virgin. So I don't even know if it's that. All I know is that I feel something. Even more so, I don't wanna let you go. I wanna continue to explore what we have and possibly watch it grow. As for the stripping thang, I don't really have a problem with that because it's just dancing and teasing men, which I've been doing both all my life. As long as I don't have to sleep wit 'em, I'm cool."

That was how I became a stripper and one of the hottest showgirls in Atlanta. By 1999, 'Sweets' was a household name throughout the Atlanta club scene. I could bounce my ass and work the pole like no other. I made more money dancing then a lot of bitches made hoe'n. I averaged five grand a week and still had yet ta sleep with a trick. Lez had five other girls that worked for her as well. We all called her Momma because she took care of us as such.

RIINNGG! "Hello," I answered the phone as I was driving down the 85 freeway, just passing the "Welcome to Atlanta, The Home of So So Def" Billboard.

"Hey Ma, meet me and the girls at Club 112. I need to talk ta yawl about something."

"A'ight Momma, I'll be there in twenty or thirty minutes." 112 was one of the hottest clubs in Atlanta. The line ta get in always stretched clear around the building. We hung up the phone as I continued driving headed towards the club. I arrived at the club around 11 pm and as always, the entry line was ridiculously long. Atlanta's finest had come out ta get krunk. I parked my 335i white on white BMW with the valet, and walked straight to the front of the line, where security was standing with his clipboard. I knew Lez had to have put me and the rest of the girls on the VIP list, because that was how she rolled.

We never stood in line like the common folk when we went out. Lez was known in the ATL. Loved by some, hated by few, but respected by all. She commanded attention when we went out. Pimped out surrounded by six girls poppin Cristal in VIP, how could she not stick out, and mugs took notice.

"Hey shawty, wut can I do for you?" The security said as I walked up and stood in front of the velvet ropes.

"Hi, my name is Sweets. I should be on the list." He scrolled down the clipboard with his index finger then said, "Yes, Sweets, you're on the list, come right in." He unhooked the velvet rope, stepped aside, and let me pass. You could see the bitches that had to wait in line, sucking teeth, rolling their eyes, and hatin. Sorry, wasn't my fault I was a boss bitch. And since I started dancing, I stopped dressing Tom boyish, and started dressing more feminine and seductive.

My line of work required fulfilling male fantasies and I damn sure wasn't finna do that in baggy jeans an Timbs. Plus I'd grown accustomed and come to love the attention that I got from men when I went out. Even though I wasn't interested in dating them, I got great joy and pleasure in teasing them. I entered the club and the place was krunk. I walked straight to the V.I.P section where Lez and the other five girls was sitting, popping bottles, and enjoying the vibe.

"Hey Momma. Hey girls. Wut, ya'll couldn't wait for a bitch?" I playfully said as I greeted Lez and the girls and gave everyone a hug.

"Hell nah we couldn't wait. You know I gotta be krunk in the club off that Crissy, but you know Momma got choo. Better late than never right?" Lez said jokingly and semi tipsy, as she waved the beautiful bartender over and ordered three more bottles of Cris. I just laughed, took off my Baby Phat faux mink, sat down, and got comfortable.

"Alright girls listen up. I invited you all because I wanna talk to yawl about a special event comin up in a couple weeks. Now yawl know how big we did it in Brazil for New Years last week. That shit was krunk and I'm sure we'll all agree that we had the time of our lives. Well, its time to do something game related ladies. Next month we're headed down to the 2000 Players Ball and give these guys a run for their money. We gone show 'em how the bitches do it."

We all got excited, because none of us ever been to a Players Ball before, but we all heard about them and knew what they were about. It was the place that pimps and hoes from all across the globe congregated to socialize and get recognition for their work they put in the game.

"Who said pimpin was a male sport? Who ever did must have never met Lez. Six deep no sleep, pockets fat and nothin cheap. 600 Benz Coupe out there in the streets, ostrich leather car interior wit my name in the seat. They can't fuck wit me." We all started laughing and slapping high fives to one another.

"Toast to the most, and Boss Bitch on any coast." Lez said as she raised her glass towards the sky like The Statue of Liberty.

"Okay, so until we make this trip I'm a need yawl workin over time & puttin it down major, so we can make back and stack some of the money we spent in Brazil. Because you can best believe one thing for certain, and two thangs fa sure, we gone be the baddest bitches in the buildin, and mutha fucka's is gone take notice." We all agreed and toasted to the situation.

"Okay, now that that's said, enjoy yourself ladies, because it may be a while before we get another chance to come out to the club and just kick it."

We ordered a few moe bottles of Crissy, got a little tipsy, and hit the dance flo. We got krunk ta about three in the morning. I had a blast. After the club let out, we went to Steak-N-Shake and got something to eat before heading home. We all knew that the next day would be back to business as usual and was tryna milk the evening for all it was worth.

$$$$$

"This is your raven pimp reporter Galaxy Glen, reporting to you live from the 2000 Players Ball and Pimp JuJu's Birthday Bash. We in the Chi baby but ain't nothing shy bout what's been taking place up in here tonight. We got some of the biggest players from around the world in the house tonight. It's definitely been a star studded event."

Our super stretched limo pulled up to the Red Carpet, as cameras flashed, and videos rolled. The driver got out and opened our door. One by one we got out in matching Louie dresses, all custom, caramel color, with the logo pattern throughout. All six of us got out first, leaving Lez to come out and make her grand entrance and pimp debut. This would be the first time in history a female pimp would attend a Players Ball. I mean don't get me wrong, there has been Madams since the beginning of time and a few so called female pimps here and their, but no one has ever took them serious enough ta classify them as a bonafide pimp. Most of them other so called pimp bitches was self proclaimed pimps with no game recognition. But tonight would change all that, at least we thought.

"Damnnn Gina! We got six bad ass hoes that just hit the red carpet ta grace our presence. I know this stable gotta belong to a reputable die hard pimp. Just look at their outfits," Galaxy Glen spoke into the mic, but when Lez stepped out the limo, his jaw hit the carpet. Lez stepped out in a three piece custom Louie suit to match our dresses. She had a chocolate color Godfather and matching gators, pimp cane & cup, custom by Debbie The Glass Lady, and Versace glasses with the 24k gold Medusa. Shit, she put some of these so called "Pimp of the Year" niggas ta shame. Galaxy Glen couldn't believe his eyes.

"Oh no, say it ain't so! A female pimp? Is there even such a thang? Well, apparently so from the looks of thangs." Everybody was in awe.

"So wuss your name pimpin?" Galaxy Glen asked as he put the mic underneath Lez's chin so she could answer.

"Lez, and that's Pimptress. As you can see, I'm not a man."

"Stevie Wonder and Ray Charles could see that, blind folded in the dark!"

"Ya dig?"

"Yea, I can dig it, let's just see if they dig it in there," he said, pointing towards the entrance of the Players Ball.

"Hey, what can I say? Loved by some, hated by a few, respected by all." With that, we walked inside with Galaxy Glen watching, still in shock with a smirk, shaking his head. The ball was live. Everybody who was anybody within the game was there. We got a table for seven in the V.I.P section in front of the stage where the entertainment and award ceremony was held. Lez ordered a few bottles of Cristal and Don P. All eyes was on us. Suga Free had just stopped performing and finished up his set when the host from TooRealForTv.com, Michael Maroy came over. Camera and mic in tow. He interviewed Lez for his next up and coming DVD he was putting out. He was the Executive Producer and brains behind the infamous "Cross Country Pimping" DVD's, which was becoming a hood classic. Watching Maroy interview Lez for his film made some of the other pimps in the place take notice. One pimp in particular was 'Supreme.' A pimp outta San Diego that owned his own escort service and record label. He was their with four of his best hoes and showing out in a real way. His brother, Ka$hanova, had just gotten out of prison for pimpin and was back at it like he never left. Apparently, his bottom bitch held it down throughout his jolt and kept him fresh while he was inside. Books maxed out and packages every quarter. She also had a big fat stack waiting for him when he came home, so as a reward, he brung her to the Players Ball.

After Maroy was done interviewing Lez and walked off, I got up to go to the bathroom. When I came out, Supreme was standing there. I put my head down and tried to walk past, but he was on my bumper like the fifth wheel on an old school Cadillac.

"Wuss up hoe? Supreme's the name and pimpin's the game. I see pussy payin pussy and like oil and water, that shit don't mix. You need a pimp that's recognized and qualified, rich, talk slick, cross country and bonafide. See all dat pussy lickin and dildo stickin got choo confused. Make your next move your best move, turn around and choose hoe." This nigga was pissin me off, but I knew the code, so I just kept my head down and continued walking back to my table.

"Yeah bitch, I don't chase hoez, but my conversation ain't gotta problem wit walkin you back to your table. If you can hear me you can feel me, ya dig? I see your so called Folks got her panties soaked and lost for words. That's what happens when a bitch try and play a male's sport. Maybe she need ta stick ta tennis and let the men handle this pimpin." I got back to my table pissed off, for two reasons. One, because this nigga was talking shit and had us on front street looking like a fuckin laughing stock. Two, because Lez wasn't saying shit, and just letting him get away with talking reckless. I just sat down in disgust. For the first time, I was ashamed of Lez. I could tell she noticed by the expression on my face and attitude I displayed. That's when she said,

"Bitch wuss your problem? You think all that slick talkin bullshit makes him any more of a pimp and me any less? Am I not here six deep to his four? Did he not get denied, tryna knock me for one of mines? Sticks-N-Stones break bones but his words couldn't knock my bitch. So why should I bust a sweat, stoopin down to his level talkin shit? When I get a bitch, I keep a bitch so fix your face and your fuckin lips. Bitch your outfit cost more than all four of his hoes put together. We're in the V.I.P.I.M.P section, center stage just like him. Poppin bottles and representin."

She was right. The more she talked, the more stupid I felt. I still kinda wished she would have said something, put him in his place and made him look stupid, but I understood why she didn't. Why should she come out of character when she wasn't the one gettin rejected or looking stupid.

"I understand, and I'm sorry for letting my frustration show," I said as I relaxed and got back to my normal self.

"It's alright. Now pop that bottle, pour us a glass, and let's continue enjoying the evening," she said, pointing at the bottle of Cris. The rest of the night went on without a hitch. All-in-all it was a good night. A lot of the other pimps still hated but a few gave us our props.

The Arch Bishop Don "Magic" Juan even said, "If Lex keeps it up we're gonna have to create a new category next year, Female Pimp of the Year."

Six Years Later...

Yeaaa, let's get it! Young Jeezy blared through the speakers in Magic

City as I graced the stage like a prom queen getting ready to accept her crown. By this time, things was changing rapidly in the ATL. Club 112 had been shut down, Buckhead was the new party spot, but the clubs no longer stayed open til 5 am due to a new city ordinance. The community was tired of nigga's shooting, fighting, and stabbing one another after the clubs let out. After the last sticking, they came with the ordinance. That just brought more people to the strip clubs. Now they were liver than ever. Ballers from all over the ATL frequent the club. This is where the D-Boys came to party and do it big, and big is what they did. But nobody did it bigger than Big Meech. Niggas in Atlanta sold dope like the 80's. When it came to trappin, Meech was as big as they came.

The modern day Nino Brown. Meech was the head of BMF (Black Mafia Family). BMF was known in Atlanta, feared and respected by all. When they came to the strip club, they shut the shit down. They were the ones who invented and introduced the infamous "Make it Rain" era to the world. They'd walk in the club with a bullet proof platinum suit case like you see in the Mob movies, with fifty to a hundred racks in all ones inside. Then all night they would throw stacks in the air and watch it rain like money ain't a thang.

These niggas kept a bitch rich. They raised the bar and status quo. A nigga couldn't get away with tryna place a single in a bitches G-string anymore. He would become the laughing stock of the club. You could best believe that everyone would know about it because the DJ would put you on blast.

"Ok, ok, seems we got a new Jack, slow baller that needs ta step to the back. Five dollars in ones ain't gonna get it here playa. This is Magic City, and the magic happens at five hunet or better," The DJ said to a nigga in front of the stage smoking a black, waving a dollar like he was doing it big. Everybody started laughing, pointing fingers and clowning. The nigga felt stupid, as he stepped away from the stage, flipping the DJ off behind the booth. At that moment, BMF entered the club in full force. They all wore black t-shirts with "BMF" on the front. On the back, it said, "The world is BMF's." They walked in the club fifty deep. Right away Meech bought out the bar, which only left the cheap liquor for the rest of the club to drink. Meech sat down in the VIP section and lit a blunt full of purp while the rest of his entourage immediately hit the front of the stage, bottle in hand, making it rain.

On any given night BMF was in the house, a bitch could clock three ta five racks a piece, easy. Also wit me being the top stripper and money maker in the ATL, you can best believe I got broken off proper. After finishing up my two song set and collecting my money off the stage that was scattered everywhere, I went to the back to cool down, freshen up, and get myself together, with one thing on my mind, workin the VIP and BMF to the fullest.

By the time I came back out, there was so much money on the floor throughout the club that bitches was sweeping it up with brooms into large trash bags, literally. I played my position and sashayed towards the VIP section. Gracefully switching my ass from side ta side like an elephant. All eyes was on me, and I ain't talkin Tupac baby. I had on my six inch heels with the custom clear bottoms, filled with tootsie rolls and small candy (sweets). Black latex leather boy shorts with, "Sweets" written across the ass, matching latex bra trimmed with diamond studded rhinestones. My natural hair was bone straight to my back, thanks to my Indian roots.

My dad was black and my mom was Indian, so I had a real unique look about myself, as well as natural pretty long hair, which always did wonders for my money.

"Hey Baby Girl," Meech called out as I stepped into the VIP section.

"Hey Meech, how you doing baby?"

"I'm good. I see you're still looking 'sweet' as ever."

"Thanks, but you know a girl gotta live up to her name at all times." We both laughed as he said, "Amen."

"So how long you staying tonight? Until the 'rain' clears up?"

"Hahahaha...that was a good one shorty. Nah, just made a pit stop before heading out to my final destination. I'm throwing a little shindig at my place in Dunwoody for my man that just got out of prison. I brought him here first, to check out and party with my favorite ladies in the ATL. He just did a six year bid in the Feds, so you know I had ta hit 'em off wit a proper homecoming now that he's out."

"I feel you."

"Here, let me introduce you. Hey Blue!" He called his homie over that was in front of the stage throwing money like rice in a wedding. "Sup homie," he said as he approached with about twenty racks still left over in his hand.

"I have somebody over here I want you to meet. Blue, this is Sweets. Sweets, this is Blue." Blue stuck his hand out and gave a slight smile, just enough to reveal his top and bottom diamond incrusted platinum grill and said, "Nice ta meet you."

I shook his hand, smiled, and said, "Nice ta meet you, too." Blue was about 5'10, medium weight, handsome, with long hair, which he wore in cornrows. He had on a Sean John fit with some all white Air Force Ones. Diamond watch by Jaccob the Jeweler with the Bezel all flooded out, in flawless VVS diamonds shinning all throughout his custom BMF chain and medallion that hung to his stomach. The nigga had "Baller" written all over him.

"So you workin all night Ma, or can I steal you away from the club for a night, on the private tip?" Meech asked. I looked at him with my playful but serious look and said, "Depends, we talkin business or pleasure?"

"Both, I want you to come back to my crib for the after party. You can be the main attraction. After you're done gettin your money, you can just kick it and be eye candy for the event. I know you don't fuck wit niggas, but still being, I feel you'll be a good look for the party."

"How much you payin?"

"Come on now Ma, don't insult me like that. You know I'm a take care of you."

"I never meant to insult you, but business is business. You don't just walk into a restaurant and eat before knowing how much the food is on the menu."

"I do."

"Oh yea, I forgot, you're Big Meech."

"Apparently you did," he said sarcastically but serious. We both laughed then got back down to business.

"Ok then Ma, name your price. Better yet, does this cover it?" He pulled out a brick shape and size amount of money from his brief case and placed it in front of me on the table.

"That's ten stacks ma, but you gotta leave now and stay for the rest of the evening."

Shit, that's a no brainer. "Deal!" I went to the back to change and get my things from the locker I kept my stuff in when I work, came back to the table where BMF was seated and said, "Ready when y'all are." When I got outside and saw the entourage of exotic cars by BMF sitting in the parking lot, my jaw dropped. These nigga's weren't rollin around in Benzes and Beamers. They were rollin brand new Lambos, Ferraris, and Bentley Coupes. Nothing under a hundred grand, and to top it off, Meech was in a Platinum Phantom, with "BMF" on the license plate. It was over a couple million sitting in that parking lot, easy. Meech took my hand and said, "You roll wit me Ma." Four other strippers from the club came along as well, and rolled with Blue, and three other nigga's I didn't know from BMF. We all got in the cars and headed to the after party. Now that was the first mistake I made that night, not taking my own car. The ten stacks had me jaded and not thinking straight like a hit of PCP. I knew better than to leave my car, but when I suggested to Meech I drive, he dismissed the notion. Stated I'd be safe and was in good hands. He said that he'd bring me back and drop me off personally.

$$$$$

"Yea bitch, shake that shit!" One of the niggas in the room yelled as a bitch name Tasha from the club made her booty hop like a six foe in a Doctor Dre video. The bitch was good but had nothing on me. I just sat back and observed and waited till the money came out so I could show this bitch and these nigga's, what a real show look like. Meech had a show room built into his house that looked like a mini full fledge strip club. It had music, lights, a stage and two stripper poles. I planned on putting those ta good use.

"Hey dog, wuss that bitches name right there," a nigga name Mad Man asked Blue, referring to me.

"Oh I just met shawty tonight at the club. I believe her name is...Sweets! Yeah, she hot!" Mad Man was a hit-man for BMF. A straight gunner, and all around crazy mutha fucka. It's rumored that he once shot a man in cold blood for getting his order wrong at a restaurant, but that was nothing compared to the countless stories of what he did to people that crossed BMF. He was heartless and prided himself on the fear and respect he commanded from people who knew him or came in contact wit 'em.

"Hell yeah she hot. I'm a have ta put a bid in and see if I can come out a winner," Mad Man said looking sinister, while eye'n me across the room.

"I think she might be on pussy," Blue stated.

"What gave you that impression?"

"I over heard Meech talking to her at the club and heard him say something about it."

"What a waste. It's always the fine ones too. Tell me, what anotha bitch gon do wit all that ass and pussy?"

"I don't know dog, but apparently something."

"Well, maybe its time foe tha bitch ta see what she's been missing." Mad Man walked over to where I was sitting and took a seat next to mines, on a stool in front of Meech's fully stocked bar.

"Hello, how you doing? My name's M&M, but you can call me M."

"Hi," I responded back and shook his hand.

"May I get you a drink, umm..."

"Sweets."

"Yes, you are." He smiled.

"Yes, thanks, I'll have a Long Island Iced Tea," I responded. That was my second mistake of the evening.

"Fa'sho, comin right up." He walked around the bar and made my island iced tea and a rum & coke for himself. He came back around the bar, handed me my drink, and sat back down. Two girls was on the stage simultaneously working the pole to a Lil Jon and Twister song. By now, nigga's was faded and starting to come out their pockets. Stacks on deck, I thought to myself. *Well, that's my cue. After them two bitches get done with their set, I'm a go handle my business like the boss bitch I am and clean house.* At that moment, my thought process was interrupted by Mad's voice. "You heard me Ma?"

"Huh?"

"I was talkin to you Ma, but you was in a daze, zoned out or something. Cause you didn't hear a word I said."

"Oh I'm sorry, I was daydreaming."

"It's ok, but what I said was, what choo gettin into later on this evening?"

"Going home to my girlfriend." I figured that answer would nicely end the line of questioning and where this conversation was headed, but it didn't. For some reason, nigga's can't never take a hint, especially "Ballers." They walk around like they own the world and can't nobody say no to them, or shut'em down. Ain't nothing worst than a nigga with money. As their pockets get bigger, so does their pride and ego.

"Oh is that right? Well, you know, three is company."

"No, that was a TV Show. In all actuality, two's company, and three's a crowd." I could tell, he didn't like that answer. I took a sip of my drink as he gave me a peculiar look and watched me closely. The look in his eyes actually sent chills down my spine. My thoughts was on, finishing up my drink and getting on stage. I took down the rest of my drink and politely excused myself.

"Well, it was nice meeting you, but if you'll excuse me, I need ta go get changed, so I can get up on stage and dance."

"Alright Ma, go do wut choo gotta do, I'll be checkin you out." I was happy to get away from him. I stepped down from the bar stool and walked towards the bathroom that I knew was down the hall, after noticing two of the other strippers using it to change into their costumes, and walking out before their set. On my way to the rest room, I ran into Meech. He was headed upstairs to his bedroom, with a yellow redbone stripper from around the way named Tay.

"Hey lil Momma, you good?" Meech asked me, puffin a blunt and leading Tay towards the stairs by the hand which lead to his bedroom.

"Yeah, I'm good. I'm just going into the rest room to change clothes and hop on stage."

"Ok Ma, if you need anything just let me know. Make yourself at home. I'll be upstairs for about twenty or thirty minutes. So just do wut choo do fa ma nigga's. I know you know how ta work your shit so as long as you keep it poppin, they'll keep the money droppin."

"Will do." Shit, that was music to my ears. I already made ten stacks just for showing up, and the way BMF nigga's loved ta floss and blow money, I could easily walk outta here with five or ten more. I walked into the restroom when all of a sudden, I began to feel drowsy. I walked over to the sink and my head started spinning. "Uhh, I don't feel so good." I ran the water, put my head near the faucet, and threw some cold water on my face. When I looked up, Mad Man was standing behind me. That's when I blacked out.

"Yea bitch, you enjoyed your drink? Daddy got choo, don't worry bout a thang. I'm ah take care of you just fine."

This dirty mutha fucka drugged me, I thought to myself as I fell in and out of consciousness. I could hear him talking, but I couldn't respond. Next thing I knew, he picked me up and took me to a bedroom down the hall. The last thing I remembered was him removing my clothes.

$$$$$

"Oh yeah bitch, I'm bout ta show you wut choo been missing in ya life." I placed her down on the bed after removing all her clothes, pulled down my pants, and began stroking my dick. The sight of her hour glass shape and perfect titties gave me an instant erection. My dick grew to its full ten and half inches. I pulled her panties off to reveal her smooth, perfectly shaven, fat monkey. I couldn't wait ta feel her insides. The bitch was passed out and incoherent, like a sedated patient in the hospital, on the operating table during surgery. I sucked on her nipples as I held her titties firm. Her body must have had a mind of its own because, even though she was passed out, her nipples still got hard. I nibbled and sucked on her breast until I couldn't take it no more. By this time, my dick was rock hard like a cement slab and needed instant gratification. I slid my hand down in between her thighs and noticed that her pussy was still dry. I pushed her legs to the side spread eagle and began to massage her pussy.

I used my first two fingers to spread and open her lips as I gently made small circles with my thumb on her clit. I spit on my hand and rubbed her pussy to get it lubricated. I couldn't wait no longer, I had to have her. I grabbed the shaft of my penis and worked the head of my dick inside her pussy and limp body. I pushed hard with enough pressure for her pussy to engulf and take my dick inside her completely. Her inner core was warm and moist.

Her pussy felt tighter than the glove that helped O.J. Simpson get acquitted for murder. I long stroked her deep and slow, working her pussy like a Marksman. The shit was feeling so good, I almost bust a nut pre maturely. I couldn't bust yet, I had ta savor the moment. I took my mind off the pussy and how good it felt for a moment ta bring down my excitement. It worked, at which time I put the pussy in over drive. I was banging up against her side walls like a "Mad Man" in a nut house, pun intended.

I pulled my dick out of her semi wet pussy and flipped her over. She was now laying on her stomach. Her ass sat up like the fifth wheel on an old school Caddi. I spread her ass cheeks opened and spit in between her crack. Her booty hole was tight and I could tell it had never been tampered with before, until now. I grabbed a hold of my dick, and rammed it in her ass, like I use ta do them punks in prison. All ten and a half inches. This semi woke the bitch out of her stupor as she screamed,

"No! Don't!" Then passed back out. That shit only turned me on more. I smacked her ass as I drilled the bitch like a tool bit, hoping she woke back up. I smacked her harder, leaving a red print on her ass, still to no avail. I was fuckin her so hard her rectum started to bleed. I pulled out, spun her around and shoved my dick in her mouth, even though she was passed out. Forcing her to taste her own ass, blood and pussy.

The shit and sight before my eyes got me excited. I felt myself finna cum. I grabbed a fist full of her hair, forcing her head back and mouth open wider. I fucked her mouth while grabbing her head with two hands and forcing her to bob on my dick like a boxer.

"Oh yeah, I'm bout ta cum bitch." I pulled my dick out of her mouth, and busted a fat load all over her face. The tip of my dick got sensitive, as I rubbed the remaining cum off the head of my dick using her drugged, incapacitated lips. After I was done having my fun with this whore, who hung like a rag doll, I knew I couldn't just leave her in my man's bed and crib in the state she was in. So I grabbed her shit, put her clothes back on, picked her up, and walked her to my car.

I placed the bitch in the back of my double R, and laid her across the seat. I walked around the front, opened the driver side door, got in and started it up. "Damn, now where am I gonna take this bitch?" I asked myself, while driving down the 75 freeway towards Atlanta. Then it dawned on me where I could drop the bitch off at. I drove and got off on the exit ta take me towards "The Underground Atlanta." Then I took the back streets to Piedmont Park where I had decided to dump this hoe off. When I got to the park, it was dark and not a person in sight.

Perfect, I thought to myself as I pulled up, stopped the ride, got out, and drugged the bitch out the backseat. The hoe was still dazed and confused. I placed her on a bench in the park like a bum sleeping the night away before the morning sun. I made sure no one was around or saw me, jumped back in my Range Rover, and bounced.

$$$$$

"Oh, I don't feel so good." I woke up laying on a park bench with a splitting headache. *What happened, and how did I get here?* I asked and thought to myself as I looked around unable to figure out, or remember what happened the night before. Last thing I remember was drinking at the bar with "M" then going to the rest room to change into my…*DANCE OUTFIT!* That's when I frantically searched for my Louie bag I had taken to the party, suddenly remembering about the ten stacks I had hidden at the bottom under my dance clothes.

"Fuck!" My bag was missing. All I had, was the clothes on my back. I tried to stand up when I felt a sharp pain from my butt that instantly sat me back down. My pussy was sore as well. When I put two and two together got four and realized I had to have been raped. I wobbled to the woman's rest room in the park, went into one of the stalls, and locked the door. When I pulled down my pants and panties to examine myself I noticed a horrid sight, blood! Blood everywhere. All along the inside of my panties like I just had my period or something. My pussy was swollen and my ass was on fire. I felt violated, used, abused and pissed the fuck off.

Whoever did this to me was gonna pay. They done fucked with the wrong bitch. I took off my panties and flushed them down the toilet, went to the sink, grabbed some paper towels and washed my ass and pussy as best I could, got myself together, and made my way home. When I came out of the rest room, I saw a guy just finish up talking on his cellphone.

"Excuse me sir, but may I use your cellphone to make a quick call? It's an emergency and I'd really appreciate it."

"Not a problem," He responded and handed me the phone. I called Lez to come pick me up, without getting into too much detail on why I was stranded in Piedmont Park without my car and no money. "I'll explain what happened when you pick me up." I told her, as I finished the conversation and hung up the phone.

"Thanks Sir," I said as I handed the man back his cellphone.

"Not a problem" he responded, smiled and walked off. I sat back down on one of the park benches as I waited for Lez to pick me up. Going over the events from the night before, doing my best to remember. That's when pictures of Mad Man entered my head, and glimpses of him raping me. Flashes of him on top of me, flashes of me screaming "NO!" as he fucked me in the ass, flashes of him entering the bathroom, standing behind me, right before I passed out.

"OH SHIT, it was him!" I said out loud as it all started to come back to me. I still couldn't remember everything, Like how I ended up in Piedmont Park on a bench. But I remembered the important shit, like who fuckin raped and used me like a fuckin dog. The more I remembered, the more pissed off I got. I never felt so violated in my life. Payback's a bitch and her name was Sweets. Lez picked me up and drove me back to Magic City to pick up my car. On the way there, I explained to her what happened to me the night before. At first she was concerned and sympathetic. Then her sympathy turned to anger the more I spoke.

"Bitch, how could you be so careless and stupid? You know damn well you never go to a party in someone else's ride and leave yours nowhere near the place the party's taken place. What the fuck I bought you a car for if you ain't gonna drive the mutha fucka when you pose to? And why the fuck you actin brand new like a bitch that don't know her shit? You fuckin know better than to be drinkin on a call, letting some other mutha fucka make you a drink, or leaving your glass unattended. That shit was stupid as fuck! But the thing that kills me the most is, you let a mutha fucka get choo foe your money. Bitch you should shoot yourself for being so dumb." After Lez finished talking, I felt lower than a three year old baby next to Shaq. What could I say, she was right. All I could do was put my head down in disappointment, like a child who had just fucked up in school and was getting scolded by his momma. This shit just fueled my anger more.

Lez turned on MLK, drove passed the Greyhound station, and pulled into Magic City. The parking lot was empty, with the exception of my car, which was still sitting where I left it.

"Look Sweets, I don't ever wanna hear no shit like this again. In this game, mistakes cause lives. You gotta be on point at all times like the Empire State Building. When you slip in this game you fall hard, so we can't afford ta fuck up. Here take this." Lez opened up and reached into her glove compartment and pulled out a shiny 38. Special. "I want you protected at all times, and if a nigga ever try ta take advantage of you again, you blow his fuckin dick off. Once you leave here, go home and get cleaned up, then go to the clinic and get checked out. Make sure you get tested for everything."

I took the gun and held it in my right hand by the handle, finger on the trigger, rotating it side ta side admiring the weapon I knew I would use to ultimately kill Mad Man. I placed the gun in my pocket, told Lez I was sorry, understood completely what she was saying, and that it wouldn't happen again. I opened the door to her 745Li and got out. Before closing the door behind me I told her, "I'll see you at the house, or later on after I come back from the doctor's."

"Alright Sweets, holla if you need me."

"Ok ma."

"Peace."

"Peace."

I watched her pull out of the parking lot and make a right towards the freeway as I walked towards my car, hit the alarm and unlock on my keychain, and got inside. I pulled down the visor ta get a look at myself in the mirror. I looked like shit. My ass was still hurting like I had just shitted out a basketball and two watermelons. I couldn't wait ta get home, and into my bathtub. *I hope this mutha fucka didn't give me AIDS or no bullshit,* I thought to myself as I placed the visor back up, started the car, and drove off.

$$$$$

2 weeks later...

"Shake wut ya Momma gave ya, Shake Shake wut ya Momma gave ya!" I hopped my ass to the music that was blaring out the club speakers. Slow grinding the stage floor while nigga's threw money. Just as I finished up my first set and stepped off the stage, I saw Mad Man walk in the club with two nigga's I recognized from BMF. Instantly rage filled my body like lava in a volcano. I went to the back and changed into my street clothes. When I came out of the dressing room my boss was standing by the door, keeping an eye on the club and making sure no one tried to sneak in the back and fuck with the girls while they were getting changed. I told him I had an emergency situation of a personal matter to attend to and would have to leave early.

He said okay, smiled and said, "See you tomorrow." I inconspicuously stepped out the club without being noticed and went straight to my car. I threw my stripper bag with my clothes in it in the back seat, opened the glove compartment, and retrieved my 38. Mad Man Killa. Yeah, that's what I named my gun, and tonight, it was gonna live up to its name. I sat back anxiously in my seat and waited for MadMan to exit the club. I waited for an hour which felt like two, due to my anticipation. *I can't wait ta peel this nigga's cap*, I thought ta myself as I watched Mad Man and his homies coming out the club, half drunk and slippin. Little did he know that he was being watched by the female grim reaper and I couldn't wait ta send him to meet his maker. I watched them exit towards the parking area. Mad Man gave his two homies dap and walked towards an all black Porsche Cayenne. The other two got in a Benz Wagon and left the parking lot.

I watched Mad Man get in his mini SUV, spark a blunt which was still noticeable through his light tint, start the engine, and take off. I started my engine as well and followed not too close behind. I made sure I stayed at least two cars back to not let on that he was being followed. We drove down the I-20 Freeway and headed towards Marietta. The entire drive, all I could think about was killin this mutha fucka. We got off Exit 17 and took the back streets through Mableton to Bankhead Courts, the Projects, also known as The P.J's. I knew that it would be hard to get him in the PJ's because there was only one way in and one way out. Not only that, but nigga's in the PJ's stayed on point and was highly active with the business. Almost everyday they were with the gun play. I knew they would recognize me as not being from around there from the jump, so I parked my car across the street in front of the entrance and chilled.

I'll just wait till he comes out and finish what I set out to do, even if it takes all night and till the sun comes up, I thought to myself as I laid my seat back and clutched my pistol in hand, eager and anxious ta peel this nigga's cap. I waited for about 45 minutes when I saw him exiting the courts. He banged a right and I followed at a safe distance. We got on the freeway headed north and got off on Paces Ferry Rd. He pulled into Steak-N-Shake and parked in the back. Not to make it obvious that he was being followed, I parked across the street.

I watched him get out of his SUV and walk inside the restaurant to order his food. This gave me time to make my move and post up. I crept in the parking lot like Dough Boy from Boyz-N-The Hood and hid behind his Cayenne, waiting ta ambush the mutha fucka that took what was sacred to me. I started to get nervous like a kid watching the clock in school before a three o'clock fight with the local bully, as I watched him leave the restaurant, burgers in tow, headed towards his truck. Just as he got close enough to put his keys in the door, I leaped from behind the SUV like a lion on a Gazelle, gun drawn and ready for murder. "Ready ta die mutha fucka?" I said, gun aimed at his forehead as I approached.

Oh shit, that's the bitch I raped the other night at Blue's Party. "Bitch who you pointing that gun at shawty? You better put that shit away before you hurt yourself."

"Hurt this mutha fucka!" I pointed the gun at his dick and balls and fired a shot. **POP!**

"Ahhhh, you bitch!" He fell to the floor clutching the spot where his penis use to lie, as blood began to soak the front of his pants.

"And watch who the fuck you call a bitch nigga. Don't worry, where you're going, you won't have any need for that little dick of yours."

"It wasn't too little when I was ramming it in your ass you fuckin hoe!" That was the last thing that came out his mouth. **POP! POP! POP!** One in the head and two in the chest. He laid in a fetal position in his own blood, clutching his dick area. At that moment I lost track of time. It seemed like everything was moving in slow motion. I got myself together and ran back towards my car. As I was just about to leave the parking lot, a police cruiser pulled up right in front of me to a screeching halt.

"Freeze!" an officer said as he got out the car, gun drawn, kneeling behind his door, using it as a shield, while aiming his gun at my chest. "Drop the weapon!" I dropped my 38. Revolver and put my hands up towards the sky like I was praising Jesus. "Get on the ground slow, lay on your stomach, and put your hands behind your back."

I complied and did as he said as his partner got out the car, gun drawn as well, approached me cautiously and cuffed me up. At that moment I knew that this was the beginning of the end of my life. Six months later I was found guilty and convicted of pre meditated murder by a jury of my peers. Lez was devastated. She felt guilty and like it was somewhat partly her fault for giving me the gun that was ultimately used to take Mad Man's life.

I didn't blame her. I told her it wasn't her fault and one way or another, with or without the gun she gave me, I would have killed him when given the chance. A week later I was sent to State Prison to serve a life sentence. When I first got to prison Lez held me down, wrote and visited me every weekend. Slowly but surely as time went on, one by one, that all stopped. First the letters, then the visits. Actually, the money was first.

She stopped sending and putting money on my books four months into my sentence. By the fifth month she had stopped writing, and by the six she had fell off completely. I guess like they say, "Out of sight, out of mind." And to make matters worse, when I first arrived to prison I took an AIDS test which came back HIV Positive. The Doctor said the test I took on the streets probably came back negative because it was too soon after the rape had occurred. So now my life sentence had turned into a death sentence. Maybe that was the reason Lez fell off, or maybe she just looked at it as she no longer had any use for me. Either way, she was no longer in the picture or apart of my life. Now I would leave the game the same way I came in...Alone.

CHAPTER 4 THE CHRONICLES OF GREEN EYES

Today was one of the worst days of my life. Up until today, things had been going great, but today was the day that my world came crashing down right before my eyes. The past five or six years I had been with a pimp named Jackpot. I met him back in the mid 90's in Hollywood one night while working the track on sunset.

I was looking for a way out of my current situation with a pimp named Payday, who was more of a gang banger than a pimp. That was a turn off for me. Not only that, but he was very abusive towards his other hoes and I knew it would only be a matter of time before I experienced the same fate. So I left Payday and chose Jackpot. Jackpot was a real pimp and took care of his hoes and business. When I met him, he had a Japanese hoe named Yuki. We hit it off right away and took the track by storm. Wifey and I prided ourselves at being top notch money makers. We rarely came in with anything under a rack. Life was good and getting better by the minute. Before you knew it, Daddy was four deep and getting money. Now it was me, Yuki, a black girl named Sunshine, and another white girl named Lisa. We were Daddy's main bitches, but through the years, things would slowly begin to fall apart. Lisa got over protective and possessive of Daddy and started to get jealous of the rest of us and our relationships. This caused a lot of petty arguments and cat fights between us. That only made things worse and ultimately ran Sunshine off. Sunshine leaving behind Lisa's bullshit pissed Daddy off and put a strain on their relationship, so one day Daddy had had enough of Lisa's bullshit, fired and threw her out.

Which brings us to the present, and like I said earlier, the worst day of my life. This morning, Vice and San Diego PD Special Crime Unit raided our house. They said they had a couple of Daddy's ex-bitches that was willing to testify against him in court and take the stand. They arrested him on pimping and pandering charges and me and Yuki for prostitution. The case against Yuki and I was weak and just a misdemeanor, so we easily made bail and got out right away, but Daddy wasn't so lucky. He was being held on $500,000 bail and had a special stipulation from the judge and prosecutor that states that he has to show proof of where the bail money came from, in the event that he was able to post it.

There was no need for that stipulation anyway because when the police hit the house, they confiscated all his money that was found to be used against him as evidence. Lucky for us, Daddy was smart enough to have prepaid a bails bondsman and lawyer with a nice size retainer just in case a day like today would ever come. Mine and Yuki's bail was only a couple thousand a piece so Daddy arranged for us to be bailed out immediately. Which brings us to here.

"Girl, what we gon do now?" I asked Yuki, standing in front of what used to be our house but was now a Police taped up, No Trespassing view of its former self.

"Exactly what Daddy would expect us to do, keep working, stack money, take care of him and business until he comes home," she responded back.

"I don't know if I can do this by myself."

"Bitch, pull yourself together. How would Daddy feel hearing you talk like that? Save that shit for them weak bitches who Daddies didn't teach 'em shit. You been in this game and family way too long ta be falling apart now."

"I know, you right. It's just, everything happened so fast and I still haven't processed it all yet. Its like we went from sugar ta shit."

"Don't worry girl, we have each other, and as long as we stick together and remain focused, we'll be alright. Come on girl. Let's go make some money and find a place to stay for the evening."

We left and made our way to the one place a bitch could go from zero to a hundred with no car in seconds flat…the track! We went to El Cajon Blvd in East San Diego (East Daygo), a prominent track where a bitch could always get money. We hit the blade in full stride and did what we had to do to maintain, take care of Daddy, stay afloat and survive.

I made $800 and Yuki made $700. By then, the vice was rollin thick and riding down hard on the hoes, see and how it was thursday…vice night! So we found a little cheap hotel off the blade and took it in.

"I'm a run down to the Mexican Restaurant and get a Carne Asada Burrito. You want me to bring you back something?" Yuki asked.

"Yeah, bring me back some rolled tacos with sour cream and extra cheese," I responded back.

"Okay, I'll be right back," Yuki grabbed a twenty out of her purse, put on her shoes and coat, and went to the taco shop. While she was gone, I jumped in the shower and rinsed the trick smell off me that all hoes have after a good night's work, got out, toweled off, put on my boy shorts and a long t-shirt of Daddy's to get comfortable. Yuki came back with the food and some weed she had copped from a small time D-Boy at the corner on her way back to the hotel. It was only a nickel, but it would surely suffice. We ate and smoked our stress away. We both missed our folks. We were grateful to have one another. The next morning, I woke up to my cellphone ringing. "Hello," I answered. It was one of my sugar daddies from Oceanside. He owned a high end car lot and paid me a thousand dollars every time I saw him, plus a weekly allowance.

"Hey Sugar. How you doing, you missed me?" I put on my seductive voice. "Yeah, you can see me today. What time you talking?" He said he wanted to meet around 3 o'clock.

"That's fine. You gotta pick me up though, because I don't have my car." He asked me what happened to my car and why I didn't have one to drive. I told him I'd explain it to him later. He agreed ta pick me up. I gave him the directions to the hotel, said good-bye, and ended the conversation.

"That was my sugar daddy from Oceanside. You know the one that owns the car lot?" I said to Yuki.

"Oh yeah, the one with all the money that doesn't look a day over thirty?" She responded.

"Yeah, that's the one. He's about ta pick me up at three. Maybe I can play on his sympathy and work 'em out of a car or something."

"I heard that, cause this bus and trolley shit ain't the move."

"Girl, you got that right. Feel like a bitch done went from peanut butter to peanuts." We both started laughing and got up ta get ready to start our day. I jumped in the shower first since I only had a couple of hours to get ready before my sugar daddy picked me up. When I got out of the shower and came out of the bathroom, Yuki was hanging up the phone. "I just got the info and visiting times to see Daddy at the county jail. They transferred him to Baily. We can go see him this weekend."

"Definitely!" The news had me excited like a kid receiving his first bike on Christmas. Two days later, we went to see Daddy. I was sad that it was behind a glass. I thought I would be able to sit, talk and touch 'em.

"How's my bitches doing?" Daddy asked, while holding two phone receivers simultaneously to his ear to talk to us both.

"We're fine," we responded back.

"How's business? I know yawl still working and gettin my money, right?"

"Daddy, you don't even have to ask. You know we got you," Yuki responded. I shook my head in agreeance.

"Ok bitches, look. Dis what I want yawl to do. My pimp patna Supreme, has an escort service. Since he owns the mutha fucka, he can set the rules as he sees fit. Now for the most part, he runs a pretty smooth and legit establishment, but since he's my patna, he's willing to do me a solid favor and let you bitches work without your escort permits, see and how you bitches got 'em confiscated by them toy cop mutha fuckas when they raided the tilt. I already holla'd at 'em so he knows wuss up."

"Cool Daddy, cause the track been real slow. I've been making most of my money from my sugar daddy in Oceanside, and Yuki's been making hers from a few of her regulars."

"Yeah I know. Right about now the blade is hotter than a firecracker on the 4th of July, and colder than the snow in Alaska and the air in a winter sky. That's why I set it up for you bitches to get that high class money that yawl already accustomed to. When yawl leave here, I want yawl to go downstairs and max out my books. From there on, make sure I have two hunet on my shit at all times. Nothing less. That's the max I can have on my books."

"Ok Daddy, we got you," I responded.

"I hope so, cuz right now you bitches are gonna have to show and prove and perform like a racehorse in the Kentucky Derby. I know yawl use ta me having the rings and holding it down, providing the much needed guidance that a hoe needs to function and maintain daily at full capacity, but shit don't stop cuz the pimp got popped. Yawl gotta think like me now. All the game that yawl soaked up while being with me, yawl have ta now implement into your day to day routine. Get money or die hoe'n cuz failure's not an option. Yawl understand me?"

"Yes Daddy," we both responded. By the time Daddy was done talking and setting forth the instructions he expected us to follow, visiting time was over.

"Ok, get ready to wrap it up. You got five minutes," blared over the loud speaker, indicating that visiting time was almost done.

"Dang, that was quick, Daddy."

"I know, Green Eyes. They only give us thirty ta 45 minutes and time flies when you're spitting game." Three minutes later, the phone clicked off and I could no longer hear my Daddy, nor could he hear me. I blew him a kiss and hug through the glass that separated the visitors from inmates and said my goodbyes as I watched him walk down the stairs that led him back to his housing unit and cell.

For the next few weeks, I was on my grind, then life took a turn for the worst. One day, my sugar daddy said he wanted me to come over because he was bored, lonely and wanted to party. Of course I told him he would have to pay to play, which he didn't have a problem with in the least. What I didn't know was what his definition of "party" was.

"Hey baby doll, how you been?" My sugar daddy, Mark, greeted me as I walked into his house.

"Fine, I can't complain."

"Make yourself comfortable, I have some pizza in the kitchen I just ordered. Would you like a slice or something to drink?"

"I'm fine on the pizza. I ate before I came over, but I'll take a glass of juice if you have any."

"How's apple?"

"That's fine."

"Coming right up." He went into the kitchen to pour me a glass of juice while I took off my coat, sat down on the sofa in his living room and got comfortable. When Mark came back into the living room, he had my juice in one hand and a silver serving platter in the other. At first I couldn't make out what was on the tray. I had just assumed it was a slice of pizza. Once he sat down, I realized pizza was what it wasn't. Mark handed me the juice and put the tray on the table. The tray had a white crystal like substance on top of it.

"What is that, Cocaine?" I asked with the *I know you don't think I'm finna do that* look and voice.

"No, this is Meth."

Shit, that's even worse, I thought to myself, as I looked at the sugar like substance in disgust.

"I told you I wanted to party."

"Well, I didn't know that was the type of party you was referring to. I'm sorry honey, but I don't do dope. At the most, I smoke weed. At the least, I drink alcohol. Anything more than that, I'm a have to pass."

"Well I don't wanna get high alone, that's no fun. What if I paid you an extra thousand dollars just for partying with me, on top of the two thousand I was already gonna give you just for coming over?" Now this was how a lot of hoes got turned on to drugs in the game. Greedy and desperate to make as much money as they could, while letting all common sense go out the window like a cat burglar in the night. And now I was falling into the same trap, because against my better judgment, I reluctantly agreed. In my mind I was thinking, *shit one time ain't gonna hurt nothing. No way am I gonna get hooked. And three thousand dollars is, three thousand dollars. What kind of reputable hoe would turn down and walk away from that much money? Shit, not me. It's hard times right now and I need it all.* I wasn't comfortable with smoking the dope, so I asked Mark if I could snort it like powdered coke. He told me yeah and fixed me up a couple lines, one for each nostril. He rolled up a dollar bill and snorted a line first, then passed the tray and bill to me. I grabbed the bill, put it to my nose, leaned over the tray, and snorted a line. It burned my nose with an instant sizzling sensation.

I felt the crystal drip down the back of my throat, a single tear left my eye like when you first wake up in the morning. I snorted the other line in the same manner in my left nostril. By the time I felt the drip hit the back of my throat again, I was high. I never felt anything like the way this drug made me feel in my life. I was amped. My heart felt like it was beating a mile a minute and before long, my mouth and body was moving just as fast. I couldn't stop talking or moving. I loved the way the crystal made me feel. From the moment I snorted that first line, just like so many other hoes before me, I was hooked. This was my first time ever doing crystal meth, but unfortunately, it wouldn't be my last.

"So, how you feel honey?" Mark asked me smiling as he watched the drug take control of my body.

"Fuckin great!" I answered back.

"Well, if you think you like it and feel good now, watch how you feel when I eat your pussy and ravage you." He stood up, stuck out his hand for mines and said, "Shall we?" I grabbed his hand as he helped me up and lead me to his bedroom. We undressed and got into bed. Now I'm a keep it real with you. I never let a trick make love, kiss, or get too personal with me. When I lay down with him. Sugar daddy or not, it's all business. But this time around, the drug had me vulnerable, doing and allowing things I normally wouldn't. Mark started off kissing my neck, which felt so good I didn't dare tell him to stop. He then proceeded to make small kisses towards my breasts. He grabbed my left tit with his firm hands and massaged it so gently as he sucked and nibbled on my nipples like a newborn baby. The meth within my body had my nipples extra sensitive.

"Ooh, don't stop! Yeah, right there. Suck my tits baby." He stuck his index finger in his mouth to lubricate it. He then pinched and played with the right nipple as he continued to nibble and suck the left. I loved the feeling of pain and pleasure. I couldn't take it no more. If he could make me feel like this just from sucking my tits, then how would it feel once he sucked my pussy? The thought alone got my pussy wet like a leaking faucet.

I pushed his head down south. The crystal had me overly aggressive. It brought out the true whore in me. Mark started off teasing me, kissing my inner thighs as he spread my legs apart like a pair of scissors and licked my pearl tongue. I arched my back as he spread my lips apart and made small circles with his tongue on my clitoris. The feeling and sensation sent vibrations through my whole body. "Oh God, yes! Suck this pussy! Ooh I'm so fuckin wet!"

He stuck two fingers inside my pussy and finger banged me like a school girl as he ate my pussy. I gyrated and threw my pussy at 'em while gripping the back of his head with both hands as he ate my pussy like a Thanksgiving dinner. The meth was bringing out the savage in me. I didn't even fuck my folks like this, let alone my tricks, but the crystal had thrown all my inhibitions out the window. I was hornier than a porn star getting gang fucked by four dudes in a porno flick. "Ooh I wanna feel your dick inside me."

"You wanna feel this dick, bitch?"

"Ooh yeah!"

"You want me to stuff my cock inside your wet pussy?"

"Yes baby. Don't make me wait much longer. I need to feel that hard dick inside me." By this point, my pussy was throbbing and aching for some "hard" attention. He grabbed the shaft of his dick and rammed it inside me. By now, we were fucking like a couple of porn stars in a XXX movie. All that making love shit went straight out the window. We were no longer in control. The crystal had taken over.

He flipped me over onto my stomach and stuck his dick back inside me, doggy style, my favorite position. I arched my back face down ass up so he could go deep. And deep is what he did! He fucked me so hard I thought I felt him in my uterus.

"Ah! Ah! Oh! Ah! Fuck me!" He smacked me on my ass so hard that it left a red hand print on my left cheek. That just turned me on more! I started bucking like a horse in a rodeo. I felt myself about ta cum. "Oh my God I'm bout ta cum! Don't stop! Harder! Harder!" He picked up his pace and started drilling me like an oil well.

"Oooooh shit! Shit, shit!" I screamed as I squirted and came all over his dick. He pulled out and sucked up my sweet nectar. He licked his lips in satisfaction and put his dick back inside me.

"Come here bitch and ride this dick!" I never saw this side of Mark before. He was overly aggressive and it was totally turning me on. He rolled on his back and I straddled him like a horse in a western, reverse cowgirl. This was my specialty. This was the position I used ta make a trick cum in sixty-seconds or less. I rode his dick like a mechanical bull in a honky tonk bar. He grabbed ahold of my waist and started thrusting his dick inside me as I made large circles with my body like I was a belly dancer or little girl playing with a hula hoop. I grinded on his dick as his pubic hairs caused friction on my clit, which allowed me to cum for a second time. By now, Mark was ready ta cum as well.

"Oh shiiit! I'm about ta cum!" He said as I watched his toes curl and his dick tighten up, jerk, throb and spit.

"Yeah cum for me. cum for your bitch." I jumped off his dick just as he was letting loose and jacked him off until nut squirted out and gushed all over the place like an erupting volcano. I played with his balls and the tip of his dick as the cum ran down the sides of my hand. By now, his dick was sensitive and he would squirm and jump every time I touched the head of his penis. I loved doing that to men after they came. I did that with Daddy all the time. What I couldn't believe was that I was doing it with him.

The drug had me stupid and not thinking straight. Not only did I just fuck a trick like he was my man, but I also didn't make him use a condom. Now how fuckin dumb was that? For the next few weeks, I saw Mark on a regular basis, and every time we saw each other, we got high on crystal meth and fucked each other's brains out.

Mark had asked me if I would like to stay with him until I got back on my feet and found my own place. Normally, I would have denied such a request. Never would I have even fathomed the thought of moving in with a trick, but by now, the crystal had taken a toll on me. I was way past the ability to make responsible decisions. I saw moving in as a way of getting high everyday. Not only that, but Yuki was beginning to get suspicious.

I had already dropped fifteen pounds and since I wasn't no big girl to begin with, it was very noticeable. I just told her it was due to the stress of Daddy being locked up. I knew she wasn't stupid and probably had her doubts, but she wanted to give me the benefit of the doubt and went against her better judgment. That's what we do when we love someone that's fuckin up, we feed ourselves bullshit and lie to ourselves like we lost all common sense and no longer know any better. But I knew it wouldn't be long before she figured out exactly what I was doing and quit second guessing herself. So I told her I was gonna move in with my sugar daddy so that I could stack more chips for Daddy and quit wasting money on hotels that could be going towards him.

I don't think she bought it, but could tell that my mind was made up, so she told me to be careful, stay in touch, and know that she was always here for me. She said since I was gonna move in with my sugar daddy, that she was gonna move back in with her ex roommate that she use to live with before she met Daddy, that way she could stack more chips and quit wasting money on hotels as well. We hugged and promised to be there for one another, stay focused and never give up on Daddy. That would be the last day I saw Yuki.

By now, I was a full blown addict. I graduated from snorting to smoking. I no longer worked to stack chips. I now worked to stay high. I had also became what is known in the tweaker world as a "picker." These were people that got high on crystal, then picked their face so bad that it began to cause sores, craters, and acne like bumps. My shit was so bad it looked like I had chicken pox or the measles. I was a mess. I knew it too, but for some reason, couldn't do shit about it.

I started to alienate myself from everyone I knew and loved who wasn't getting high for fear that if they saw me, they would judge me and pull my coat to what I was doing. I wasn't ready to look myself in the mirror and face what I was doing wrong. I hadn't seen Yuki in weeks. The last time I saw Daddy, he knew I was fuckin up right away. He asked me if I was on dope, but I denied it. I felt so ashamed. That was the first time I ever lied to my folks. After that visit, I knew I could never face or sit with him in the same room again. Not while I was on drugs. So after that visit, I never went back to see him. I feel bad about it now, but at the time all I cared about was myself. Me and me only. Well, not just me. Me and my best friend, Crystal. Crystal Meth. I was a full blown tweaker, in the worst way. All I did was smoke dope all day, and even more at night. I would go seven days straight with no sleep before my body finally gave in and crashed.

That's when I would fall in a coma like sleep for three days, wake up, and repeat the cycle all over again. I was killing myself slowly, on a collision course to hell and early grave. I was in an airplane with no pilot or parachute and going down fast. The straw that broke the camel's back was the day I got caught in a stolen car with a trick and a half ounce of dope.

"Shit, shit, shit! The cops are behind us!" A trick I had just copped some dope from said as he looked into his rearview mirror. Before I could react or think what to do with the dope, the police had turned on the cherries and ordered us to pull over.

"Turn the car off and throw the keys out the window, then slowly put your hands out the window," the officer ordered, gun drawn, speaking through the bullhorn. The trick turned the car off and did as he was ordered.

"Driver, take your right hand and slowly open the door from the outside while keeping your left hand in the air." Once again, the trick did as he was ordered.

"Now, exit the vehicle slowly with your hands above your head and walk backwards towards my patrol car." By this time, three backup police cars had arrived to assist in the arrest. The trick took about eight steps back before the officer said, "Okay, stop right there. Now get down on your knees and lay flat on your stomach with your hands spread in front of you." He did as instructed. Next, the officer put me through the same drill and ordered me to do the same. He then walked over, cuffed us up, then threw us both in separate cars. At this point, I still didn't have a clue as to what we were being arrested for. After they placed us in the squad car, they searched our vehicle. That's when they found the half ounce of crystal. I left it in my purse in the front seat, not thinking to hide it somewhere better when we got pulled over. A place that wouldn't have linked it directly to me.

Shit, why didn't I just stick that shit in my pussy, I thought to myself, but in the heat of the moment, one never thinks fast enough when it comes to the po-po's. Just look at them fools on "Cops" that get pulled over and start telling on themselves long before the cop even asks the first question. I knew better than that, though. Once the cop told me I had the right to remain silent, that's exactly what I did.

"Ma'am, did you know that you was riding in a stolen vehicle?" the officer asked me as I sat in the back seat of his squad car cuffed.

"No, I didn't sir."

"How about the bag of crystal we found in the purse in the front seat with your ID in it?" Conversation over. From that point on, I was silent. They transferred me to Los Colines County Jail in Santee, and the trick to Downtown Central Booking. Come ta find out, the trick had stolen the car from his ex-girlfriend a week ago because she was seeing and dating someone new. You know how it go, sucka for love ass square shit. That slit your wrist over a bitch shit.

At first they tried to charge me with grand theft auto as well, but once the facts came out and the trick cleared me of any wrong doing, they dropped the charge. But as for the dope, that one stuck. Seeing how they found it in a purse with my ID inside, directly where I was sitting on the passenger side of the vehicle. Shit, wasn't no way I was gonna beat that shit. Ray Charles could see I was guilty, blind folded in the dark with Stevie Wonder to back him up. No way could I go to trial. There wasn't a jury alive that wouldn't convict me. I just had to sit and wait my chance to cop out to a good deal.

This was my first offense and in Daygo, you usually get a get out of jail free card on your first offense. Typically a program, probation, or community service. Sometimes, all of thee above. But the next time you catch a case, its county jail or the state pen. One thing good about being locked up was a drug addict could detox. It was better than any program or NA because there wasn't no leaving after a meeting and getting high. It was sit in your cell, lay on your bunk, and think about whatever you did to get locked up.

I sat in jail for three days before I got my first court appearance. I didn't have enough money to bail out so I had to stay until my next court date, which was in about a month. During my time locked up, I began to gain my weight back. As my weight was coming back, so was my mind. I started to return to myself, the person I was before I started tweaking. The more I got back to my normal self, the more guilty I felt for abandoning my folks when he needed me the most. I decided to write him a letter. I knew it was a long shot, but thought fuck it. What could it hurt? If he didn't write back, I would understand completely.

Daddy was still locked up fighting his case. When I wrote him, I came clean about my drug use and told him I was too ashamed to come around him while I was in the state I was in. To my surprise, he wrote back saying he could forgive, but would never forget. From there we reconciled and started writing each other frequently. Things began to feel like old times. It felt good to have my Daddy back in my life. A couple of weeks later, I went to court and was happy to find out that the DA was willing to drop my drug charge to a simple possession instead of sales and send me to an outpatient program which meant, if I took the deal, I'd go home today.

As I'm sure you know, that was a no brainer. I signed quicker than a crack head's check at the first of the month, thinking about all the crack he's gonna buy after it's cashed. That night I was released and back on the streets. When a person gets released from jail or prison, the feeling you have inside is indescribable. Its like being reborn, experiencing new things that the average person takes for granted day ta day like it's your first.

Simple things like smelling a flower, walking to the park and watching the sunset, or enjoying a cold ice cream cone. Yeah, when you're fresh out, you realize for the first time in your life that it's the little things that count, but one has a funny way of forgetting all that once you've been home for a while. You tend to forget that your worst day on the streets was better than your best day in prison. So needless to say, after about a week back on the streets, I was back getting high and fuckin up, until one fatal day it all came to a tragic end.

"Come on people, hurry up. We're losing her…CLEAR!" The doctor placed the electric probes on my chest and shot enough electricity through my body to jump start my heart, but was unsuccessful. "Turn it up!…CLEAR!" My body jumped off the operating table and back down as he shot me with another volt of electricity, still to no avail.

Two hours prior, I was at a friend's house getting high, speed balling for the first time. Speed balling is when you mix cocaine and crystal together. I was on a good one. So good that my fragile little 120 pound body could no longer handle the abuse and finally gave up on me like I gave up on life. My heart beat became irregular. Next thing I knew, I was over dosing. I fell to the floor, pipe and drugs still in hand. Tweakers are some of the most scandalous drug users on the face of the earth. The friends I was getting high with panicked when they saw me fall out and eyes roll into the back of my head.

"Oh shit! The bitch is finna die!" One said as they ran out the house; not ta get help but for fear that they might get arrested on some type of charge once the police and paramedics arrived and realized everyone was getting high. He didn't even call 911 once he got outside. Now if that ain't scandalous, then I don't know what is. Lucky for me, the other person I was getting high with had enough decency to call 911 and give them the 411 before abandoning me as well. And these was supposed ta be my so called friends.

Unlucky for me, it didn't really matter either way if they called 911 or not because I was slipping fast. I saw my whole life flash before my eyes. From the time I was a little girl to my dying day. I could see it all like a clear picture on a movie screen. I started to get a sense and feeling of peace, a feeling I haven't felt in a long time. I then saw a big cosmic tunnel form with a bright light at the end of it.

I began to feel my soul escape my body with a feeling of relief. Everything seemed to happen so fast. I could hear the doctors trying to revive me, but I didn't wanna go back. For the first time in a long time, I was truly happy and on my way home. As I began to walk towards the light, I could feel my past life fade away like a distant memory or night's dream. I heard the doctor pronounce me dead as I continued walking. I was now going…going…going…GONE. **BEEEEEP!** Flat line.

CHAPTER 5 THE CHRONICLES OF BAMBI

"Fuck me! Yea that's it, right there! Stick your dick in my mouth! Oh, you're so big!" I loved the way I was getting banged by three guys at the same time. Every hole simultaneously stuffed at once. I could take it however you could dish it. I was a nympho. I loved sex more than life itself. When I was in high school, I was known as the school whore. Senior year I fucked the entire football team.

I had a bad rep and gave a fuck what anybody had thought of me. I had an insatiable hunger for dick, and one was never enough. I loved having trains ran on me. It made me feel dirty, but in a good way, if there is such a thing. "Suck this dick, whore!" I deep throated the 10 inch black dick with no gag reflex all the way down to the balls. While I was satisfying my lust and appetite for dick in my mouth, his friend was exercising his eight and a half inch dick in my asshole, drilling away like a jack hammer. "You like the way my dick feel in your ass bitch?"

"Em Hmm." And I did, too, but nothing felt better than when his white friend, who surprisingly had a big dick as well, stuck his dick inside my pussy at the same time as his friend was ramming my ass. I could feel both dicks inside me rubbing against each other, separated only by that thin skin and flesh that separates ass from pussy. I took it, and even bucked back to let 'em know they weren't fuckin wit no punk bitch. I was the real deal.

"Fuck this pussy and ass you big dick mutha fuckas!" I bit my lip and looked back over my left shoulder, dick in hand, as I made eye contact with my pussy executioners.

"Bitch, don't stop suckin this dick now. Put that shit back in your mouth." I turned back around and looked up at the voice that was making demands.

"Yes, Daddy. You want Momma ta finish suckin that dick?"

"Bitch, you already know." I spit on the head of his dick and went to work. Up and down, on his dick like I was bobbin for apples at a Halloween party. I let my saliva build up until his dick was dripping wet and spit was running down my hands, before I took his dick out my mouth and sucked his balls. I gave each scrotum equal attention as I jacked him off seductively. The veins in his dick were huge and throbbing. I could sense he was about to nut. I put his dick back in my mouth and started sucking faster. I knew he was about ta erupt like 'Old Faithful'.

"Yea, nigga, cum for me. Cum for me Daddy." I cheeked his dick to the side of my mouth like a lollipop. You could see his dick print on the side of my face from the outside as he grabbed my head and hair and forced his dick down deep until his dick completely disappeared inside my mouth. I felt a shot of cum hit the back of my throat at 10 mph. I hurried up and took his dick out my mouth so that he could finish coming over my face. I gripped his dick like a microphone at a hip hop convention. He busted all over my face as I milked and sucked the remaining cum out his dick and swallowed. When he was done coming, I wiped his cum off my face with my hands and sucked my fingers. Now it was time for my other two male suiters to cum. I felt the dick in my ass begin to swell, an indication that he was about to cum as well. I pulled his dick out my ass and turned around to face it as the white boy pulled out my pussy and stood side by side with his boy, dick in hand, stroking the shaft as I approached them both.

I got in the middle in between them both, dick in each hand, and simultaneously stroked them both off until they busted a fat load all over my face and mouth, just how I liked it. This was my life and I loved it. Everyday was an adventure. I loved dick more than I loved food. I didn't do drugs. Sex was my high, and it didn't matter what you looked like either as long as you had a big dick. Teeny weenies need not apply. I would tell a nigga in a heart beat you're not big enough, you need to be at least "this long" ta ride this ride, with my two index fingers stretched out the size of a ruler.

I would meet guys every night and fuck 'em; in clubs, bars, the beach, swing clubs, supermarket, laundry mat. It didn't matter. Any place was fair game. I truly put the "Ho" in nympho. I been hot in the twat since I was 16 and in high school. Funny thing is, I used to be a tomboy before I discovered my sexuality. I'm now 22 and legal with a high appetite for sex. The freakier the better. I even had a threesome with two guys that was bisexual. Now that was an experience.

The one thing I like about bisexual men is that they have no inhibitions or limitations. They know what they want and aren't afraid to explore ta get it. Men can't seem to resist me. They say I look very young and innocent for my age. It's how I acquired the name Bambi. Now men call me their chocolate bunny. I'm thick in all the right places. I have nice big natural Double D titties, an ass that a put most Georgia peaches to shame. Shoulder length hair, pretty smile, smooth skin with a chocolate complexion. I was born and raised in Texas and moved to San Diego when I was twenty.

I was ready for a change of pace and scenery. I always dreamed of living in sunny California. Laid out topless on the beach getting fucked by a stud or Mandingo. Yeah, as you can see, "Everything" always falls back to sex. My whole world revolved around it. I moved to San Diego in 2003 with a thousand dollars and two suitcases. I met a guy on the internet that was infatuated with me and said if I came out to California, I could stay with him. So six months later, I packed up my shit and took him up on his offer. Within two years, I had planted my feet, got grounded, and moved out on my own.

I wasn't the monogamous girlfriend housewife type. I need to be free as a bird. To soar and spread my wings, but the longer I stayed with old dude, the more possessive, jealous and clingy he got. Which was obviously a big turn off. So now I have my own place in Hillcrest, the gay district of San Diego. I work at F St, an adult bookstore located downtown across the street from Horton Plaza.

"Hello. Welcome to F St," I greeted a handsome young man as he entered the store. He had a mustache and goatee, bald headed, Gucci eyewear, sports coat and jeans with Gucci sneakers on his feet. A fat pinky ring and a Rolex watch with the iced out bezel. The nigga was fine. When he turned around to face me, I noticed the four karat canary yellow diamond earrings in his ears.

"Hi, how you doing?" He responded back. The sound of his voice made me weak at the knees and wet in the panties. I eyed him and watched his every move as he went to the section where we kept the condoms and lubrication. "Where y'all keep the Magnums at Baby Girl?"

He asked while holding the Trojans that were obviously too small for his size.

"Right here. We keep those behind the counter." He placed the small Trojans back down on the shelf and walked over towards me and the front counter.

"Hey sweetheart, let me get two jumbo boxes of those Magnums and this K-Y Jelly."

"Two boxes, huh? You doing it like dat?"

"Most definitely. I thought you knew."

"Well, now I do but I'd love ta see and find out first hand."

"Is that right? Well, we may be the two but I ain't the one. I don't just go around tricking my dick off Baby Girl."

Oh hell nah! I know this nigga didn't just turn me down. Ain't a nigga alive that can turn down this pussy. "Oh is dat right? So what a bitch gotta do ta get wit a nigga like you?"

"Show me some class instead of her ass, be true to the game and bout her cash."

"Oh really?"

"Yeah, really. See here, Baby Girl, let me learn you something and pull your coat to a few things. I'm not your run of the mill, sniffing under your dress, stalkin the pussy like it's gonna fall off the face of the earth tomorrow ass nigga. I'm truly cut from a different cloth than most. No offense, sweetheart, but its money over pussy wit me."

"No offense taken." I never met a nigga that would turn down a night of no strings attached sex. Shit, I never met a nigga that could turn "me" down. This was a first, and believe it or not, it actually turned me on. "I feel where you're coming from. I like your style. My name is Bambi."

"My name's Ka$hanova, but you can call me Ka$h."

"Nice to meet you Ka$h."

"The pleasure's mine."

"So is it possible for us to get together outside of my job and get to know each other a little better?" *I can't believe I'm "chasin" this nigga and asking him for his hook-up. Shit, it should be the other way around.*

"Fa'sho. I think you might need a man like myself in your life, too."

"Is that right? And what makes you think that?"

"Call it a hunch, but my senses are usually never wrong. Not only that, but I have a lot to offer, bring to the table, and introduce you to which may benefit us both. I'll speak to you more in debt about it when I give you a call."

"Well, you can't call me without my phone number."

"I know smarty. That's why you're finna give it to me." He said serious and confident with a slight smile on his face which showed off his sexy dimple.

"Oh you just know I'm a give you my number, huh?"

"I knew the minute I walked into the store."

"So you're conceited, huh?"

"No Baby Girl, confident and assure of myself which is far from being conceited. See when you're conceited, you 'think' you're the shit, but when you're confident and assure of yourself, you 'know' you're the shit."

"I heard dat, good answer. Well, here's my number." I took out a pen and wrote my cellphone number on the back of his receipt after ringing up his condoms and lubricant, which if I had it my way, we'll be putting to good use sometime down the line in the not so distant future.

"Alright then Bambi, I'll get at you."

"You do that." I handed him his purchase after placing it in a discreet bag as he thanked me and walked out the store.

$$$$$

It had been two days and Ka$h still hadn't called me. For some reason, I couldn't get him outta my mind. I knew from the moment he spoke that it was something special about him, something very different from any other man I've ever known or came in contact with. They say you can think a person or situation into existence, and it must be true because no sooner than I had Ka$h on my mind, my phone rang…"Hello."

"Hello. May I speak to Bambi?"

"This is her."

"How you doing? Dis is Ka$h."

"I know. I recognized your sexy voice." I didn't really recognize his voice. He actually sounded more sexy on the phone, but I knew it wouldn't hurt ta stroke his ego.

"Girl, save that crap fa someone else. I bet you say that to everybody."

What the hell? This nigga sharper than a block of cheddar cheese. I can't put nothing past 'em. Still being, I lied. "Nah ah. I did recognize your voice, and no I don't tell everyone that."

"Ok I'm a let you tell it, but anyway, wuss good wit'cha?"

"Nothin, just doing my nails and watching soaps."

"Is that right?"

"Yep."

"What choo got up for the night?"

"Chillin with you hopefully."

"Is that right? I like a female quick on her toes. Ok then Baby Girl, then your wish is my command. Would you like to accompany me to The House Of Blues? Katt Williams is performing tonight and I have tickets."

Hell yeah, I thought to myself, but played it cool and said,

"Yeah, that sounds like fun."

"What area do you stay in?"

"Hillcrest."

"Gayville huh?"

"Yeah you're not homophobic are you?"

"No, I'm secure enough with myself that I don't have to sweat shit like that. Gimme your address and I'll pick you up at seven." I gave him my address and directions to my house, spoke for about five more minutes, then hung up. It was 3 o'clock, which left me four hours to get ready before he was here to pick me up.

My nails were already done and I had an outfit in my closet that was still brand new and never worn that I was saving for the right moment and special day. So that just left me with my hair, which was cool because it would take at least three hours to set up an appointment, then wash, rinse, and style at the last minute on short notice. Lucky for me, I had a regular stylist and knew she would fit me in at all cost when I called. Soon as I hung up with Ka$h, I called my stylist and set up an appointment for 3:45.

$$$$$

Knock! Knock! Knock! I went to answer my front door, but not before taking a look in the mirror and doing a double take to make sure, I looked good and was on point. I had on a one piece form fitting Apple Bottom bodysuit with some leather all black with the gold plated heels and beaver fur around the top rim, Apple Bottom boots to match. My MAC lip gloss and make-up gave my lips and eyes definition, while my hair was styled to perfection. As I looked in the mirror and gave myself the once over, I thought to myself, *you's a bad bitch!*

"Who is it?"

"Ka$hanova Tha Mack, your Royal Highness and Daygo's Finest!" I opened the door and said,

"Mack huh?"

"Girl, you better believe it! I thought you knew." Damn this nigga looked good. He was shining from head to toe. If I had to describe it, it would be Thug Casual. He had on a button up with french cuffs and 24 karat gold cuff links, an Italian multi print tie, a sport coat with a matching handkerchief, semi baggy Sean John jeans and Gucci sneakers with a fat watch. Big earrings and a fat pinky ring to set off his attire. The nigga put the "F" in fine.

"Emm, you look and smell good. What's that you wearing?" I asked as I moved to the side and invited him in.

"Egyptian Musk, and you don't look too bad yourself. I'm feelin those boots."

"Thanks."

"Well, you ready ta get outta here?"

"Yeah, let me juss go grab my coat." I went into my bedroom closet and took my Apple Bottom short length leather and fur coat that displayed my stomach off the hanger, put it on, turned out the lights, and headed out to start our evening. The comedy show was live. Katt Williams is a fool. He had me crackin up all night. Ka$h couldn't stop laughing as well. It was definitely a perfect first date and good way to start the evening. I had a blast an d didn't want the night to end.

"So what would you like to do now pretty lady?" Ka$h asked as we left The House Of Blues and walked towards his car. "The night is still young, so if you like, we can go get a bite ta eat in the Gaslamp, and maybe even a few drinks. I'm not much of a drinker, but we can definitely do the champagne thang."

"That sounds good to me," I responded back.

"How's Friday's sound?" He asked.

"That sounds good."

"Ok then, pretty lady, Friday's it is." We headed back to Ka$he's 320 bubble eye Benz sport and got inside. The car was black on black and rimmed up with the peanut butter guts. The inside had that new car smell in it, like he had just bought it or got it detailed.

"I was meaning to tell you, I really like your car."

"Thanks. I just got it last week." Well, that explains the new car smell.

"I wouldn't mind having a car like this. Maybe one day, if I strike the lotto or something."

"You don't need ta hit the lotto to roll in no Benz."

"Well, I damn sho ain't finna be able to buy one on my salary workin at F St."

"Exactly, so what does that tell you?"

"That it'll a take a miracle, or me hittin the lottery to ever be able to afford to buy one."

"No, it means you just need to aim higher and never settle for less in life. This ain't the Middle East or some third world country, this is America. Home of the free. Where dreams come true everyday. You just gotta be willing to do whatever it takes to get it. Keep your eyes on the prize until the deal is met and the prize is won. You have to utilize and take advantage of all your resources. Never give up. Stay focused and keep a mindset like failure's not an option. Only the strong survive, but the hustler gets the money. You gotta have hustle in your bones and a never settle for less attitude."

"Wow that makes so much sense. I never thought of it like that. You should be a motivational speaker or something."

"I am."

"No, I'm serious. You really should. Cause just that little bit you said got me thinking and feeling like I could do more with my life."

"I'm serious too. Remember when I came to your door and said it was Ka$hanova Tha Mack? That's what I was talking bout when you asked if I was a Mack. You was being sarcastic, but I was being serious. I am a Mack, a Master Applying Correct Knowledge. Some say I dress slick and talk quick, but everything I speak about is real spit. I'm from a whole different breed. When I speak, I want it to uplift the masses or with whomever I'm speaking to at the time."

"Ok I feel you on that." Just then, we pulled up to Friday's and valet parked in front. The Gaslamp District was always crowded and active. This was the Downtown Club and Bar scene. Back in the day, it was the drug spot and hoe stroll, but now it was party central. Due to the fact, finding a parking space close, if at all, was always a chore. So the smart move was to valet park your vehicle whenever possible.

"May I have your keys, Sir? And here's your ticket," the valet attendant said as he held our doors open to get out and handed Ka$h a claim ticket to retrieve his car when we were done eating or ready to leave the Gaslamp. Ka$h handed him the keys, a $20.00 tip and told him, "Now make sure you take care of my Baby. Stay out of my glove box and park it up front where I can see it, and I'll give you another $20.00 when I come out."

"Yes okay, will do Sir." I loved Ka$h's take charge attitude. It was a real turn on. Women love men who know how to take control. We walked inside and was seated at a booth by the waitress. We sat down and ordered our meals and drinks. The waitress smiled, picked up our menus and said, "Coming right up."

As we sat waiting for our orders, we recapped on some of the jokes we heard from Katt Williams, laughed and talked. "You know what? I never met a man like you before."

"Yeah I hear that all the time. What can I say, I'm one of a kind."

"Okay there goes that conceitedness I should have known would surface again."

"Not conceited Baby Girl, convinced. You can't argue with facts, baby. It is what it is."

"Yeah and I'm sure it does what it does." We both laughed. "Boy you crazy."

"So what about me is so different from all the other men you met in your life?"

"Juss your whole get down and vibe. For one, you seem to have your shit together. You have swagger and confidence, but it doesn't come across as cocky. Two, just from the short and very little conversations we've had, I can tell that your visions and outlook on life is a lot different from most, in a good way of course. And three, you don't seem to have your mind on sex or getting pussy 24/7 and that's definitely a first and new one on me. Most guys I meet and come across only have their minds on one thing and one thing only…gettin laid!"

"Well, see Baby Girl, that's because most men are sucka's for love and don't know how to use their top head ta control their bottom head. Most nigga's and people in general be on some square shit. While I be on some true playa shit. I don't move, maneuver, and make decisions with the heart and emotions. That's the type of shit that'll make a nigga go O.J on a bitch. Instead, I make conscious and calculated decisions with my mind."

"See, that's what I'm talkin bout. Guys don't talk like that and they damn sure don't think like that."

"Well, maybe you've just been running into the wrong guys."

"I guess so because I damn sure would have remembered you or anyone like you."

"Fa'sho. I can dig it."

"So, what's your definition of a square?"

"A person that sees the world through western eyes. A civilization that can't think on its own and always go with the status quo. I'm a leader, not a follower. A chief, not an Indian. But most of society needs ta be lead. The government does most of the thinking for them. If Johnny Law tell you it's wrong or illegal, then it's wrong. Even if it has nothing to do with anyone else and everything ta do with you.

For example, its illegal to have more than one wife in the United States and you could actually be arrested and jailed for doing so. But what if three people just so happened to be in love with each other. Just like an average couple, and wanted to spend the rest of their life together? Why should they be denied the benefits and opportunities? Who are we to say and judge what's right and wrong? Love is love, ain't it? Who are we to force our views on someone else? That's crazy, but that's the world we live in. The shit makes no sense like play money in Monopoly, pun intended.

"See, we live in a Democracy and sometimes that comes back ta bite ya in the ass. I feel a person should be able to think, feel, and do whatever you want in life, as long as you're not inflicting pain, harm, or hardships on someone else. Life's too short and it's your life to live. So one should be able to live it as they see fit. We're all very different individuals, so how can I say what's good for me has ta be good for you, or what's good for you has ta be good for him? That's that square shit. So I cut the corners of life out the box with me and became well rounded. I'm a free thinker.

"I don't believe because you say it's right, then it's right, and no matter how much I may disagree or feel uncomfortable, I'm wrong. Yeah that's what the Pilgrims did to the Indians and look what it got them. The world is a scandalous place and built on corruption. History has proven such. Only the strong survive. So how you gonna survive in a scandalous world being weak minded and passive? You can't. So long story short, cause I can go on and on with this topic, that's my definition of a square. And believe it or not, that's the short version."

"Wow. I mean, what can I say but wow? I never looked at life like that, but once you put it all in perspective, I have to agree with you 100% Even when thinking about my own life. I was always considered the 'fast' girl. The easy girl in High School that would sleep with you on the first date."

I couldn't believe I was being so opened and forth coming with him, not that I was ashamed, but I knew most men would judge and probably couldn't deal with a woman as myself for anything other than sex or a one night stand, and usually I was cool with that, but with Ka$h, it was different. I really wanted to get to know him. He intrigued me. For some reason, I felt like I could totally be honest with him and he wouldn't judge me in the least, and if he did, then fuck 'em, it wasn't meant ta be.

"All through life, I let sex define my being, and thought the rest of the world saw it as a bad thing, I never did. I felt like I'm a grown ass woman doing grown ass things and if I like it and it feels good to me, then why should you care?"

"I feel you. Shit, if you like it, I love it!"

"I'm very much in touch and tuned with my sexuality and I never much cared how anyone else felt about how I carried myself or what they thought or heard about me. Shit, I wasn't doing nothing more, then most men did everyday. The only difference was they were considered cool and I was considered a tramp. You know how the double standard go. A man can sleep with whoever he wants. Thousands upon thousands of women, and no one finds anything wrong with it. But let a woman do the same thing and everyone a look and treat her like yesterday's garbage."

"No doubt, I feel you on that. That's the square shit and type thinkin I was talkin bout. See I feel like when it comes to sex and sexuality in America, we still have a long way to go. Just look at television in other countries and then compare it to ours. Their light years ahead of us with the type of shit they be showing and doing on TV. Same thing with prostitution. Most of America still looks down and frowns upon prostitution, even though it's the oldest paid profession, and the very same people that push and pass laws ta make it illegal, can't seem ta keep their dicks out of the whores they're persecuting.

"You go to other countries and it's not like that. Actually, it's the total opposite. The one thing in this world you can say is 100% yours, which you've owned since birth, you can't sell. But you can sell that boat, house and raggedy car that you don't have a clue of who built it, or where it came from in the least. Once again, that's that square way of thinking and hypocritical justification of a law that needs to be changed."

"Yeah, I agree. Why should one care what two consenting adults are doing behind closed doors?"

"Exactly, but you have ta be a free thinking, non-bias, outside of the box type person to look at it like that. That's why I call most people in the world square, because it takes squares to form a box and once formed, most squares live within the box they created. I feel in order not to be considered square, you have to live and take yourself 'outside the box,' not to sound too confusing."

"Not confusing at all. That makes perfect sense." By now, our drinks had arrived. Shortly after, our food. We ate, drank, and talked for the next two hours. The more Ka$h talked, the more I was feeling him. I knew I didn't want this night to end no time soon.

"Ticket, please." Ka$h handed the valet ticket stub to the valet attendant to get his car. Not that we had to walk far, seeing how the car was parked right in front of the restaurant. The valet went and got the keys to the car off the clipboard where they kept all the keys to the cars that were checked, opened the door for us ta get in, and handed Ka$h the keys. Ka$h thanked the attendant and gave him the $20.00 tip as promised, for keeping his car straight. "So you enjoyed yourself Baby Girl?"

"Very much so. I'm not ready for the night to end."

"Well, we're not that far from the Harbor. Would you like to take a walk through Seaport Village? Its pretty cool at night."

"Yeah, I'd love to." We drove down to Seaport Village, which was about five to ten minutes from the Gaslamp, parked, got out and took a stroll. "It's nice out tonight," I said as we held hands walking above the edge of the water, on top of the walkway which separates Seaport Village from the ocean.

"Yeah it is, ain't it?" He responded back as we both looked at the moonlight shimmer off the ocean, like diamonds on a rapper's necklace.

"So, I never asked, what you do for a living?" I asked in a curious and genuinely interested manner.

"I'm a gentleman of leisure. I make money the player way. I give guidance to the misguided and get paid well for it. I show a bitch how ta make a way outta no way. Give game where game is needed."

"So you're a pimp?"

"No, I'm something like a pimp, but more like a Mack."

"Wuss the difference?"

"There's a big difference. A pimp accepts any kind of money, but a Mack accepts the right kind of money. Any bitch a do for a pimp. If she's hoe'n, then she's going. But a Mack is only gonna have the best of the best. Not only that, but a pimp pimps hoes, a Mack pimps everybody. I don't just limit myself to the track and escort services. I'm playin for big stakes out here, so if one of my bitches or a bitch I fuck wit can get money some alternative way, and it's lucrative, like getting married to a trick that done fell in love with her only to divorce his rich ass down the line and get him for half his shit, you can best believe the bitch is going. That's the difference, Baby Girl."

"Wow!" I mean, what else could I say? The last thing I thought he was gonna tell me was that he was a Pimp or a Mack, as he liked to call it. I would have thought he was a D-Boy before a pimp because he didn't have or act like the stereotypical super flashy, no respect for women, slick talking and clown suit wearing pimps I had always seen on TV, or the streets. He was actually someone I could see myself with. Pimp or no pimp. Something about him was just special. I knew it the first time we spoke, that night he walked into my job.

"So does that shock you?" He asked.

"A little bit."

"In a good way or a bad way?"

"No way in particular. Just shocking."

"Right, I feel you. Well, you know I pride myself in keeping it real at all times. Take me as I come or don't take me at all. You know wut I'm talkin bout?"

"Yeah."

"That's why I never judge a person for what they do because what goes around comes back around and I would hate for someone to judge me, even though the truth of the matter is I'm being judged everyday. But fuck what the next person thinks, either pay me or pay me no attention. Period!"

"So do you currently have girls working for you?"

"No doubt, I have two out here, one in Atlanta, and three in Texas."

"Like dat?"

"Hey, I don't play wit the game Baby Girl. I'm in it to win it."

"I see."

"Let me learn you something Baby Girl. It's crowded at the bottom, but lonely at the top. I'm not tryna be smothered in a pot wit a bunch of crabs tryna pull me down. Everybody who's somebody doing it big is at the top. The haters, Pimpetrators, and hoe fakers are on the bottom. It's as simple as that. When I aim, I aim high. When I shoot off, I'm firing towards the sky."

"I like how you analyze and put things. I really like you Ka$h, but where could this possibly go? You already have six women. Where would I fit in that equation?"

"Right in your position. I'm always taking and reviewing applications for those that's qualified and wanna be by a Mack's side. My doors is always open like 7-Eleven, 24/7. If you've been liking what you hear, then have no fear. I got you as long as you got me. Together we have each other. You said you were in tune and in touch with yourself, so let me help you use that to get in touch wit some money. If you come fuck with me, I guarantee you'll make more money in a month then you made all year. You got nothing to lose, but everything ta gain."

I can't believe I'm actually considering doing this, but shit, how much of a stretch is it? I was already fucking for free, and a lot, mind you. So why not try something different and actually get paid for once. Shit, why not get paid for something I love to do for free? That's like someone paying you to breath everyday. "Okay, so if I decided that I wanted to give it a try, what would I have to do?"

"Just choose up wit a reputable nigga as myself and let me handle the rest."

"And there's not gonna be any drama between me and your other girls when you bring me home, right?"

"Come on now Baby Girl. Don't insult me. This is pimpin and hoe'n, not simpin and bone'n. A bitch is gonna respect this or reject this. A hoe of mine is gonna fall in line every time. Either you're with me or against me and I don't fuck with bitches with larceny in their hearts. So if I bring you home, they know it's for the good of our family and our common cause. Which is get money and stack paper."

We talked for forty-five more minutes about the game. He told me experience would be the best teacher, but until then, listen and do everything he tells me, and then once I knew the game, still listen and do everything he tells me because he always knows best and would never tell me anything wrong. I agreed and as you say in the game, "Chose Up." That night, Ka$h took me back to his house and to my surprise, still didn't sleep with me.

He said, "From this point on, just as you no longer fuck fa free, neither do I so until you lay your first bankroll into my hands, I will not sleep with you." And that nigga meant it, too. He really didn't and had no intentions on sleeping with me until I made him some money. The crazy part is it actually turned me on and made me wanna get his money faster.

I couldn't wait ta make his money so I could feel his hard dick inside me for the first time. Shit, if his dick was anything like his brain…fuck that…his 'game,' then I was in for a wild ride, and I couldn't wait! Sitting down on his black leather sofa, I asked him the number one question that all bitches wanna know when they first decide to hoe and enter the game…"How much money do I get out of this?"

"None."

What? I must a heard wrong. No, this nigga didn't just say none. What bitch in her right mind would have sex with a man for money, fuck 'em, then receive no compensation? "Not even half?"

"Not unless you wanna receive half of this Mackin. See, look here. Let me learn you something. From this point on, I'm your everything. Your teacher, lover, big brother, shoulder when you need one to cry or rely on. Your financial broker, manager, accountant and banker. Bitch, from this point on, I'm your everything."

Bitch? Oh I know this nigga ain't just call me outta my name. And what's this banker shit? Nigga I can take care of my own money. I ain't feeling that shit. He must have read my mind because no sooner than I was thinking what I was, he said,

"I can tell by your expression that you're not feeling that, and you probably even got upset that I called you a bitch."

Bingo nigga! Two for two.

"So let's just deal with them topics both and elaborate fully so I never have to explain myself, nor do we ever have to talk about it again. First, let's address me calling you "Bitch." Bitch, you're no longer square, nor do you go around functioning like one. In our world, 'Bitch' is like a term of endearment. It's not used in a derogatory sense. Shit, you're my bitch, the most loyalist creature to man on earth. Name anything on this planet more loyal to their master than a 'bitch.' And I'm not talking about a female or human being. You can't. You know why? Because it doesn't exist. So think nothing of it when I call you a bitch because throughout our time together, you're gonna be a lot of 'em. You're a hoe now, not a square. We done cut the corners off you and rounded you out. Don't sweat the small shit. Square shit. Square shit no longer intrigues you, deceives you, or misleads you. You're not my girlfriend. You're my hoe, my bitch. You understand?"

"Yes." I really didn't, but fuck it. Guess it's something I'm a have to get used to.

"Also, from this point on, I'm Daddy to you, not Ka$h. My friends call me Ka$h but my hoes call me Daddy."

Daddy? What, this nigga ain't my father. Lucky for him, I actually like calling my man Daddy. It made me feel subordinate and my man dominate. It was a complete turn on.

"Now, as for the money, let's keep it real. You know how women do when it comes ta money. They have no sense of control. If there was a nail and hair salon in the check cashing place when they cashed their checks, half of their money would be gone before they even left the building. Females like spending money more than they like stacking it, proven fact. And if you don't think so, I'll prove my point if you promise to keep it real." He stopped and looked at me for reassurance and confirmation.

"I promise." I assured him to see where he was going with this.

"Ok let's take you for instance. I just met you a couple days ago and hung out with you today. Still wit that being said, I bet I can predict your life and spending habits before I came into the picture."

Yeah right. Shit, this gonna be good. This nigga don't even know me like that. How he gone tell me how I spend my money? Watch this nigga clown himself. I thought to myself before saying, "Ok then, shoot."

"Typical payday. Friday comes around, you get your paycheck, run straight down to the check cashing place, cash your check. If you still got time, get your hair and nails done. If not, definitely getting done the next day. Buy an outfit for the club later, and of course, no outfit is complete without a nice pair of shoes. Later on, hit the club or hang out with the girls, either way, money's gettin spent. If you drink, you're buying alcohol. If you smoke, you're buying weed, and if you do both, then by this point, your check is already more than half gone. Now it's Monday, time to get back ta work, and the little bit of money you have left has ta last you the rest of the week until next payday. And the only thing that may alter this program and cycle is the first of the month when you have to pay bills, or that rare day or weekend you just don't feel like hanging out with the girls or going to the club. Am I correct?"

What the fuck? How he just gonna pull my card like that? Who feeding this nigga information about my life because I ain't never met a psychic before. "No." I lied.

"Yea, right. I thought we were gonna keep it real?" He said seriously but with a slight smile on his face. I couldn't do nothing but laugh.

"Ok you got me. You happy?"

"No, I'm just showing you that there's always a method to my madness and good reason why things are the way they are. I don't spend money, I spend racks. Other than that, I stack. You ain't gonna want for nothin fuckin wit me. I'll buy and get you whatever you need in life. You're now a reflection of me, so I ain't gonna have you out here on some bum shit. When you look bad, I look bad, cause you're representing me. Now if for nothing else, that would be bad business on my part, and I've worked too hard to build my empire just ta watch it fall down and crumble behind stupidity and not taking care of business. So when I'm slippin, you trippin. So as you can see, slackin in my mackin is not optional."

"Okay."

"I stay true to the game so that the game rewards and be true to me. It ain't nothin I can't ask the Mack God ta provide for that he won't answer my prayers and give to me. I play the game fair and treat people the same way I would want to be treated, in or outside the game. It's all about respect and as long as we respect each other, we'll never betray each other."

With that being said, I felt a lot more comfortable with the situation. "Well, that makes me feel a little better about it. Just something I'm a have to get used to. I never had to pay a man before and I've always taken care of myself so it's just an adjustment."

"Fa'sho. This whole situation and transformation is gonna be an adjustment, but within time, it'll all become second nature to you. Like wiping your ass after you shit."

"Ewww Daddy, you so gross."

"See bitch, you learn fast." That night, Daddy put me up on game to the fullest. He said he would introduce me to my wife-in-laws after I made and turned in my first "trap" (money).

"I'm gonna make you proud tonight, Daddy," was all I said before I got out the car to pull my first date. Last night, Daddy revealed to me that he half owned his own escort service that he ran with his brother, $upreme. The way the calls would work is, a client would look up the service on the internet or the Yellow Pages and call in. Then they would state what they wanted and what type of girl they were looking for. I don't know who they had answering the phones, but I know it was a woman. I know this because after the calls came through and got booked, she would then call me or one of the other girls that worked for the service and dispatched us out. She never sold sex on the phone. It was just nude entertainment and companionship, but once we got to the call and confirmed that it wasn't vice, it was up to us hoes ta work our shit and make that real money.

"Hey, how you doing? I'm here to see Rick."

"I'm Rick. Come on in." I walked inside the house of my first call and introduced myself. "I'm Bambi."

"Nice to meet you, Bambi."

"Likewise."

"Would you like a drink?"

"No thank you. I try not ta mix too much pleasure with business."

"Well, it's definitely a pleasure to have your business. You're very beautiful."

"Thank you, and the pleasure's all mine." I didn't have to worry about him being vice or this being some type of setup or sting because the call took place in a house. Vice never used a house to do stings unless it was recently confiscated in some type of bust, then they're allowed to use it for 48 hours, some places 72. Daddy said he wanted me ta get the feel of turning an actual date without the added pressure of tryna check and figure out if the trick was actually vice, so he made sure my first call was a house call. Vice did most of their stings in hotels and would occasionally bust females "in-call" spots, which basically meant the hoe was working out of her own home or hotel. Just a sitting duck waiting ta be gaffled.

"So what do I get for the $200 service fee?"

"Well, for that you get companionship, but for $500 more you get me."

"Wow, that's pretty steep."

"So is Mount Everest but it doesn't keep people from tryna climb it." I was a natural. "Good things are worth paying for and I guarantee you I'm worth every penny."

"Oh really?"

"Really!"

"So what guarantee do I get with that?"

"I guarantee that after you get done fuckin this pussy, you'll be worn out and satisfied or the second rounds on me."

"Wow! Well, how can I say no ta that?" He gave me the $500 on top of the $200 he had already payed on his credit card when he called the service, just for me to show up. I put the money in my purse and made sure that I left it in eye sight of my view at all times.

"So would you like to come with me to my bedroom," he said more like a statement than a question, with his hand extended for me to grab and follow. I took his hand as he lead me to his bedroom. Once we got into his bedroom, I went right to business. Time is money and I had no time to waste. I unbuckled his pants for him as he removed his shirt. He had a chiseled chest but a semi gut, like he might have been swoe in his prime. Still all in all, he wasn't bad looking. He looked ta be about 40 and spoke with an Italian accent. He was handsome for his age which made the date that much easier for me to conduct. I actually lucked out for my first date, but it wouldn't take long before I found out that most of my dates wouldn't look or be like him, but actually the total opposite. I dropped his pants and boxers to reveal his semi hard dick standing at attention looking me eye to eye. He had an average size dick for a white boy. About six inches. I took a condom out of my cleavage with two fingers, opened it up, and took it out.

I placed the condom in my mouth, like I had done so many times before in my freaky fuck for free days, stroked his dick ta get it all the way hard, and placed the rubber on using nothing but my mouth. My prior sex life was making my transition into prostitution a lot easier than most. I was a pro at this shit. I wrote the book on sex, sensuality and seduction. I just wasn't getting paid, but other than that, I was a bad bitch. I even prided myself in being able to take it in all holes. I had no limitations. I wasn't one of them prissy fragile bitches that didn't, and wouldn't get down low for the dough.

I had my mind set on being the best bitch Daddy had. I was black but knew I was capable of getting white girl money. I wasn't like most black bitches. I loved to suck dick, swallow, and take it in my ass. When it came to sex, it was like I was a white girl trapped in a black girl's body. "You ready to take the ride of your life honey?" I said in my most seductive voice.

"You better believe it."

I placed his dick in my mouth and sucked it long enough to get it lubricated. "That was on the house," I told him as I took his dick out of my mouth, spit on the head and shaft, and stroked him. I could tell he was feeling me. I laid on my back as I slid up top his bed resting my elbows as he took my panties off to reveal my perfectly shaving pussy and sweet scent of Victoria Secret Body Lotion. I took off my shirt and unsnapped the back of my bra to unleash "DD," the twins, with the dime size nipples. I brung one of my twins to my mouth as I licked my own nipple and got it aroused. I used my other hand to play with my pussy and get it wet.

"Can I taste you?" Now let me tell you something. Most hoes do the bare minimum with their clients. The less they have to do, the better in their eyes. It was all a job. A lot of them didn't even like their job, which is usually why they always made shitty money, got bad reviews and no repeat clientele! But I was a nympho. So for me it was different. I loved fuckin, getting my shit ate, and bringing men to their knees when I sucked their dick, tea bagged their balls, and licked their ass. I was a nasty bitch. As long as they were clean, I was down for anything.

"You wanna lick Momma's kitty?"

"Em hmm." I grabbed the back of his head and guided him towards my pussy until his face disappeared in between my legs. He placed his tongue on my clit and made small circles until it grew twice in size. If there was one thing white men knew how to do, it was eat pussy. He took both of his hands and spread my pussy lips apart to reveal more of my clit. He then sucked and nibbled on it until I felt a sensation that brung me to an instant orgasm. As I came, he continued ta eat and suck my pussy like it was the last supper. I gripped his head so tight he must have thought I was tryna suffocate 'em wit the pussy. It just felt so good I couldn't let go. I could tell it turned him on because he started moaning and getting into it. He damned near licked me dry, if there ever was such a thing.

"Ooh, I wanna feel you inside me!" He raised up from in between my legs and sat up over me on his knuckles like a gorilla. I grabbed his dick with my right hand and guided him inside my pussy. Even though his dick wasn't that big, my shit was still tight. I used my pussy muscles ta make it even tighter as I watched his eyes roll into the back of his head.

"Yeah, you like the way dis tight pussy feel on your hard dick. You feel how wet I am for you?" "Yes, hmmm. You feel so good." I grabbed his ass cheeks for support as he started to pump and hump away.

"Oh yeah, fuck me! Fuck dis pussy!" I could tell my pussy was too much for him when I felt his dick throb like he was about ta cum as his toes curled. Normally, that would have been a good thing, the quicker the better, but this was my first date and I had a guarantee to fulfill. By the time I'm done with him, he'll be begging me to stop and let him rest. I pushed him off just as he was finna cum and said, "Not yet honey. You don't cum until I'm ready for you to." I turned around and got on my knees, reached under my pussy and ran my finger from my ass to my clit, using three fingers to massage my pussy aggressively in big circles.

"Now stick that dick inside this pussy and fuck me like you mean it." He stuck his dick inside me, grabbed my ass, and fucked the shit out of me. "That's wut I'm talkin bout! Fuck this pussy! Uh uh uh! Yeah, yeah. Right there! Fuck dis pussy! Fuck me harder!" He was now deep up in my pussy. I could feel his balls smack up against my clit with every stroke.

"Yeah bitch. You like that? You like when I fuck you like a whore?"

"Oh yeah, talk dirty to me! Smack my ass and pull my hair!" That turned him on when I said that. I knew all this extra shit was winning me points. I knew he never had a hoe come through and work it like me. I'm a make sure he never forget me or this pussy for as long as he live. I gripped his dick with my pussy and made small circles with my hips and ass. I could tell he was about to cum. This time I would let him. By now he was in such a fuck frenzy and zone that he was sweating and pounding away at my pussy like a mad man.

"Fuck dis pussy! Let me feel you cum fa Mommy."

"Yes, I'm bout to cum!" I gyrated my ass like a stripper in a Luke video.

"Oh fuck! Your pussy feels so good!"

"Cum fa me! Cum for this pussy!" He came as I felt his dick pulsate inside my pussy. Ten-seconds later, he was flat on his back breathing heavy and exhausted…Just as I predicted.

"Oh my God, that was the best pussy I ever had in my life." I smiled with the, 'I told you so' look on my face, grabbed my clothes, and went into the restroom to clean up. When I came out, Rick was on the edge of the bed in his boxers counting out some money. "Here you go, baby doll." It was a three hundred dollar tip. "You're worth every penny." I thanked him, grabbed the money, gave him my number and told 'em, "Call me anytime," as I left his house eight hundred dollars richer than when I went in.

"How'd you do Baby Girl?" Daddy asked as I got into the car and closed the door.

"Like a bad bitch suppose to!" Ok I didn't really say that but it sounded good right? I wanted to say that but instead just handed him the money and said, "I'll do better next time." He took and counted the stack of twenties, fifties, and hundreds, then said, "Bitch you did good, especially for your first day."

"Thank you Daddy, but next time I'm a make a G"

"Fa'sho Baby Girl. Always aim for the clouds. I'm proud of you. Keep up the good work."

That was my first call, but it was far from my last. I got three calls that night. The next call I did, I made six hundred and the last call I made a thousand. So all in all I made twenty foe hunet. Not bad for a first day's work, and from a black bitch! Eat dat you Snow White bitches. They ain't never met a hoe like me. I was really feeling myself. Until Daddy took me home to meet two of my wife-in-laws and I saw how pretty, and the amount of trap they had waiting for Daddy.

"This is Jennifer and this is Gina. Say hello to yawl new wife-in-law,

Bambi."

"Hi!" They both smiled and said in unison, happy as all outdoors, like they just hit the lotto. Jennifer was white, slim with pretty eyes and long hair. She was petite and sweet. She kinda resembled Alyssa Milano, the girl from 'Who's the Boss' and 'Charmed.' Gina was Mexican, thick, and had that Latin sex appeal about her. I could tell she was a money maker right off the back.

"Here goes the money we made last night Daddy," Jennifer said, handing him two separate stacks.

"This one I made and this ones Gina's." Daddy counted Jennifer's first. It came out to thirty two hunet. Next, he counted Gina's. Hers was twenty eight hunet.

"Wait, Daddy. I have more. I just pulled a quick date before you came over. I got five more," Gina said, then handed him the money.

Dammn! These some money makin bitches here. I need ta step my bars up and get in the three thousand club. I knew Daddy was getting money, but I didn't know he was getting money like this. I had a new found respect for him. I got along with my wife-in-laws great. And two days later, I had my first three thousand dollar night. I was on cloud nine. From that point on, me, Gina and Jennifer called ourselves "The Get Money Crew." Three of the baddest hoes in Daygo.

$$$$$

It's been a week since I chose up and I yet ta fuck or feel Daddy up inside me, even after I made the three racks. Truth be told, I hadn't had the time anyway. I been busy working my ass off every night and sleeping through the day. I usually came home when the sun was coming up. When most people are just waking up to go to work, I'm laying down to go to sleep. Real shit. But I was now in need of some Daddy dick. I needed to feel my folks up inside me for the first time. I needed to show him what his bitch was made of. I needed ta taste his dick inside my mouth. Shit, I just needed my Daddy in every way imaginable, period! And to my surprise, today would be the day.

"Baby Girl, you been doing good. Every day your work is better than your last. You continue to step it up. You've proven yourself through actions. I told you once you broke luck and brung me some cash, I would sleep with you. Well, to say you surpassed my expectations would be an understatement. You've consistently brung me a fat bankroll and took ta this hoe'n like fish ta water. Its time to consummate this relationship and make it all official like a referee wit a whistle."

He took my hand and led me to his bedroom. I sat down on the bed as I watched him remove his shirt to reveal his chiseled chest and flat stomach. He was cut up with that bedroom physique. Like he did a term and just got out of prison. My pussy got wet just from the sight of him. He illuminated like a man with the confidence of a lion as he took his pants off to reveal an eight and a half inch bulge behind his boxers. I bit the side of my lip with anticipation of what was yet to come. I removed my mini skirt, baby tee and boy shorts ta unleash my kitty cat that was purring for instant gratification.

I assisted Daddy with his boxers and took 'em off as his soldier popped out and stood up at attention. I gently grabbed the shaft of his dick and licked the tip of his head in order to taste the pre-cum from his one eye anaconda, as he continued ta get aroused. I sucked on the head of his dick like a school girl with a lollipop. I felt the veins in his dick enlarge as the penis grew to maximum length. I began to stroke and take him completely in my mouth, bypassing the gag reflex and going deep. I made his dick disappear and reappear at will. Daddy grabbed the back of my head and fucked my mouth as I used my left hand ta play with my pussy, and my right hand ta play with my tits.

"Ooh my pussy is so wet for you, Daddy." I took his dick out of my mouth and sucked the two fingers I used ta play with my pussy. I looked up at Daddy seductively with my "cum and fuck me" look. He picked up on it and took his cue as he pushed me back onto the bed and spread my legs open. He teased me with the head of his dick. Barely tapping the pussy until I was damn near begging him to stick it in. "Fuck me Daddy. I wanna feel that big black dick inside me."

"Oh you gonna feel it bitch." After placing on a Magnum rubber, he stuck his entire dick inside me in one smooth motion. My pussy hugged his dick like a condom on a bull.

"Oh your dick feels so good, Daddy!" He was long stroking the pussy and made every thrust count. He was so deep inside me I could feel him in my stomach. He started making small circles as his dick rotated and bounced around my sugar walls. I wrapped both my hands around his neck and my legs around his waist like I was tryna hold on for dear life. As he humped and fucked me, I pumped and fucked him back. I threw the pussy at 'em like a baseball in the World Series.

"Yeah, take this pussy! Fuck this pussy Daddy! Fuck…this… pussy!" I emphasized every word as I threw my pussy at him. He grabbed my legs and put 'em both over his shoulders so he could fuck me deep. He drilled my pussy like a jackhammer, hitting my

"G" spot with every stroke. The dick felt so good that my eyes rolled into the back of my head and I started talking in tongues like the bitch on the 'Exorcist'. He then pulled out and stuck his dick in my mouth, making me suck and taste the juice from my own pussy.

"Yeah bitch, you like the way that taste?"

"Em hmm Daddy. I love the way my pussy taste." He then scooted down a little lower and placed his dick in between my titties. I grabbed my tits with both hands and sandwiched his dick in between. He titty fucked me while holding my head up so that his dick could slide directly into my mouth with every stroke. I kept my mouth open and hollow with a lot of spit to make it easier for his dick to slide through my tits and into my mouth. He then grabbed my head with both hands and a fist full of hair and fucked the shit out my mouth. He fucked me so hard I couldn't help but gag a few times.

"Yeah choke on dis dick, bitch." He stopped fuckin my mouth and rolled over on his back.

"Bitch, get up here and ride your folks." I rolled over and did as I was told. I loved Daddy's take charge attitude. It was a fuckin turn on. I climbed on top of Daddy like a horse in a John Wayne movie, grabbed his dick from behind my ass, and placed it into my pussy. My kitty cat was so wet it just slipped in. I tightened up my pussy to give it a tighter fit. I grinded my pussy in a wave pattern and small circles as Daddy's pubic hairs tickled my clit. The sensation made me cum instantly.

I closed my eyes and threw my head back as a stream of creamy nectar released and flowed from my pussy. I started to ride his dick like the stallion he was. I raised up to watch my pussy juice run down the sides of his dick as he palmed my ass. I leaned down so that my breast was low enough ta touch Daddy's face and placed my tits in his mouth. He sucked on my breast like a newborn baby. My nipples was so hard and sensitive.

"Pinch my nipples Daddy. Pinch 'em hard." I loved getting my nipples pinched. The mix between pleasure and pain turned me on. He gently bit my nipple and I came for a second time. He then spun me around reverse cowgirl without ever having to remove his dick. I rode him backwards as he stuck his thumb in my ass and grabbed my tits.

"Ooh yeah Daddy." I started pounding away on his dick and thumb until both completely disappeared.

"Pull my hair Daddy." He grabbed my hair and forced my head back as I worked his dick like the joystick from Atari.

"Oh yeah! Fuck! Your dick feels so good up inside me!"

"Yeah bitch, dis is what you get 'fa keeping Daddy rich. Good hard dick!" He pushed me forward so that I was on all fours and got behind me. "Bitch, lift your ass up."

"Yes Daddy." He stuck his dick in my pussy from behind and fucked me so hard I could barely hang on to the bed. He held onto my left ass cheek with his right hand and pulled me into him as he pushed inside me. He did this all with the same finesse and swagger he possessed on the streets.

"Oh fuck this pussy, Daddy. Fuck me! Yeah! Ah! Ah! Ah!"

"Yeah bitch, this wut you been feenin foe?"

"Yes Daddy."

"You like the way Daddy dick feel inside you?"

"Ooh yes, it feels soooo good!" He spread my cheeks apart and stuck his thumb in my ass.

"Ooh Daddy, fuck me in the ass! I wanna feel your big dick in my tight ass! Hurt me Daddy!" He pulled his dick out my pussy and stuck it in my ass. I could tell he was surprised and shocked how easily it went in and I took it. I was a pro and now it was time for Daddy ta know so.

"Oh, my nasty bitch like it freaky and rough, huh?"

"I thought you knew Daddy."

"I see why you bringing in so much loot now." He shoved his dick deep into my ass until I let out a scream, a good scream. I tightened up my ass muscles and took his dick, bucking like a horse tryna be broken.

"Damn bitch! Like that?"

"Fuck yeah!" He started pounding harder and faster, especially once he realized I could take it however he dished it. Shit, dis is what I do. The rougher, the better. "Harder! Harder! Harder!" We were now both in a full sweat. He closed my legs, pushed me flat on my stomach, and continued to fuck my ass." I knew in this position, it wouldn't be long before he came. Just as that thought came to mind…

"Oh shit bitch! I'm finna cum!"

"Me too, Daddy." I felt that feeling you get right before you're about to cum. My body started to tremble as a wave of sensual vibrations and pleasure went through my body. "Oh yeah fuck! I'm coming for you Daddy!" This was the big one. The other two orgasms I had was just a prequel to the real thing.

"Yeah bitch, I'm bout ta cum."

"Cum in my ass, Daddy. I wanna feel you bust in my ass." I was coming nonstop. I felt my body tingle from my head to the toes on my feet. I never came this hard in my life. At the same time, I felt Daddy's dick swell up then release into the condom in my ass. The warm fluid sensation felt so good, even through the condom. I looked back at my Daddy to see his face as he came. He tried ta play it cool and maintain his composure, but still couldn't keep from eyes rollin into the back of his head and toes curling to the ground. It's alright, I can deal with that. At least he didn't scream like a bitch or let out some funny sound like a lot guys did when they came.

"WOW," was all I could say as we laid still, exhausted in bed completely satisfied from the night's endeavors. That was truly the best dick I ever had, and believe me, I've had a lot of dick. That was the kinda dick that got a bitch sprung. I finally met my match. My Daddy really knew how ta work his shit. All that and didn't even have to eat the pussy. Wow! Daddy rolled a blunt of Purple Haze and smoked it with me as I rested on his chest. We got high as a kite with propellers on it, then went for round two. After that, we both couldn't take anymore and passed out in a coma like sleep. That night was everything I dreamed it would be, and then some. If I wasn't hooked on Daddy before, I damn sure was now! Money, respect, "AND" good dick. What more could a bitch ask for? I was now married to the game.

CHAPTER 6 THE CHRONICLES OF LISA

Ok, so I had a very different life prior to hoe'n. Hoe'n wasn't even on my resume…

Summer 1991

I was born and raised in Cleveland, Ohio. I grew up poor in a single parent household with very little money. My father died when I was young which threw my mother in a state of depression. This caused her to have, and go through bipolar mood swings at times. My mother received a check each month for her condition.

The lack of a strong male role model and father figure caused me to run wild and take to the streets at an early age. I was seventeen going on twenty with the way I was living and the type of shit I was doing. I was in the fast lane of life. Out of control doing 120 with no breaks. I lost my virginity when I was 13 playing "Spin The Bottle" and "Truth or Dare" at a ditch party when I was in Junior High. I fell in with the wrong crowd early on in my youth. I was white but always felt like I had more in common with the blacks. I listened to the same music, hated rock and liked the way the blacks carried themselves with style. And six months after I lost my virginity and slept with my first black, like they say, I never went back.

At school I was the token white girl that hung with all the blacks. This is how I discovered a lot of game. I looked like your average ditzy blonde white girl, but I talked and conducted myself like a bitch with IZM. On the weekends, I would go to this hip hop club called 'The Jump Off.' It was 21 and up but I always got in with my fake ID. Yeah that's right, fake ID. I had one ever since I was sixteen. The Jump Off is where I met my boyfriend, JayDee. He was twenty-two and a baller. He had Ohio sold up. Whatever you needed he had it and if he didn't, he knew where ta get it.

I couldn't believe he chose me to be his girl. When we first met, I lied about my age and told him I was eighteen. Two weeks later, he discovered my real age after calling my house one day. Mom answered the phone. Wondering why this grown sounding man was asking to speak to her 17 year old daughter. She said,

"Are you aware that Lisa is only seventeen?"

"Yes, ma'am." He lied.

"And how old are you, if you don't mind me asking."

"Not at all. I'm eighteen. I'll be nineteen in two months." He lied again.

"Sorry but you sounded older."

"Not a problem, ma'am. I understand."

"Let me get her. Can you hold on for a second please?" My mother yelled for me to pick up the phone from downstairs.

"Hello. I got it ma, you can hang up." Mother hung up the phone, then I continued to speak. "Hello."

"Wuss up? How you doin?"

"Alright, who's this?"

"Jay Dee silly. Who else is it pose ta be?"

"I know. I was just messing with you."

"Yeah right."

"I'm serious."

"So you're 17 huh?"

Uh oh. Busted! "Huh?"

"If you can huh, you can hear girl."

"Yeah well, age ain't nothing but a number anyway."

"And I agree, but I also believe that honesty is the best policy. I was always taught that if you lie, you'll steal. The two go hand in hand."

"Well, I'm not a thief."

"But you are a lier," he said sarcastically.

"No, I just didn't think that you'd talk to me or give me the time of day if you knew my real age."

"Ok, well is there anything else I need ta know about?"

"No, that's it. I promise."

"Alright then, with that being said, we're gonna start fresh, no lies, clean slate, and keep it real with each other at all times." I agreed, and from then on, everything was cool. From that day forth, we did everything together. We were inseparable. Jay Dee would drop me off in the mornings and pick me up in the afternoons from school. I was the envy of the school with the other kids, as they watched Jay Dee pick me up everyday in his 600 big body Benz.

Six months into our relationship, I was head over heels in love. There wasn't nothing I wouldn't do for Jay. That's what I called him, "Jay." Everyone else called him Jay Dee. "Well, baby, school's out," he said as he picked me up on the last day of school.

"Yep, and now I have the rest of the summer to just lie around and kick it."

"Did you pass all your classes?"

"Yes, I just made it. Barely, but I passed thanks to you. I got three C's, one C- and a B." Jay pushed me to do good and go to school. Before I got with him, I would ditch every other day. School bored me. I just didn't see the point in knowing when Christopher Columbus discovered America when it came to living everyday life in the here and now. Was knowing who the first President of the United States was, gonna help me make $100,000 a year or better when I graduated? I think not. So school never really interested me. The only class I took seriously was Math, because I felt like it was universally fundamental and beneficial. That's the class I got a 'B' in.

"Good job, Boo. I'm proud of you."

"Thank you Babe."

"Where would you like to go to celebrate?"

"Your place."

"That's a given, but where would you like to go before that?"

"I don't care. You pick. Whatever you decide is fine with me."

"Okay, I have an idea. How about I take you to the mall and get you something nice, then take you out to eat before capping it off at my place?"

"Sounds good to me." Jay took me to the mall and bought me six outfits from Neiman Marcus with the shoes ta match. He spent over $2,000.

"Nothing but the best for my baby," he said as we left the shopping center. One of the outfits he had me put on in the dressing room and wear it out. Jay always spoiled me like this and it was something I was really starting to get used to.

"Thank you boo. So where we going?"

"I thought I'd take you to a nice comedy club on the West Side. We can get some laughs and eat as well. The food there's pretty good."

"That's cool. I've never been to a comedy club before. Sounds like fun." Jay was looking handsome as always in his Karl Kani denim thug wear, freshly corn rowed hair and butter Timbs. He had a nice build and sexy body. He sorta resembled LL Cool J with braids. He even licked his lips like him, in that sexy way that only a woman could love and appreciate. I was dressed to impress as well, in a Donna Karen Limited Edition two piece set and open toe heels which showed off my perfectly manicured feet. We went to the club, ate, laughed, and had a blast. Later on, we took it back to his house and made love for two hours.

Two Years Later…

By now, I had been with Jay so long that I was every bit a Hustler's Wife. I was down for my man like no other. Jay moved me outta my mom's house and into his. A nice three bedroom condo with top of the line furniture and appliances. I had become his Ride or Die bitch. Death before dishonor. In the two years we'd been together, I'd tucked his gun for him numerous times when we got pulled over. Hid drugs in my pussy, helped him cook, weigh and bagged up work, and stood by his side like a down ass chick was supposed to. I loved Jay so much, that there was nothing I wouldn't do for him. One day after a long night of passionate fuckin, he asked me to do something that would ultimately change my life forever.

"You love me Boo?" He asked while laying down smoking a blunt with one arm rested behind his head and me laying on his chest. I looked up at him and said,

"You know I do."

"Would you do anything for me?"

"Of course I would. Haven't I already proven that?"

"Yeah, so far you have."

"Then why you ask, babe? Is there something you need me to do for you?" I looked in his eyes and asked sincerely.

"Actually, there is. I need you to do something for me that I really need done and can only trust you to do it.

"What you need me to do Boo?"

"I need you to go outta town and drive back wit some work I got already rigged up in secret compartments. So even if you was to get pulled over, you'll still be safe. You ain't got nothin to worry about. You know I would never let anything happen to you, or have you do something that fuck up your life and puts you in danger, unless I was a thousand percent sure you'd be alright."

"I know, but do you think I can do it alone? I'm kinda scared to go by myself."

"You'll be straight. The Police would never suspect a young white girl driving alone to be transporting drugs." He passed me the blunt then finished talking.

"You're only driving from Seattle back to Ohio, the same route that you've taken a dozen times before with me. I already have everything worked out. Remember Hector, my connect?" Hector was Jay's connect for the weed in Seattle. I knew this because I met him a year back while making a run with Jay. He had me come along so that we would just look like a couple on a road trip, if we were to get pulled over. I made the trip with Jay about a dozen times. So like he said, I knew the route pretty well.

"Yeah I remember him."

"He has the car you'll be driving back already hooked up and ready to go. He's already expecting you. All you have to do is fly to Seattle, meet up with Hector, and drive back to Ohio."

Really, I didn't feel comfortable with driving back alone, but I felt even less comfortable telling Jay no. So reluctantly, I agreed.

"I got you, Boo." He smiled, kissed me on the forehead and said,

"I knew I could count on you," then finished the blunt.

$$$$$

"Okay, Boo. Have a nice flight and remember what I told you."

"I know Babe. Call you when I arrive in Seattle and let you know that I touched down safe, and the same after I pick up the car to head back home. I got it." ***Now boarding Flight 1436 to Seattle. Final Call!*** Blared over the loud speaker.

"I love you! See you when you get back."

"I love you too." I said, picked up my Louie carry-on bag, gave Jay a kiss and hug, then boarded my flight.

"Hola! Como Estas?" Hector greeted me as I walked towards him from my gate terminal.

"Fine, and how are you?"

"Bueno, and you're still looking lovely as ever Bonita La Señora."

"Gracias."

"Shall we?" He reached for my hand and led me towards the stretched limo that was waiting for us outside in front of the airport.

"So, how's my good friend Jay Dee doing?" He asked as we drove down the freeway to his mansion in the Hills.

"He's doing well and sends his love."

"Jay's a good man. Es una hombre de honor." We arrived at Hector's mansion, which resembled Tony Montana's house on 'Scarface.' Armed guards surrounded the compound. They all looked like Secret Service men dressed in black with transmitter headphones in their ears. We drove up the long driveway and parked in front of the mansion. The driver got out the limo first, then walked around to Hector's and my side of the door to let us out. I called Jay to let him know that I had arrived safe and was okay. He spoke with Hector for a couple minutes, got back on the phone with me, and said to call him when I was about ta leave and head back home.

The plan was for me to drive back the same day I arrived in Seattle, but Hector insisted that I stay the night in one of his guest rooms and leave first thing in the morning. That way I was well rested. That's what he was talking to Jay about on the phone, which Jay agreed. I didn't mind staying the night because Hector was a complete gentleman, and I could use the rest. So, as long as it was cool with Jay, it was cool with me.

The next morning, Hector had the maid bring me breakfast in bed, a fresh robe, towel, washcloth and said, "Feel free to shower when you're done, Señora. El cuarto de bano es right this way," she said as she pointed towards the bathroom.

"Thank you," I said, with a smile, ate my food, washed up, then got dressed and ready for my long drive back to Ohio.

"This is the car you'll be driving, volver, regresar su casa Señora Lisa," Hector said as he pointed to the blue 1993 Nissan Sentra. The weed was hidden in a spare tire in the trunk. At first and second glance, you couldn't tell. You would have to remove the tire completely from the trunk and thoroughly examine the inside after removing the rim, which a Patrol Officer shouldn't do for a basic traffic stop.

I didn't need to see the tire to know where the drugs were, because Jay had already told me everything on how the deal was taking place and going down. Not only that, but I've been with Jay plenty of times before, making the same run in the same manner. "Cool, this actually look like a car you'd find a white girl driving. Not too old. Not too flashy. It's perfect."

"Mi sentimientos también Senora Lisa." He handed me the keys, gave me a slight hug, and wished me well on my journey and trip back home. Fifteen minutes into my trip back, before I was even able to merge on the freeway, **Bloop! Bloop! Pull over!**

"Oh shit, it's the Cops!" I looked into my rearview mirror and saw a convoy of unmarked vehicles with red and blue lights flashing behind me. "Fuck! Fuck! Fuck! This can't be happening." I pulled the car over to the side of the road.

Turn off your engine and exit the vehicle slowly! Blared through the bullhorn of one of the Officers. As I opened the door, fifteen or so Police Officers and D.E.A agents rushed and surrounded my vehicle. They ordered me to the ground, guns drawn, cuffed me up, and arrested me. I was taken Downtown and booked on charges of Possession with Intent to Sell.

I didn't know it at the time, but would find out later that the Feds had been on to everything. They'd been watching Jay for about a year, and had hope ta catch him slipping, but had got me instead. The Sentra was impounded into evidence and stripped down. Finding the weed in the tire wasn't a problem because they already knew what they were looking for. My bail was $200,000 and my first court date was in three days.

"*Collect call from*…Lisa. *Will you accept?*" I called Jay to let him know what happened.

"Yes."

"*This call is being made from a County Jail Facility. Your call may be monitored. If you do not wish to be recorded, hang up now…*" **Click!** Dial tone. I called back figuring something must have gone wrong with the phone. This time, Jay didn't even pick up at all. I couldn't believe it. No, hell no! He would never do this to me. I tried all day getting ahold of him. Sometimes he would answer, but never accept. By the next day, the phone was disconnected. I was hurt and very confused. I couldn't accept the truth so I let my mind play tricks on me. I went into denial and fed myself bullshit.

I made every excuse in the book for why I couldn't get ahold of Jay and his phone was disconnected, except the truth. That he shook me, wasn't taking my calls, and left me for dead to rot in this cell. Days turned into weeks, weeks turned into months, and months would eventually turn into years. The Feds and the DA tried ta get me to roll over on Jay. He was the one they really wanted. I was just a pawn in their game. And even though Jay did me dirty, I kept it "G." Stayed loyal, and never told a thing. So six months down the line, I was tried, convicted and sentenced to six years in State Prison.

I got lucky on a couple of factors: 1. There was only twenty pounds of weed in the trunk. Had it been cocaine, I'd been doing a lot more time; 2. I never crossed state lines with the weed so I was able to do state time instead of Fed time; 3. I was a female, white, and it was my first offense.

Now here I was locked up in prison behind a man who showed and proved that he really never gave a fuck about me. I grew a strong hate and resentment towards men while being locked up. The more time I did, the more animosity I developed. One year into my sentence, I started experimenting with women. Ninety percent of the females in here was bisexual or gay. I met a bitch named Porsche who was locked up for check fraud doing a three year sentence. I thought she was very beautiful and knew I had to have her.

Being with women was a lot differently than being with a man. It was a lot more sensual. A bitch knows what feels good to another bitch, where a man learns from trial and error. It took me six months to break Porsche down and turn her out and after one lick of the twat, she no longer thought about cock. "You got a visit today?" I asked Porsche as I watched her walk through the gates back from the visiting room.

"Yeah, my mother came to visit me. Today is her birthday."

"Oh, that's cool. Its good you got ta see and spend time with her for her birthday."

"Yeah, but I always get sad once the visit's over. Especially when you watch them go through the door that leads back to the free world, and you're going back ta the one that leads to hell. I mean, don't get me wrong, I can do the time, I have no choice, but I just hate being locked up like a fuckin animal."

"I understand. You just gotta do the time without letting the time do you. Use this time to figure out what you wanna do when you get out. Sit and write down your goals and game plan while you're in here. That way when you get out, you already have a jump start on what you wanna do in life. From there, it's just about executing and seeing it through."

"See, that's why I love you so much. Cause you always have the right thing to say." We walked back to the dorm, made a spread which was a meal that consisted of top ramen noodles, with any and everything you could imagine in it. From sardines, tuna, chicken and fish steaks, to potato chips, oysters, squeeze cheese and rice. On a good day, all of thee above. I know you're probably thinking gross, believe me, I was too when I first arrived here. But like everything in prison, you get used to it real fast. And truth be told, it's really not half bad.

After eating our spread, we played Spades for a couple of hours, watched a little TV, then called it a night. Once I got settled into the day to day routine of prison life and started programming, my time began ta fly. I tried writing Jay a few times throughout the years I was down, but the letter would always come back "Return to Sender." Eventually, I just gave up and forgot about him. That was my past and I was now looking towards the future. When I was with Jay, I had suppressed my inner sexuality. Remember, before I met him, I was pretty wild. Now that I discovered how much I liked women, but still craved a hard dick inside me, I knew I would never be the same. I loved being with the best of both worlds. Being in prison brung out the whore in me. There was a C.O. named Thomas that worked the late shift. Rumor had it that he was sleeping with some of the inmates. It had been awhile since I had some dick and made it my business to find out first hand.

I knew Thomas was scheduled to work tonight, so tonight I would make my move. Thomas was a handsome young black man in his early 30's, nice body, bald headed and tall like Jordan, with big hands and feet like Shaq. I had to have 'em, at least for a night that is. And to make sure he took the bait and couldn't resist, I brung an added bonus to the table, Porsche.

"Okay, here he come. You remember the plan, right?" I whispered to Porsche in a low hush tone.

"Yeah, I got it." It was count time in the dorm. Most of the girls were asleep in their racks and the dayroom was closed. Porsche slept above me on the last bunk in the dorm which sat off to the corner in a blind spot. It was considered a cadillac bunk because you could get away with just about anything without being seen. Everybody wanted it. You had to pay, bribe, take or wait your turn in line when the former owner went home to get one.

As Thomas was rounding the corner with his flashlight and notepad, me and Porsche went to work. Porsche was sitting on my bunk with her hands on my tits and mines on hers as we both began passionately kissing each other.

"Count time ladies," Officer Thomas said with a wicked grin on his face like the 'Grinch That Stole Christmas.' I could see the bulge between his correctional uniform appear as he bit his lip and massaged his crotch.

"Would you like to join us?"

"Does a bat have wings?"

I started rubbing my pussy and flicking my clit like a guitar string, legs spread to reveal I had no pants or panties on.

"I'll be back as soon as I finish up count."

"Okay, but don't keep us waiting too long. As you can see, we already started without you," I said, then stuck my tongue deep into Porsche's mouth as she kissed me back then sucked on my tongue like a Jolly Rancher.

"Oh, don't worry about that. Yawl can start, but I'm a finish," he said with a slight smile as he walked off to finish count. I laid down in my rack flat on my back and let Porsche eat my pussy like an All-You-Can-Eat Buffet. She had me wetter than a faucet as I ran my fingers through her naturally long hair. She sucked on my clit and slid two fingers inside my pussy. I moaned and purred like a kitty cat to her sensually aggressive touch, warm tongue and soft lips.

"Emm, eat that pussy Mommy." She loved when I called her that. Porsche was Puerto Rican. She had a fire tongue and a fiery appetite for sex. Officer Thomas came back to find us entwined like a pretzel, sexing each other like two professional porn stars in a Triple-X flick. Thomas started rubbing and caressing Porsche's hair and back, down to her butt, in between her legs and massaged her pussy as she ate mines. He played with her pussy until she got wet. I slid from under Porsche as she laid flat on her stomach, eyes closed and biting her lip. I sat up and began to unbutton Officer Thomas' pants.

It's been awhile since I had a big black dick in my mouth and I was feenin for a taste like a crack head for rocks. I opened his pants after zipping down his zipper to reveal a 9 inch one eyed snake fully erect and ready. My pussy got wet just looking at it. I licked my lips and placed him into my mouth. I sucked and stroked his dick, simultaneously gagging in between strokes as I took him deep into my mouth. It been a while since I sucked dick, but I refuse ta let it show. I spit on the head of his dick and sucked it like a lollipop. Porsche got up and walked around Thomas, bent down and licked his ass. I watched him tense up as she spread his cheeks and stuck her tongue inside his booty hole. I turned around, bent over and stuck his dick inside my pussy. It's been so long since I had any dick that my pussy was tighter than a small condom on a black man. He pushed as I guided him inside me. I placed my hands on the bunk as he fucked me standing up from behind. It hurt so good, if that makes any sense.

Porsche stood up, then placed her tongue inside Thomas' mouth, forcing him to taste his own ass. He was so caught up in the moment that he didn't give it a second thought. She then bent down, licked and sucked his balls as he fucked me. I pulled his dick out my pussy and turned around to join Porsche as we double sucked and tag teamed his dick together. I sucked on the top of his dick as she sucked on the shaft. I played with his balls gently and passed the dick to Porsche. Porsche was a deep throat specialist. She could make a dick disappear like a magician.

Porsche took Thomas' dick so deep into her mouth that her nose was in his pubic hairs. She pulled his dick, dripping with spit, out of her mouth and laid in the bunk on her back. I opened her legs to reveal her pink kitty cat. I dove in head first, like a kid at a swimming pool. Her pussy tasted so good I didn't come up for air. I couldn't if I wanted to anyway, the way she had her hand palmed behind my head, forcing me to eat her shit. I didn't mind though, especially when I felt her gyrate her pussy on my lips and cum in my mouth.

I moved to the side so Thomas could fuck her and feel her sweet tight pussy on his dick. He placed the head of his dick in her pussy and teased her until she couldn't take it anymore and bucked back. Ramming her pussy up against him, forcing his dick to enter her deep. He fucked her so hard she couldn't hold back her moans. I bent over and sucked her tities like a newborn baby. I climbed on top of Porsche while Thomas continued to fuck, pump and thrust. Our titties met as I laid on top of her and tongue kissed her in the mouth.

She caressed my back and held me tight. Nice, close and licked my neck. She nibbled on my ear and stuck her tongue inside. I looked up for a split second and saw another female across the dorm taking in the free peep show, laying on her rack playing with her pussy. I smiled with a devilish grin and went back to work.

Thomas took his dick out of Porsche's pussy and stuck it in mines as she grinded in small circles using her hips. Officer Thomas went back and forth from my pussy to hers and back to mines as we took turns receiving his dick. I turned around and got in a 69 position. Porsche and I ate each other out while Officer Thomas watched and stroked himself. He then came over and placed his dick inside of Porsche's pussy while I licked and sucked on her clit.

This made Porsche go crazy with emotions as satisfaction penetrated her core and forced her to have multiple orgasms back to back. As I felt her body tremble and tense with satisfaction. Thomas pulled out and placed his pussy wet dick into my mouth ta taste the aftermath of Porsche's orgasm. I sucked his dick long and hard. I was ready for him to cum and I wanted to taste every drop.

I bobbed my head and stroked his dick simultaneously, causing the necessary friction and sheer pleasure of emotions to bring him to cum. I felt the veins in his dick swell up, an indication that he was about to cum. He grabbed the back of my head and started fuckin the shit out of my mouth at a vigorous rate. I choked, gagged, and sucked as I felt his cum hit the back of my throat and tonsils. I swallowed his cum drop for drop as I came as well from the continuous action of Porsche eating my pussy. She stuck three fingers inside me and finger banged my g-spot until I came back to back and couldn't take no more. I collapsed on top of Porsche. Exhausted thinking to myself,

that was a much needed fuck session. For the remainder of my time, this would take place every weekend until the day of my release. I had done three years out of my six year sentence and was being released early for good behavior. Porsche was sad to see me go. I was too, but not as much. I knew once I hit the streets, I'd get over it. There was too much dick and pussy on the streets for me to be stressing and worrying about one behind bars. Sorry, I know that may sound harsh, but it is what it is.

Today was my release date and boy was I happy to go! It's been three long years and I was more than ready to hit the free world. The girls I was cool with in my dorm and on the yard threw a big spread for me the night before my release. I gave all my stuff I had accumulated throughout my incarceration away to Porsche. I got everyone's hook up and promised ta keep in touch. Something that everyone does before leaving prison, only to renege upon getting out and totally forgetting about everyone you made promises to. And I was no exception.

The day I left prison and walked out them razor wired gates, I never looked back. I was released at ten in the morning, given two hundred dollars gate money, and driven to the Greyhound bus station. I had nothing but the clothes on my back. The same clothes I had on three years prior when I went to prison. Isn't it funny how things come full circle? But I wasn't tripping because I was out.

Free. Free to do what I want, when I want. Free to move and eat freely. Never will I take life for granted again. Never will I let another man get to my heart and put me in a cross. Prison had made me a lot smarter. Men would be at my mercy from now on. I'll play the fool to catch a fool. I walked to the counter and bought myself a ticket to Ohio, then sat down and waited for the 3 o'clock bus. As I sat there waiting, a nice looking well dressed man walked up to me and said, "How you doing Baby Girl? My name's JP..."

CHAPTER 7 THE CHRONICLES OF JENNIFER

"Bitch, I don't wanna be nothing less than a Mack jumping out a Cadillac wit six or seven singing hoes saying Daddy, handle that." Suga Free blared out the Escalade speakers of Daddy's SUV as he drove down the blade to drop me off for work.

"Ok bitch, look here. I don't want nothin less than five and you really need ta shoot for a rack today. You been slacking in your hoe'n lately, which is why I bumped you back down to the basics and where it all started. The Blade!

Bitch you done came full circle. You took that internet shit for granted and got lazy. That's wuss wrong with you hoes today. Instead of going out and gettin some money, yawl waiting for the phone to ring for someone to hand you some. That's all well and good, but when the shit gets slow, the bitch gone hoe. There's no such thing as a broke hoe because pussy a sell when cotton and Jeri Curl kits won't. You need to blow the dust off that pussy and get money. I been outta town checkin traps and stacking racks while you been in the house being lazy. You know better, but now you're bout ta do better."

He pulled into the parking lot of Pep Boys off the track on El Cajon Blvd and let me out.

"Bitch, remember what I told you. Nothing less than five, make it seven for every day that you was sitting around broke, being lazy while I was gone."

I was pissed, but what could I say? I knew I was wrong for not having some money waiting for Daddy when he came back in town from his trip to New York. I mean, don't get me wrong, I had some money for him, but nowhere near as much as I should have had. I was a thousand dollar a day bitch and here I was with only twenty-two hundred dollars waiting for my Folks for a full week's worth of work.

I knew I was wrong and there would be hell ta pay, but I had been going hard for months and just needed a break. Shit, even a teacher gets two to three months off out the year, but try telling a pimp that. It'll be like tryna convince a Priest that Hell is cold and Heaven's hot, or a three year old kid that his teeth a rot if he keeps sucking lollipops. So I just sat back and did what hoes do in this situation, shut the fuck up, let Daddy's words go in one ear and out the other, and took my punishment. Oh yeah, and told him what he wanted ta hear,

"Yes Daddy, I understand. I'll have your money." I got out of the SUV, closed the door and went to work. As I walked up and down the blade, I thought to myself, Damn, I can't believe I'm back out here. It's been two years since I worked the Blade. I had elevated my hoe'n to the internet. I had my own webcam site where I got paid five dollars per minute or more, depending on what the trick wanted to see. I also took calls and sold videos of my amateur porn.

To top it all off, I had a personal ad up on Eros, CityVibe, and SanDiegoExotics.com. Tricks would log onto the site where girls like myself would have their picture and contact numbers posted, along with a brief description of their do's and don'ts, likes and dislikes, and how much they charged. Then when the trick found a girl they liked, they would contact, speak with her, and negotiate a price. It was hoe'n in the 21st Century. And now, I'd been bumped back to this primitive, bedrock, on the stroll hoe'n. Oh well, a bitch gotta do what a bitch gotta do.

Everyone knows that when a pimp's away, a hoe's gone play. Some more than others. I met my folks three years ago in San Diego at the Super Bowl in February 2003. I was standing on the corner of 5th and Broadway behind the bus stop, when a 600 big body Benz pulled up and stopped at the light in front of me. I was amazed at the fact that the car was still, but the rims was still spinning. I never saw rims like that before. The passenger side window rolled down and a handsome black man in the driver's side said,

"Hey Baby Girl. Can I holla at you for a second?"

I was a little reluctant to approach his car. I usually didn't speak to guys who didn't at least have the decency to get out of the car and holla at me properly, but of course, I broke the rule, seeing how he was handsome and his car was so tight. At the time, I was still square and green to the game, but one thing I longed for was ta be with a baller or a man that had his shit together. I knew early on that I looked way too good to be with a lame, especially one with no game and brains.

I was white and black, light skin, long curly hair, smooth complexion and cat eyes which made me look exotic. I was a dick magnet. I grew up in Southeast San Diego and graduated from Lincoln High School in '02. Lincoln was gang bang central. You had niggas from Lincoln Park Bloods, Skyline Piru, Little Africa Piru, 59 Brims, Emerald Hills, shit all in one school. It was a predominantly blood school to say the least, with a few Crips that snuck through the cracks sprinkled here and there.

I was never into the gang members cause all they wanted to do was set trip and kill each other. Plus, I be damn if I was gone catch a stray bullet sitting in the passenger side of his ride. Or parked with my nigga while another nigga from a different set that had beef with him, got ta shooting and shit tryna kill my nigga, only to miss him and hit me. Never that! So I always talked to the ballers and nigga's tryna get money. Especially the D-Boys because they were the ones in High School already driving their own whips.

"So wuss up Baby Girl? You gone let a nigga holla or wut?" The handsome nigga in the Benz said smiling, showing his dimple while eyeing me through his Versace shades. I walked over to his car, kneeled down enough to the point that we were eye ta eye and said, "Wuss up?"

"Nothin much, just seeing wut a nigga like me gotta do ta get to know a sweet looking lady like yourself." He stuck out his hand and said, "They call me Get'It." I shook his hand and said, "Get'It, huh? Well, why do they call you that?"

"Because there's never been anything on this earth that I've ever wanted that I couldn't get."

"Is that right?" I was turned on by his confidence.

"Yes ma'am. And your name is?"

"Jennifer."

"Well, Jennifer, I can already feel the vibe and slight connection between us which I'm sure, if I can feel it, then you must feel the same. So with that being said, we only have a few more seconds before that their red-light turns green and I gotta put foot to petal. So how about we exchange hook ups so we can finish this conversation a little later where we leave off now?" I took out my eyeliner pen and wrote my number down on the back of a receipt I had in my purse. No sooner than I handed him my number, the light turned green.

"Alright Jennifer, I'm ah hit you up."

And that's how I met Get'It. The next day, Get'It called me and asked if he could take me out to dinner and a movie. I said sure.

"Alright then, how bout I pick you up at six, that way we have enough time ta eat and catch the late movie."

"Sounds good to me." I gave him my address and directions ta get to my apartment, hung up the phone, then got ready for our date. Our first date was cool, but our second date was better. For our second date, Get'It rented a twelve passenger speed boat at Mission Bay and had a picnic basket with bottles of Moet, and an ounce of weed.

None of that square cheese and cracker bullshit, or feed me grapes out the picnic basket. This was some real "G" shit. Blunts and Moet on a speed boat. Yeah this nigga was the business. This was the first step of him gaming his way right into my heart. And let me tell you something, it worked.

"I never been on a boat before," I said as Get'It helped me onto the boat.

"Well, pretty lady, there's a first time for everything." I took a seat on the long sofa like seat that wrapped around the back of the boat and got comfortable while Get'It placed the picnic basket down on the floor board. We cruised the bay and shoreline while sipping Moet, enjoying the atmosphere and San Diego sunshine weather. We cruised under the Coronado Bridge while smoking a blunt of Humble Kush.

We finished the blunt and cut the engine to the speed boat and just floated outside the horizon of Mission Bay. The sway of the rocking boat on the open sea was relaxing. Get'It walked over to me and sat down. He placed his arm around me as I leaned into his shoulder and rested my head. For about five or ten minutes, we just sat there silently and enjoyed each other's company. No forced conversation, just a comfortable silence. This was the best date I ever had in my life. Never have I ever felt so good in the arms of a man. Something about him captivated my essence and inner core.

The more time I spent with him, the more I wanted to be with him, and not just because he had money. Even though I can't lie, it helped. But it was more about his style and the way he carried himself. His confidence and way he went about doing things. Like he owned the world, and this was just our second date. That very moment, on the water sitting in his arms, I knew I had to have him. A woman knows within the first five minutes of meeting a man if she's feeling him or not, and within ten if she a sleep with him, and this situation was no different. I was feeling Get'It the moment he rolled and pushed up on me at the stoplight. All he was doing at this point was getting me more intrigued. He had me wide opened and the look on his face signified he knew it, too.

"You enjoying yourself, baby?" He asked.

"Extremely! This is the best date I ever been on."

"Good and this is just the beginning. I'm a make sure everyday of your life is an adventure."

"Is that right?"

"Oh that's more than right. This is the lifestyle I live, love and like, while only dealing with the finer things in life. I live life to the upmost. I never settle for less. Why should I? This is America. Home of the Free. Where dreams come true. The place where you can do anything you want with a little hard work, hustle and determination. There's no excuse for being broke in America. Now maybe if we were in a third world country or some shit, and even then I'd make it. when You could drop me off in the middle of Tijuana and I'd stand on the corner slanging burritos and pinata's until I came up on a bomb ass Señorita. See, this shit is in you, not on you baby. Either you got hustle or you don't. A true hustler can always make a way outta no way. The type a nigga that can roll down a one way street and still find two ways to his destination. No cars, clothes, and jewelry and still have a way to come up. You feel me? That's the makings of a true hustler. You feel wut I'm tryna learn you to?"

"Yeah I feel you."

"Well, you're too close not ta feel me, but do you hear me?"

"Yeah I hear you."

"I got plans for us Baby Girl. I got visions."

"So wuss your plans?"

"Well, if you listen, I'll tell you and after I tell you, I'll show you. See, I know it's a no brainer that I get money. Shit, you could see that in the dark with both hands covering your eyes. But like they say, behind every great man is a great woman, and let me tell you now I'm one of the greatest. Now, all I need is a woman that's bonafide, fine, qualified and wanna be by my side. A female that likes ta get it like I get it. I want a bitch that's money motivated like myself. One that does whatever it takes ta get paid and succeed in life. Now I know you love money just like I do, if not more, because I saw the way your eyes lit up the other day when I pulled up on you in my big daddy Benz, and that was before I rolled down the window and you got a good look at me."

Shit, nothing gets past this nigga.

"Yeah Baby Girl, I don't miss a beat. You wouldn't be able ta get something past me on a conveyor belt in a Coke factory. I'm very observant and a good judge of character. But its cool baby. This is one of the things that I like about you. You have a pay me or pay me no attention attitude like myself."

"Yeah, but it's not just about that. It's not like I'm a gold digger or anything. I just know that I look too good and have too much to offer ta be settling for less or fuckin wit a bum ass broke nigga, no car still living with his momma. I could do bad all by myself. So why drag a nigga along to do bad with me, or vise versa."

"I feel you. I agree 1000%."

"Well, I'm feeling you and I really like you so I'm down for whatever."

"Is that right?"

"Yep! Business over bullshit. I feel like you're the whole package. You look good, carry yourself well, and got money. Wut moe can a bitch need or want, except some good dick?" We both laughed. "Real shit, doe."

"I got you, Ma. Keep it funky then."

"So if you're asking me if I'm down ta get money, shit ain't no question."

"Well, I didn't ask you nothing yet. Before you jump the gun and fire the pistol, you might wanna check what ammo's being used. I say all that to say, do you know how I get my money?"

"No, but I have a pretty good idea."

"Oh is dat right? So wut you think I do?"

"Not that I mind, but I'd say you was a D-Boy." He laughed.

"D-Boy? Nah Baby Girl, I'm a P-boy, not a D-boy. I ain't never sold drugs a day in my life. Including the short stint I worked at CVS and Walgreens when I was sixteen."

"Ah P-boy? Wuss dat?"

"That's a pimp, Baby Girl. Man of the night, Gentleman of Leisure, Paper in My Pocket and all around Playa." Okay, so I didn't see that one coming. I got blind sided like a runaway truck on the wrong side of the freeway. I took my head off his shoulder, looked him in the eyes, and said,

"So you want me to be your hoe?"

"I want you to do like you said and be down to get money. I want you to use what you've been using all your life to manipulate men, whether you realize it or not. I wanna show you how to get that big pot of gold at the end of the rainbow, and I ain't talking about Lucky Charms either. I wanna convert you from a square to a bonafide hoe wit game. From basic to cable. I wanna introduce you to the lifestyle of the rich and famous without Robin Leach."

Now I know I said I was about my money and down for anything, but this was one thing I never even thought about doing. The weird part about it all is that, I didn't feel offended, upset, tricked, misused, or gamed on in the least. Get'It had a way with words. The way he put things made it not sound so bad. He made shit sound like it made perfect sense. He had me open like a garage door to new ideas. A new found way of thinking. Like it was two different worlds on one planet. Those that made shit happen and those that waited for shit ta happen. Cats and dogs, squares and lames, pimps and hoes.

Ta make a long story short, I was a little reluctant ta take Get'It up on his offer at first, but needless ta say, by the time our date was over, he broke me down and turned me out. My time working and breakin luck was on the Blade. Get'It said he was gonna start me from the bottom up. That way when I reached the top, I would appreciate where I was at and knew where I came from. He said hoes that never worked the Blade and just fucked with the internet and escort services was too lazy. Then they get boogie and start turning their nose up ta Blade Runners. Like they're too good to work the track. Like they're more high class or better than the hoes that work the Blade just because they're in an escort service. When all the while, the business is the same, just the store front is different. We all selling pussy.

So for the first six months, I worked the Blade. At first, I was extremely nervous and didn't know what to expect. My main concern was getting kidnapped or raped. Get'It gave me a stun-gun and mace to protect myself. The mace was hidden inside a fake pen so that a person wouldn't suspect or see it coming when you pulled it out and sprayed him. My first night out, I made $600.00 and was instantly hooked. It was like something was awakened inside of me. This is why they say once a hoe, always a hoe, because once you realize and get used to making money with your pussy. The only thing you can sell over and over and still own, there's no way in hell you'll ever go back to being broke again. Shit, at least not no self respecting real hoe. What other job could I get at twenty making $600 a day? You tell me that. The fuckin President doesn't even make that kind of money. The more I hoe'd, the more money I made. The more money I made, the more addictive it got. After I made my first thousand, there was no turning back. I didn't make my first rack until Daddy put me in an escort service.

My first night working, I made twelve hundred dollars. Never in my wildest dreams did I ever think I could make that kind of money. I was so proud of myself. I couldn't wait ta break myself that night and show Daddy how much I made. The escort service was a lot easier to wok than the track. A bitch could sit around in her night clothes with her hair and face done just chilling at the house waiting for the phone to ring. The way it would work was, a trick would call the service and request a certain type of female, black, white, blonde, brunette, whatever. The service would negotiate a price depending on how many hours the trick wanted to spend. The going rate is between $150/$300 an hour, depending on how high class the service was. The better the girls look, the better the service. The better the service, the more money it cost.

After the service booked the call, they would contact one of the girls that worked for the service and dispatch her out. The service and girl would split the initial fee 50/50 or 60/40, in favor of the service. That was just for showing up. Upon arrival, the trick and the girl would negotiate a price for anything extra he would like to do outside of talking and companionship. This is where the girls made their real money. This was considered a tip and girls didn't have to split tips with the service. That was 100% their money. So a bitch could walk away with $500.00 or better just from one call.

On average, a bitch a get at least three calls a night. Some nights were better, some nights were worse. Either way, you do the math. Sometimes, I would get back to back calls all night until the sun came up. This was considered a good night, because as long as the calls came in, a bitch was gonna make her money. Sometimes, no calls came in at all. These were the days when Daddy would be walking around upset with his lips poked out like a kid that didn't receive the present he wanted for his birthday.

Those was considered bad nights. Those was also the reason why a lot of pimps talked shit about the service and hoes who only worked them, because on the blade there's no such thing as a bad day or day off. But a smart pimp does the math. On the blade, you're lucky to clear a rack, and in order to make a rack, you're gonna have to fuck and suck a lot more tricks for a lot less dough. In the service, you can make three times the amount you'd make on the blade in one night. On the track, you have a high chance of getting raped or going to jail. In the service, they screen their calls, take down and verify their personal info, and vice don't do stings as regular.

So you don't have to know calculus to be able to do the math, just common sense. But a lot of greedy pimps just don't understand or get it. Then the end result is their bitch is hotter than a firecracker. Overworked, underpaid, with a bunch of hoe cases. Like Forrest Gump said, "Stupid is as stupid does." I only had one bad experience working in the escort service. It was about a year ago, one cold winter night in Daygo.

Ringgg! Ringg! "Hello!" I answered the phone on the side of my nightstand a little after 4am. I wiped the cold from my eye with the back of my hand and clicked on the Playboy Bunny lamp to my left. "Hi Jennifer, this is Cindy. We have a call for you," the receptionist from Exotic Playmates, the escort service I worked for, said as I answered the phone.

"Okay, let me get a pen." I picked up the pen off the nightstand along with the notepad I use to write down my calls.

"Okay, I'm ready."

"His name is James Gray. He's supposed to be in the Military so check his ID when you get there. The address is 1455 Hill St. in Oceanside." *Damn, I hated driving all the way to Oceanside, especially in the middle of the night.* Oceanside was forty-five minutes away from Daygo and sometimes you get all the way to the call and for whatever reason it doesn't go through. Maybe you wasn't the trick's type or what he expected. Maybe he didn't have enough money to do anything extra. Or maybe another escort beat you to the call because a lot of times, a trick would call a few escort services at the same time and then pick the best or first girl that showed up. So driving for forty-five minutes at four o'clock in the morning for nothing was not something I was looking forward to. Anyhow, I was about my money and a bitch gotta do what a bitch gotta do.

"His number is (760) 555-3506, in case you get lost. You can MapQuest the directions. I told him $200.00 for an hour, plus $50.00 traveler's fee."

"Okay, that's fine. Sounds good," I responded, with the phone resting on my shoulder and ear as I wrote down the directions. "I'll be there within the hour."

"Okay honey, call me when you get there to check in so I know you arrived safe and are alright."

"Will do." I hung up the phone, jumped in the bathroom and took a quick shower, did my hair, got dressed and was out the door. A real hoe, or should I say, a "good" hoe, should be up and out the door within five minutes or less. At least that's what my Daddy taught me, and now I live and stand by that. I can go from a dead sleep to up and ready out the doe in five minutes flat, and tonight was no different.

I made it to the call in record time. 38 minutes. I was speeding like a supped up Honda on The Fast-N-Furious. **Ding-dong!** I rang the doorbell and patiently waited for James to answer. The door opened slowly to reveal a Navy Seal looking type a man standing before me. He was white, in his early thirties and in great shape. He had that stereotypical Military crewcut flat top and stood straight up like he was always at attention or had a stick up his butt.

His only real flaw was that he was ugly as fuck. I could see why he had to call an escort service to get some pussy. "Hello, my name is Jenna." That was my work name.

"Hi Jenna, I'm James. Nice to meet you." He shook my hand then stepped to the side to let me in. "You're very beautiful. May I take your coat?"

"Thank you and yes you may." He helped me take off my coat and placed it on the coat rack by the door. Of course, I got right to business. "May I see your ID to verify who you are, and use your phone to check in with my service so they know that I'm here and safe?"

"Sure, not a problem dear." He took his Military ID out of his wallet and showed it to me. The picture and name revealed he was indeed James Gray. I then called my service and let them know I had arrived and was safe. They said alright and would give me a courtesy call in an hour to make sure I got out okay. After I hung up, I collected the service fee, which in fact I should have done first when I walked in, right before I asked to see his ID. That way if there was some bullshit in the game or the call didn't got through, I'd still have the $250.00 service fee and could just walk away with that. Oh well, shoulda coulda woulda. I got it now so that's all that matters.

I put the money in a secret spot in my purse out of sight and plain view, closed it up, and sat down on the love-seat next to James. We talked and got comfortable for about fifteen minutes. I always tried to talk as long as possible to stretch the hour out, that way, by the time we got down to business, there wasn't much time left. The trick would have to do one of two things; cum fast or pay more, which was both fine with me. After fifteen minutes of small talk, we got down to business.

"So lovely lady, how much do you charge for full service?" I loved dealing with regulars. I could tell he was one just by that statement. He wasn't expecting to get anything other than conversation for that $250.00 service fee. That was just for me getting up out my warm bed at four in the morning. New clients always expected the works for that bullshit ass service fee, and that's when you took a risk of the call not going through. I couldn't stand cheap tricks. Like I always told em, you get what you pay for. I was always taught to start high and negotiate your way down. Why start low when its possible you can get more?

So I said, "$1,000.00 for full service, $500.00 for half." He didn't hesitate pulling out his money and counting out ten $100 dollar bills. He handed me the rack and I placed it in my purse along with the $250.00 he gave me earlier.

"Shall we?" He stood up and pulled out his hand, reached for mines, and guided me to his bedroom. I brung my purse with me knowing to always keep the money close. I placed the bag down on his dresser which was in eyesight and reach from his bed. I took my clothes off as he did the same and placed them at the front of the bed. We were now both completely naked. His dick got hard and rose to the occasion as he eyed my perfectly shaped body, firm breasts, and shaved pussy. I took a condom out my purse on the dresser and walked back over towards the bed. I opened the condom, ripped off the wrapper with my teeth, and placed the rubber on James' dick.

James had a pretty nice sized dick for a white man. I was able to roll the condom down to the serial numbers. If you don't know what I'm talking about, then its probable because your dick is too small. I placed his dick in my mouth and swiveled my tongue around the head of his penis. I worked my mouth full of saliva, spit on his dick and got it slippery. Tricks loved when I did that shit. I sucked his dick like a popsicle while stroking the shaft all in one continuous motion. I took his dick out my mouth, looked up at him and said, " How do you want it?"

"From behind. I wanna fuck you doggy-style." I climbed on the bed facing the headboard on all fours and that's when it happened. **BOOM!** The bedroom closet door flew open and a man jumped out like a DEA agent in a raid. Before I knew what was clearly going on, I was pinned to the bed on my stomach with James on top of me holding me down. I tried to struggle but couldn't move. The weight of James 200 lb. plus muscular frame had me stuck. I was helpless.

"Quit struggling bitch," James said as he held my arms down outreached by my wrists. I tried to scream, then saw a flash and stars, then everything move in slow motion from the blow and force of the other man's fist hitting my face.

"Shut the fuck up whore," the mystery man said after punching me in my face. I felt a small stream of blood run down the side of my face from a slight cut under my left eye.

"Why are you doing this?" I asked through blood teared eyes.

"Because we can bitch! Now shut the fuck up and enjoy the ride," James said as I felt his penis enter me from behind. By now I was dry as well as his dick, so when he entered me, it hurt like hell. Not to mention he rammed his shit into me like a linebacker on NFL Sunday. The pain of his dry dick pumping inside me had me in tears. I was just praying that the condom didn't break. The other guy that busted out the closet started stroking his shit, put a condom on, and broke out some KY Jelly. That's when I knew the situation was about to go from bad to worse. James got up and held my hands down while the other guy climbed behind me.

"Let's see how you like this bitch," he said then stuck his dick inside my butt. A burning sensation went through my rectum. The pain was so excruciating I almost passed out. It felt like he was ripping my insides from behind. I tried to scream but James silenced my cries with a dirty sock by stuffing it in my mouth. The man behind me fucked me in the ass for what seemed like eternity.

I couldn't wait for this pain to end. Finally he pulled his dick out my butt and pulled off the condom. My ass was bleeding and on fire like salt on an open wound. Just when I thought it was over, they switched positions. James got behind me and stuck his dick inside my pussy while the other man held me down. Then the man grabbed a fist full of my hair and jacked off in front of my face. I never felt so used and humiliated in my life. I was just hoping James would hurry up and finish so I could get the hell out of there.

No sooner than I had that thought, James came. While James was getting his last few strokes in, the other guy ran through my purse and took their money back. "You won't be needing this, bitch," he said as he showed me the $1,250.00 he just took back, then he threw my purse at me which landed on the bed right beside me. That's where he fucked up at. I reached inside my bag and got ahold of my stun gun and mace. First I sprayed James in one motion turning around as he pulled out of me, He instantly covered his eyes and started screaming. His boy tried to come to his rescue but was too slow. I sprayed him as well. Now they were both naked and blinded by the mace. I used that time to my advantage and re-group. I knew the mace would wear off soon so I grabbed a hold of my 500,000 volt stun gun and went in for the kill.

"Mutha fucka! Yawl wanna rape and rob me?" I took the stun-gun and shocked James in the balls as he tensed up and screamed like a bitch. He hit the floor like a sack of potatoes. I ran over to give him another jolt but realized he was passed out. I then ran over to his friend and gave him the same treatment.

"Yawl fucked with the wrong bitch tonight!" I picked up my clothes, took back my money, and spit on them both on my way out. That was my first and last time being raped. Now I'm a lot more cautious when it comes to tricks. I go into every situation mace in hand and leave nothing to chance. I put nothing past nobody in this game. That's how you stay alive and survive long. Even though that situation happened to me in the service, the odds was still better than the track. On the track, bitches was getting found in dumpsters.

There was a serial killer that had been raping and killing hoes since the early 80's that still hadn't been caught. This guy had the blade hot and the hoes shook up. He was dubbed the "Dumpster Dive Killer" for the way he killed and left all his victims in a dumpster. He had killed over fifteen women in a twenty-three year period and was still out there. Another reason Daddy had me work the service and not the blade at that time. Daddy would tell me the story about his dad who was an ex pimp that went legit and opened up his own car audio and tint service. He told me that back sometime in the 80's, his dad had a hoe named Tina who fell a victim of the Dumpster Dive Killer. She was found strangled to death in a dumpster behind a warehouse not too far from the track. The story had made headlines and really affected his father. He said his dad hadn't pimped a hoe since. He told me that he felt like his dad still blamed himself for what happened to Tina all those years ago. Anyhow, by 2003, the killer had yet ta be caught. In 2005, the killer slipped and found "himself" a victim, after trying to abduct and kill a prostitute that wasn't going down without a fight. Somehow she got ahold of a knife and stabbed him thirty-two times all over his body. DNA recovered from some of the other killings matched up with his and pinned him as the Dumpster Dive Killer. Headlines read, **"25 Year Old Serial Killer and Murderer of 15 Women Finally Caught."**

After that day, the track was wide open. It was like a curse was lifted from the blade, and in some aspects it was. Hoes could get back to getting money without the fear of being found strangled and dead in a dumpster. In the beginning of 2006, Daddy introduced me to the webcam and internet aspect of the game. This raised my stock ten folds. I was wondering why he hadn't introduced me to this a lot sooner. He said, "Everything in time. The longer you're around, the more you know. As long as you stay down, you'll continue to grow." That was his answer. At the time I didn't understand. I thought it was money over bullshit and get it while you can, but once I saw so many bitches come and go and Daddy cop-n-blow, I understood what he was saying.

Game was valuable and profitable. So why give it "all" away for free to the undeserving? Why show your whole hand so another mutha fucka can cut it off? You got choosey bitches that get with a pimp so that they can soak up as much game as possible, then once they feel like they know all they need ta know, be on the first thing smoking out the doe. So, in the beginning, all Daddy taught a bitch was the basics. Yeah my folks was smart, but shit, he had a pimp for a daddy and a hoe for a momma. How could he not be sharp? Daddy always said, "If game's ta be sold, not told, then no one would be able to afford it because the game is priceless. Which is why it should only be told to a chosen few." Real words spoken by a real pimp. I love my Folks.

CHAPTER 8 THE CHRONICLES OF SUNSHINE

"Bitch, Im a need five hunet moe wit dat. I don't give a fuck how slow it is out there. I want a thousand dollars every night. Nothin less. Yadada mean? If it take you fourteen hours plus, and twenty two hunet fucks, then that's wut it do. I wouldn't give a rat's ass in a trap wit his tail stuck behind his back. Rain, hell, sleet or snow, you always have my doe. Understand wut I'm talking bout?"

"Yes, Daddy."

"Now get out their bitch and get the rest of my money, and I don't wanna hear no moe bout it's slow shit. If it's slow then hoe faster." Mackadamian finished up as I got out the car on MacArthur to get the rest of his money. I been with Damian for about a year, ever since I was eighteen. He actually turned me out on my eighteenth birthday. At first everything was all good. Damian was my high school sweetheart, or should I say my high school fantasy. I had a crush on Damian ever since the ninth grade. I was just a freshman and he was a sophomore.

Damian was the most popular kid in school. He didn't play sports, but had a way with the girls. For some reason, females would just lose themselves and go crazy over him. Even when he got caught cheating, he would flip the script and make it seem like it was their fault or they did something wrong by snooping, being nosey, and being all up in his business. There were numerous cat fights between girls over him.

By Senior year, he had girls holding "his" books, giving him lunch money, and taking his SAT and Finals for him. I never thought he noticed or paid me any mind until I ran into him at a graduation party a year after he had already graduated, which was being held for my Senior class. It was an old school kegger house party. The kind you saw on "Sixteen Candles." Or more like the movie with Kid-N-Play. It was a pajama jammy jam. Everybody in the party had on their PJ's and house shoes.

Damian was across the room looking fine as ever, two stepping to the music with a couple of his homeboys. I couldn't take my eyes off him. He was the finest nigga in the party. I guess he felt my eyes on him because he looked up and spotted me across the room checking him out. I tried to turn away but it was too late. I was cold busted. Next thing I knew, he was walking through the crowd, headed in my direction. He introduced himself to me, like I didn't already know who he was. Shit, I been checkin him for four years, unbeknownst to him. I told him my name, we chopped it up with one another, and the rest was history.

Two months later was my eighteenth birthday, and believe it or not, by then there wasn't nothing I wouldn't do for him. He turned me onto the game the same day I blew out my eighteenth candle. I didn't come from a broken home, I was never molested by my dad or family member. I wasn't a runaway chasing a dream only to get caught up and turned out by a pimp. No, I didn't fall into none of that stereotypical shit you hear about when a lot of females explained how they entered the game. I just did it for my love and trust for Damian. Like I told you, he had that type of affect on women and I was no exception.

It's been almost a year since I got with Damian. We've been together for ten months. In the beginning, everything was lovely and straight, but lately he's been poppin a lot of X pills and playing with his nose. He liked snorting heroin and that shit was starting to affect his pimping. I started to lose respect for him. It pained me to see him destroy himself. That "X" shit took the Bay by storm. Everybody and their momma was thizzin, poppin peels and bumpin Mack Dre. I have to admit I liked the way Damian fucked me when he was thizzin, but the drawback was it made him talk too fuckin much. I bet he thought he was spittin game, but really he was just running his mouth about any and everything that came ta mind. That shit was like truth serum. It could make or break a nigga's game because by the end of the night, you'll know exactly how he feels about you.

So the X I didn't mind as much, but the heroin was something else entirely. I didn't like the effects that it had on him. Moving slow and nodding out. That shit had him looking like a feen. Sometimes he'd be so high he couldn't even keep his head up long enough to count his money. That's when some of his other hoes started taking advantage of him and started clipping money. When I noticed he didn't notice, that's when I really started to lose respect for him.

I'd come home from a hard day's work and just see him passed out, leaning like the Tower of Pisa. Nodding out, clowning himself. I'd just shake my head in disgust, drop the money I made in his lap, wash up and go to bed. I was beyond fed up with him and now it was starting to reflect in my hoe'n. I didn't care if I made my quota or not. Why should I? All he was gonna do is snort it up anyway. Fuck dat! I wasn't hoe'n ta support a nigga's drug habit, but let him tell it, it's pimping. I was at my breaking point and ready for a new situation. When the right nigga came along and presented himself correctly, I was outta here.

"Hey girl," I said to Kat, a black hoe that worked for a pimp named F.A.B.

"Hey Aleesha, how you doing? I saw your folks just drop you off," she said as we walked up the track tryna pull a date.

"Yeah he talkin bout I gotta make some moe money before I come home. You know it's never enough wit these niggas."

"Girlll you ain't never lied. My folks be on that bullshit, too. If I make too much too fast, he feel like I can make more. So you know what I started doing? If I have a really good night, anything over five hundred I tuck away. Then if he tries to sit me back down or make me stay out longer, I go post up in a restaurant or something not too far from the track for a couple hours. Then I just kill time for an hour and call him like "I made some more money" and just give him the money I had tucked away ta begin with. Tricks may think with their dick but these nigga's think with their bankroll."

"Girl you crazy." You see how scandalous hoes can be? I was never one to put shit in the game, but I also knew how a nigga mis-pimpin, over pimpin, or not pimpin enough could lead a bitch to do all sorts of foul shit.

"Crazy Hell! Shit, if you let these niggas do you any kind of way and accept it, then you're the crazy one. If you can't appreciate what I do for you and the type of money I bring, then find another bitch."

"I feel you girl, but shit goes both ways. If you ain't happy and satisfied with how a nigga's handling his business, then leave."

"Yeah that's easier said than done. Good pimps are hard to find. Bitch might go from bad ta worst."

"Yeah I feel you on that."

"Not to mention I got too much invested in this relationship. I been with my folks for six years. You don't leave a Fortune 500 company because your boss is an asshole or working you too hard."

"Well, I guess if you put it like that, but still, I'm a firm believer in if you're true to the game, the game a stay true to you. You get back exactly what you put into this shit."

"Okay I can tell that's some shit your folks must've spoon fed you. And you done swallowed it like the morning's breakfast or yesterday's dinner. Tell that shit to all the hoes that busted their ass foe their folks, kept it trill, and still got shit in return. I'm sorry Aleesha, but I been in this game too long and seen too much. You're still a newlywed to this game. Come talk to me when you got five years plus invested in this. Trust me girl, you'll have a different aspect and outlook to the game then. When I first got in the game, I believed all the dreams and big pot at the end of the rainbow shit that was told to me. I bought dat shit like a buyer on the Home Shopping Network falling for the latest gadget. Only to find the actual product didn't live up to the advertisement. And girl, this shit is like fishing, once you're hooked, the game got you."

"Yeah I feel you to a certain degree. That's why I don't plan on being with a bunch of different pimps. Hopping in and out the game from Mack to Mack like a jackrabbit. I'm actually looking for a new situation now, but you can best believe when I choose, Im a choose wisely."

"Girl, you know my folks is always taking applications."

"I ain't tryna fuck with your crazy folks. Shit his name say it all, Fuck-A-Bitch. That'll be like jumping out the frying pan and into the fire." We both laughed.

"Well, shit you know I had ta try. I wouldn't mind having you as a wife-n-law."

"No, when the right nigga come along, I'll know. Until then, Im a hang in there and stick wit my Folks." See that was one thing about the game. A pimp never knew when a hoe was fed up or ready ta shake it and break camp. One day everything could seem cool as a fan and fine as a model and the next the hoe could be gone without a trace. A hoe was unpredictable like a pitbull in a dog fight. I'm sure this was one of the reasons they kept us broke, because a hoe with money was more subject to leave than a hoe with no money.

All that, "They need all the money because a hoe don't know how ta stack" shit sound good. If you're two years old, blind deaf, dumb and ignorant. Shit, pimps blew more money than a hoe ever could; $1,200 Gators, $3,000 suits, $40,000 cars, $20,000 jewelry, you do the math. Then they preach to us that we're gonna blow the money on our nails, hair, and new outfits.

Shit, it ain't that much clothes, nails, and hair in the world. With dat kinda money, I could get my hair and nails done everyday for the next 365 days and still have change left over after I'm done. But let a pimp tell it, this is why they gotta keep all our money. Yeah, like I said, sounds good. I wasn't that dumb or naive. I never gave my money to my folks because I had to, I gave it to him because I wanted to. That's why when a hoe is tired of paying a pimp, she leaves. No matter how good the dick is, how big his name is, and how good he treats her. In this game, its money over everything.

"Well, girl let me get ta work and make dis money before I be out here all night," I said as I waved at a passing trick that looked like he was looking for some sexual healing. I watched him go up the street, make a u-turn, and double back.

"Okay I need to get ta work myself before my folks roll up and see me talking instead of working. I'll be in the dog house for real then.

Literally!" We both laughed.

"Girl you crazy," I said as the trick pulled up to the curb not too far from where we were walking. I walked towards the car and Kat walked towards the corner to pull a date of her own.

$$$$$

Two Days Later…

I was working the blade like any other normal day, when I noticed two new girls on the track I never saw before. I liked their style because they carried themselves with a class most blade runners lacked in the game. They had designer hoe clothes on and high end heels instead of the usual swap meet knock-offs and cheap shit. One was White and the other was Asian, which you rarely saw on the blade in Oakland. I could tell right away they weren't from around here.

I watched how they worked. They were in and out of cars left and right. They were seriously bout their money. They were putting the rest of us hoes to shame. You could tell too, by how upset and jealous the other hoes got watching them hop in and out of trick's cars getting money. I wasn't a hater though. I respected their hustle. They had that drive and dedication that a hoe has when she's still new to the game, but had the know how and money making capabilities of a Vet.

I wondered who their folks was. Whoever he was, he must have been doing something right because these hoes looked happy, and ain't nothing better than a happy hooker. You could see that get money glow on their face that only another hoe or true pimp could recognize. While all the other hoes was on the track hating on them, I was walking up to introduce myself and congratulate them.

"Hi, I'm Aleesha," I said as I approached them, hand extended in a greeting like manner.

"Hi, my name is Yuki and this is my wife-n-law Green Eyes," the Asian one said smiling as we shook hands.

"I haven't seen you guys around here before and thought I'd introduce myself."

"Yeah this is our first time in Oakland. I'm from San Diego and Green Eyes is from LA."

"Well, then let me be the first to welcome you to Oakland."

"Thanks." We talked a little more. I gave them the Ins and outs of the blade. Which vice was crooked, which pimps to watch out for, what times was best to get money on what streets, and other hoe shit that was beneficial to know when you was in the game. I liked Yuki and Green Eyes. They were pretty down to earth. Later on that day, a man I believe to be their pimp, pulled up in a rental and picked them up. He was handsome, young, and carried himself cool as hell. I'd never seen him before on the blade or with any of the local pimps from around the area, which to me was a good thing.

I was tired of Oakland pimps. They were some of the most cut throat nigga's you'd ever come in contact with. And playing with your nose and poppin X was like the thing to do. All I did was smoke weed and even that was just on occasion, so that heroin shit was a complete turn off. The next day, I saw Yuki on the blade and we started talking. "Hey Yuki."

"Hey Aleesha."

"I saw you and your wife-n-law get picked up yesterday by that handsome young man in the rental. Was that your folks?"

"Yeah his name is Jackpot but everyone calls him JP."

"Oh really? He seems nice."

"Yeah he treats me good. He's the only pimp I ever had or been with and probably ever will. He never hits me, always spoils me, stacks his chips, and you never see him blowing money. That's why he was in the rental because he been just stacking to get a big house when we go back home, as well as nice cars for everyone else, not just himself. He's very considerate and really takes care of business. Why, you looking for a new situation or something?"

"Yeah, sorta. I have folks at the moment, but the thrill is gone. Not to sound choosey or nothin. I mean, I been wit my folks for almost a year. He was my first and only pimp. He was the one that turned me on to the game, but lately, he been doing too much drugs and slacking in his mackin, which I'm sure you know is a complete turn off to a real hoe, and now I'm just at the point where I'm over it. I been hoe'n for this nigga for almost a year, made well over a hundred thousand and still don't even have a car of my own. Just little shit like that."

"Yeah I understand."

"I wouldn't trip if he was just stacking, and that was the reason he hadn't bought me a car yet. Shit, a hoe can respect that, but that's not the case. I feel like all my money's going to the dope man. I my as well choose him cause dat's who got my money."

"Yeah I feel you girl. I wouldn't want my folks high 24/7 or my hard working money going to the dope man either."

"Your Folks sound cool. I would like ta meet him if you don't mind having another wife-n-law in your family."

"I don't mind. I like you. You're pretty cool. I think you'll fit in with our family well, but let me tell you, my folks puts loyalty over money. Death before dishonor. If you're not willing to be in this for the long haul, then don't choose him. His motto is, 'Till Game Do Us Part' and he lives by that to the fullest."

"Yeah I can dig dat, I'm wit it. I'm not no choosey bitch. That's why I been just waiting for the right person to come along to choose up with."

"Well after work, we'll call 'em, that way if you decide ta choose up, you'll have some money to give him."

"Alright, sounds good to me." We went back to work and continued hoe'n throughout the day. I was working hard to make as much money as I could incase I chose up with Jackpot. I knew the more money I came with, the better it would make me look in his eyes. I had to prove that I was an asset, and not a liability. That I could get it just like his other two hoes. I was a black girl that made white girl money, so I buckled down and hoe'd my ass off. By the end of the night, I had $846.00. Yeah I know that's an off number. But hey, a bitch got hungry. Yuki called her folks.

"Daddy, we're done and I have a girl that wants to meet you."

"Is dat right? Dat's wuss up. I'll be there in ten minutes."

"Okay Daddy, see you then." She hung up the phone and said, "He'll be here in ten minutes." We waited at the bus stop so the police or vice wouldn't harass us, and made it look like we were just waiting for the bus. Two minutes later, Green Eyes pulled up with a trick and got out the car. She'd just finished up a date.

"Hey girls!"

"Hey Green Eyes," I said and waved with a slight smile. She smiled, said hi and gave Yuki a hug. "I called Daddy. He said he should be here in ten minutes. That was about two minutes ago."

"Cool, then I guess I'm right on time. I just made my quota, too." Just as Green Eyes finished talking, Jackpot pulled up in the rental. We hurried up and got in, after surveying the area to make sure no cops was around or prying eyes. Yuki got in the front and Green Eyes and I got in the back.

"Daddy, this is Aleesha. Aleesha, this is Daddy," Yuki introduced us.

"Hey how you doing pretty lady? My name is Jackpot. You can call me JP for short."

"Nice ta meet you."

"Likewise."

"I heard a lot about you, all good things of course."

"Is dat right? Well, it seems you know a lot about me but I know nothing of you. So how bout we go sit down somewhere, get something ta eat and get ta know each other better."

Even though I wasn't hungry, I agreed. "Sure." We drove to Denny's, seeing how everything else was closed, and got a booth in the back for privacy. Yuki and Green Eyes must have been starved because they ordered enough food to feed the four of us between them two alone. We all joked and laughed about it afterwards. I really wasn't that hungry so I ordered a salad and small appetizer. JP ordered steak and eggs and a large orange juice. Yuki pulled the money she made out her purse and handed it to JP. I watched as he counted it. She made $700.00. Inside, I was happy that I made more. Green Eyes pulled a stack of money out her bra and handed it to JP as well. She made $600.00

This really had me anxious ta pull out the $846.00 I had made and hand it over to him. I felt good knowing that I could hold my own and make just as much, if not more money as Yuki and Green Eyes. These were some top notch bitches. Straight money makers, and this let me know I was right up their wit 'em. The average hoe only got $500.00 or less off that blade, and here it was all three of us made over that. I knew then I would fit in this family just fine.

We all talked and got ta know each other better. We all had a lot in common. I liked the fact that JP wasn't over the top with his pimpin. It was like he knew how to turn it up or down at the right moment for the right situation. In a square atmosphere, he conducted himself low key instead of drawing a whole bunch of attention which never leads to nothing good. But in our world, he was a die hard pimp through and through. By the end of our meal and conversation, I was ready to choose.

I handed him the money I made and said, "I choose you, Daddy."

"That's wuss up Ma." I smiled as he counted the money I gave him. I was proud of myself.

"Welcome to the family," Yuki and Green Eyes said and gave me a hug.

"Look at that smile on you could light up a room. Matter a fact, from here on out, your name is Sunshine," Daddy said as he welcomed me into the family as well. "Let me get your ex-folks number so I can serve 'em some news." I gave him Mackadamian's number and sat back as I watched him use the pay phone to give 'em a call.

"Hello, may I speak ta Mackadamian?"

"Dis him, who dis?"

"Well, it ain't Walter Cronkite but it is a pimp right. Call USA Today and tell 'em stop the press cause the news is your bitch Aleesha, no longer belongs to you. She clicked her heels three times and came home to dis pimping."

"Is dat right? Who dis I'm talkin to?"

"Jackpot Tha Pimp, Daygo's finest, your Royal Highness."

"Alright pimp, I can't do nothing but respect dat."

"Glad ta see you handling it like the gentlemen we are. I'm a set the bitch back down tomorrow and give you action at her because I respect the game as such and ain't into hiding and harboring no bitch."

"That's pimps up."

"Alright then P, keep it mackin and cadillacin."

"All the time." He hung up the phone then said, "come on hoes, let's bounce." The next day Jackpot set me down on the blade. He told me that if I saw or ran into my old folks to put my head down, turn around and keep it moving like a 747. As expected, about two hours later, Mackadamian hit the track.

"Hey hoe, So what it is, you making a mad move on a pimp?"

I put my head down, turned the other way and started stepping as instructed.

"Bitch you can put your head down but I'm a still be around. Hoe, I made you so let me catch you outta pocket so I can break you. Hoe don't know she got it good until she hop over the fence thinking the grass is greener and land on all wood."

I crossed the street, head down in tow tryna shake this nigga like a pair of dice in a crap game.

"Hoe you can keep it moving but I'm a stay on your heels until you start choosing."

Well, it's gonna take more than them corny ass lines and nursery rhymes for me ta ever fuck wit you again. Shit, what did I ever see in this nigga?

"Bitch, on some real live shit, come home now and I can look over your insubordinates. If you're unhappy, then talk to a pimp so I can make you happy. We pose ta be in this together like Batman and Robin, assisting each other to do great. It pose ta been me and you against the world. I made you from a lump of clay and molded you into the hoe you are today. How can you turn your back on your creator and still live with yourself? How can you pay another mutha fucka without thinking bout me? The game is ran like pure cane sugar, and when it eats you up and spit you out, remember who was really there for you to the fullest. I'm done following you up and down these streets hoe, cause I ain't never met a bitch worth chasin."

Good, then maybe you'll stop talking and walking behind me cause all you're doing is wasting your breath like a drowning man with no oxygen tank underwater tryna breath, I thought to myself as I crossed back over to the other side of the street for the last time. This time he didn't follow me, thank God. He walked back up the street, got in his Cadillac, and drove off. That was the final nail in the coffin of mine and Mackadamian's relationship. I was officially Jackpot's bitch.

For the next two months, we stayed in Oakland, then headed out to Seattle. We were in Seattle for a few weeks before Daddy knocked a new bitch. Her name was Lisa. Apparently she had just gotten out of prison for drug trafficking. I didn't like her off the back. I couldn't put my finger on it, but there was something shady about her. The smile on her face said one thing, but the look of deceit in her eyes said another. Women have a way of seeing what men can't. Call it women's intuition. Still being, I kept my feelings to myself because I didn't wanna come across as jealous, a hater, or start no shit.

Plus, there was a slight chance I could be wrong about her so at least I'd give her a chance. Everyone deserved that. I believed in letting a person shoot their own foot off, then when they can't walk anymore, the only person they have to blame is themselves. So needless to say, I as well as Yuki and Green Eyes, welcomed Lisa into the family with open arms. At first, everything was great. We all got along, money was rolling in, and everyone was happy. We were Daddy's main four bitches. A lot of other hoes came and went, but we were the main four. We went cross country hitting every main track in the United States, from the Big Apple to the Pineapple.

Daddy bought a mini mansion in Bonita, an upscale neighborhood in San Diego. We all lived with him and had our own separate bedrooms. This was three years from the day I chose. 1999 was the year. In 2000, we brung in the millennium in Las Vegas, the same year we did it big at the Player's Ball and Daddy won Pimp of the Year. That was a great year for us. By then, we all had exotic cars, nice clothes and a big home with Daddy. But it was also the beginning of the end of a situation I knew was bound to get ugly and fall apart.

"Bitch, I'm so tired of your shit!"

"Then do something about it hoe," Lisa responded to Yuki's statement. This had been going on for a while now. There'd been a lot of tension in the house lately. Mainly because of Lisa. My suspicions of her were finally starting to manifest itself. She was like a dark cloud in the house. She been constantly getting into it with everyone, but mostly Yuki. She was jealous of Yuki because of the type of relationship her and JP had, and the fact that she was with him first and could probably never measure up to Yuki. At least, that's how she saw it. So for the past few months, they been getting into it a lot and fighting. I never really got into it with Lisa as much because I don't think she saw me as a threat. Maybe it was because I was the only black girl in the family. I don't know, but whatever it was, she never really came at me too crazy.

"Yeah Im a do something alright." Yuki got in Lisa's face and smacked the shit out of her ,like an outta pocket hoe at a pimp convention.

"Bitch, you don't never put your fucking hands on me!" Lisa grabbed Yuki by the hair and threw her to the ground. They were now rolling around on top of each other in a full fledge cat fight. Yuki started swinging for the fences and hit Lisa in the face. Still holding onto Yuki's hair, Lisa started scratching up her face and ripped the front of her shirt, revealing Yuki's breast as they popped out like Janet Jackson's titty years later at the Super Bowl. Yuki punched Lisa in the stomach which made her let go of Yuki's hair and clinch her stomach.

"Take that bitch," Yuki said then punched her again in the face. Lisa screamed like a mad woman in a crazy house.

"No bitch, take this!" Lisa leapt at Yuki like a lion in the wild. In one motion, got ahold of her leg and bit her. She bit her so hard she broke skin and drew blood.

"Ahhh! Let go of my fuckin leg!" By then, me and Green Eyes jumped in and pulled them apart.

"Get this bitch off me," Yuki said as we broke 'em up. Lisa bit Yuki so hard she had ta get five stitches. When Daddy came home, he was pissed. He made them both stand in the corner with one leg up like a flamingo for five hours. By the fourth hour, they were begging Daddy to just beat their ass rather then stand in the corner any longer. Shit was coming to a head like puss in a pimple and staph in a bump.

Life was good for three years, but now things was going downhill quicker than a go-kart in San Francisco. Still being, my loyalty to JP kept me around longer than I wished too. But by 2001, I was fed up and couldn't take it anymore. I felt like the walls were closing in. My intuition told me disaster was about to strike. Lisa was out of control and doing all kinds a scandalous shit. She was evil and I knew it was only a matter of time before Hurricane Lisa wrecked havoc on our situation and destroyed the family, and as much as I loved JP, Yuki and Green Eyes, I refused ta stay around and watch that happen.

So I packed up my stuff one day when everyone was gone, wrote Daddy a note explaining how I felt about things and why I was leaving, and left. Never to return again. It was one of the hardest decisions I ever made, but one I knew I had to make. When I left JP, I moved back to Oakland where I ran into Kat.

"Hey girl, long time no see," I said as I approached Kat who was walking towards me on the blade.

"Hey girl! How you been? I haven't seen you in ages."

"Yeah I know. I been living in San Diego for the past five years, but now I'm back."

"What brings you back here?"

"Just a change of scenery."

"Well, ain't shit going on down here. You heard about what happened to your ex folks Mackadamian?"

"No, what?"

"Girrrl, he a straight dope feen in the worst way. After you left him, he started going down hill. At first, he was doing okay, then slowly but surely, he started losing bitches and got knocked for the rest of his stable one by one. He then went from snorting to shooting up. That's when things really got bad. It was like he fell so hard he wasn't able ta pick himself back up. He hasn't had a whore in over a year. You'll see him around here chasin dope, looking bummy, or nodding out on a crate behind some alley somewhere. Girrrl, you wouldn't even recognize him."

"Damn is dat right?"

"Yep, but hey you're looking good. That pimp of yours must really be taking care of you."

"He was, but I ain't with him no more."

"Wuttt, is dat right?"

"Yeah girl, it was good while it lasted, but I had ta leave that situation. That's why I came home, for a fresh start."

"Well, girl you know my folks have always been interested in you."

"Yeah and I like said before, I ain't tryna get with your crazy ass folks."

"Oh girl, he's changed a lot. He doesn't put his hands on me no more. Unless I do some real outta pocket shit. Which I don't, so I don't get beat. And he stepped his game up major. You saw us at the Player's Ball."

"Yeah I have to admit he did look good and you guys did look happy."

"Girl, you should give him a chance. What could it hurt? I promise you won't be disappointed."

"Girl, you missed your calling. You should have been an Army recruiter or some shit." We laughed. "I'll think about it. Like you said, what can it hurt? If I ain't happy with the situation, I'll just leave."

"Exactly! Nothing lost, nothing gained."

Once again, I was about to go against my better judgement and intuition. I knew better than to fuck or get with F.A.B, but in my mind, I truly felt like *what could it hurt?* I could always leave if I wasn't happy, but anybody in their right mind with just an ounce of common sense would know that leaving JP and going to F.A.B was like leaving Heaven and going to Hell. But what can I say? Bitches don't always make the right decisions and hoes were no exception. Later on that evening after work, I went home with Kat.

F.A.B was surprised ta see me. He knew I used to belong to JP and was one of his main bitches and extremely loyal. When I walked through the door, he had a look on his face like he had just hit the mother load. Like he had just gotten ahold of one of JP's prized possessions, and in some ways, he did. It was like walking into your house and finding the Mona Lisa hanging on your wall.

I chose up and for a while everything was good. F.A.B did everything in his power to keep me happy and for a while I was. But the more he catered to me, the less he paid attention to Kat and his other hoes. And just like the Lisa situation, this started to cause jealousy amongst the other females towards me. I was starting to realize how Yuki must have felt with Lisa always tripping and hating on her. It hadn't gotten as bad yet, but I could see it was coming.

It wasn't to the point of cat fights yet, but the bitches was getting petty. Little stuff like tripping on who sat in the front seat of Daddy's car when we went out, what days one would spend with him. Like for instance, if I got to spend a Friday or Saturday with him, then they got upset because they had to spend a Monday or Tuesday. You know, little shit like that. In the beginning of 2002, we went to the AVN Awards and Porn Convention in Vegas.

"Pimps up, Playa."

"Pimps up wit cha," F.A.B greeted another pimp named "Too Much," who had two white girls on his arm, cane and pimp cup in tow. Too Much was from San Diego. I remember seeing him in Horton Plaza shopping with his hoes and a few times on the blade when I was still with Jackpot.

"Just came down ta see if a young Oakland Mack like myself can knock one of these big titty snow bunnies, yadada mean?"

"Yeah, I can dig it baby. I just came from Daygo ta make my presence known as well. Hoes on arms, diamonds in charm. Know wut I'm talking bout?"

"Yadada!"

"Yeah it's winter time, but even in the summer I make it snow everywhere I go. The only time you see it snow in Daygo is when I hit the stroll wit foe, five hoes, you feel me?"

"Yeah I feel you, P."

"So I see you looking good as well pimp. Hoes looking like a reverse Oreo wit them two white bitches and that black one in the middle."

"Oh yeah, them just the ones I gave the day off too. I got a stable bigger than Godzilla on the back of King Kong climbing the Empire State Building."

F.A.B brung me and two of my wife-n-laws to the convention because we made the most money last month. That was our reward. While everyone else was working, we got to take the night off and enjoy the Porn Convention. Everyone was there, from old school porn stars to the new. Ron Jeremy was there promoting his new book and Screech from Saved By The Bell had a booth selling his own personal amateur porn DVD. Everybody who was anybody in the porn business was there.

"Yeah I heard you was doing it real big pimp"

"Well, you sho heard right, pimp suit. You know pimping gunning for that Pimp of the Year at the Daygo Ball Pimpsy throwing in June."

"Yeah you know my man's renting out a yacht and the whole nine. He got Maroy from Too Real for TV coming out to film it and everything. Yeah it's gonna be real live Jack." I just sat back ear hustling, listening to Too Much tell F.A.B about the up and coming Player's Ball that was taking place this summer in Daygo.

"Alright pimp juice, I'm finna keep it moving and grooving and see if I can come up on a choosing."

"Fa'sho, playa. pimps up!"

"Hoes down," Too Much said as he walked off with both his hoes trailing behind head down, as they passed F.A.B I went over to one of the porn booths to have a look at their display and when I turned around, I got the shock of my life.

"How you been Sunshine?" Oh my God! It was Jackpot!

"Wuss up baby girl? You ain't got love for a pimp no more?" All I could do was what I was supposed to. I put my head down, walked over, and stood behind F.A.B I could see the shock and disappointment in Jackpot's face. I knew he was hurt, even though he did his best ta hide it and keep it pimping. I felt bad, but this was the game. We both knew the rules. Him and F.A.B were like sibling rivalries, ever since last year's Player's Ball where Jackpot won Pimp of the Year and F.A.B came in second. So I know to see me with his arch rival had him extremely disappointed. He probably could have stood seeing me with anybody other than F.A.B, but what could I say? That was the game.

I looked at F.A.B and saw him smiling at JP like a man that just slept with his enemy's wife. F.A.B raised his pimp cup and bowed his head in a "keep it pimping" type way. JP looked at me in disgust, then back at F.A.B and greeted him back out of respect, then walked away.

"Ha! Ha! You saw the look on his face when you put your head down and he realized who you was with?" F.A.B said to me smiling, sipping from his pimp cup. I didn't respond. I didn't feel good about what happened. JP was always good to me. In a different world, one minus Lisa, I could have seen us together forever. Seeing JP sparked up a few old emotions within side me. Some of the good times we shared together flashed before my eyes like life before death. I tried not to let it show but F.A.B picked up on it right away.

"Wuss wrong wit you bitch? You still got feelings for a nigga or something? Wut'choo looking all sad and shit for? Like you lost your best friend or something. Shit, if the nigga got choo feeling like dat, maybe you need ta run after him and catch 'em."

Shit, you better watch wut you say, suggest, and ask for. "I'm not tripping off him." I lied.

"Then fix your fucking face and quit acting like you are. I'll be damned if you're gonna disrespect this pimping tripping off another nigga." Sometimes I felt like I made a mistake leaving JP and getting with F.A.B but there was no way I was about to tell him that. So I told him what he wanted to hear.

"I don't care about him Daddy. It's all about you." Yeah pimping wasn't the only ones who knew how to play mind games. Shit, hoes had ta play them everyday on tricks. So you could best believe when backed into a corner, we'll use what we learned in the field at home. Sometimes we get away with it, sometimes we don't. Either way, a hoe gon try.

"That's more like it," F.A.B said, buying my line. Biting hook line and sinker. I smirked inside and thought to myself, *if you only knew.* Truth is, I was just about tired of this situation as well and was ready to leave F.A.B. Sure, being with him had its good moments. Being with a pimp always did. Just like having an abusive husband who sometimes is sweet and nice. But just like an abusive husband, F.A.B had the tendency to get violent at times.

He never hit me but I saw him beat the other girls numerous times. Now I also didn't give him reason to put hands on me, but I knew if I ever did, he was more than capable of taking it there. I stayed with F.A.B for about six more months before I finally had enough and was ready to leave. I found out through the grapevine that Jackpot had been arrested and charged with Pimping and Pandering. He was in the county jail and was facing a lot of time. Word also had it that Lisa was no longer in the picture. She was spotted in Vegas with a pimp named Holiday. I felt bad for Jackpot and decided that I wanted to go back to him and help him in anyway I could. I felt like I owed him that much. Even if he didn't want me back, I'd understand and respect that, but still would help him. I packed my stuff up in my Louis Vuitton luggage and wrote F.A.B a quick note.

07-02-02

Dear F.A.B

I'm very sorry I had to leave this way but I'm no longer happy. I haven't been for a long time. I know I should have said this to you in your face, but I know how mad you can get and what you are capable of. So I felt this way was easier, but even more so, was safer. I didn't be scandalous and take anything that I didn't deserve, so the same way I came in is the same way I'm leaving, with my clothes and luggage. I wish you the best,

Love SunShine

I placed the note on the coffee table where I knew he'd find it, grabbed my stuff, and got ready to leave. Just as I was reaching for the door, I heard keys on the other side. *Oh no, he's home,* I thought to myself in a panic as I watched the door knob turn slowly. A chill went through my body like a white girl in a horror flick as the door opened to reveal F.A.B standing before me.

"Wuss up girl? Where you going with all that luggage?" He asked with a puzzled confused look on his face. I dropped my luggage down on the floor to the sides of my legs and said, "We need ta talk."

"Bout wut?"

"About me. I'm not happy here anymore and I wanna leave."

"Oh is dat right? So you were just gonna sneak out and leave like a thief in the night?"

"No, it's not even like that."

"Yeah right. Then how is it bitch? Hoe you got me fucked up." He closed the door and glanced at the coffee table. That's when he noticed the note I wrote laying there on top. He went and picked it up, then read it. I was feeling more and more scared by the second. He finished reading, crumbled up the note, and threw it in my face. The balled up note hit me on the tip of my nose and fell to the floor.

"Bitch! Who the fuck you think you is? You gon leave me a note like I'm some sucka ass nigga or something? Like I'm a square boyfriend you tryna break up with or something? Bitch, I'm a pimp and you ain't going nowhere hoe till I say so! Bitch, I own you! Hoe you really got the pimping fucked up."

"But I thought this was by choice, not force, and if I chose ta leave, then I could."

"Well, that's what you get for thinking bitch. And yeah you right, it is by choice. My choice ta keep you or leave you, not the other way around."

I started to say something but never got the first word out because no sooner than I opened my mouth, he back hand slapped the shit out of me. I saw stars as I fell to the floor and started to cry.

"Bitch, shut the fuck up!" He walked over, spit in my face, and kicked me in the stomach.

"Ahhhh!" I yelled out a loud cry as I clenched my stomach in pain. Spit dripped down the side of my face and onto the floor as F.A.B kneeled down and grabbed my hair. He pulled my head back forcefully and said through clenched teeth,

"The only way a hoe ever gon leave me is in a body bag bitch!" He slammed my head down on the floor and busted it open like a sledge hammer to a melon. I never been in so much pain. Blood ran down the quarter sized gash in my forehead as I pleaded for him not to kill me. "Please, Daddy, don't do this!"

"Don't do wut bitch? Hoe, you did this to yourself. Bitch can't never be satisfied with wut she got. Ain't never enough, is it? The stupidest shit make a hoe unhappy and the minute the bitch unhappy, hoe wanna pack up and leave pimping. No problem hoe. You wanna leave, you can leave." He stood up, walked into the bedroom, and came back out with a .38 special.

"No Daddy! Please don't kill me! I'm sorry. I'll stay." I pleaded for my life and said whatever I had to ta calm the situation and possibly spare my life.

"Nah bitch, you wanna leave. Don't start breaking it down now that you got a gun in your face."

"I'm not Daddy. I promise. I'll never try and leave you again."

"Too late, hoe." He walked over, pointed the gun to my head, and said, "Death Before Dishonor!" **BOOM! BOOM! BOOM!**

CHAPTER 9 THE CHRONICLES OF MYA

"Hello beautiful. You working?"

"Only if you're dating," I said with a seductive smile.

"How much for a blow job?"

"Let me see your dick and I'll tell you." The trick in the beat up Mazda pulled his dick out to signify he wasn't a cop. The trick looked to be about fifty. He was white, about 250 pounds, with salt pepper hair, beard and receding hair line. Typical looking trick. Once he showed me his dick, I was satisfied that he wasn't Vice, I opened the door and got in the car. "I don't like to negotiate in the open so I hope you don't mind me helping myself to a seat in your car?"

"Not at all pretty lady."

"Okay, for a blow job I charge $100, but I'll give it to you for eighty."

"Sounds great." He gave me a hundred dollar bill and said,

"keep the change. But if you're not as good at blowing my cock as you are at looking pretty, then I want my twenty back."

"Deal!" I placed the hundred in my bra and directed him to a spot about a block up I used to turn dates. I was twenty-two years old and been hoe'n since I was eighteen. I came down to Daygo from Oakland three years ago after my ex-folks went to prison for shooting one of his hoes that wanted to leave him. That ordeal traumatized me from fucking with pimps and I haven't had one since.

I make a lot of money in the game because of my exotic look and unique appeal. My parents are from Egypt so I have that Middle Eastern sexy look, the type of female that you would find in a Harem with a bunch of other pretty women. I was very slim, with a cat shaped face and slanted eyes. Long natural curly hair to the middle of my back, with a naive and innocent look about myself. The only thing I didn't like about me was my nose, but ask the average female anywhere from the Middle East and most of them will tell you the same. American men loved me though, because I didn't look like everyone else and I used that to my advantage.

"You can turn right up here at the next corner," I pointed and said as I directed him towards a back alley I used to turn dates, not too far from the track. He pulled into the alley and said,

"Perfect."

The alley was dark with only one streetlight at the end in the far left corner. There was only two ways in, that was either in front of us or behind us. Either way, you could see if a car was pulling up, or someone was coming from behind. Great for spotting vice before they spotted you. I pulled a condom out my handbag and ripped it open with my teeth. The trick unbuttoned his pants and pulled out his dick. I placed the rubber on the head of his penis and rolled it down. He laid his seat and head back as I placed my mouth on his dick and went to work. I was an expert on making a trick cum fast and I had every intention of doing so now. I stroked the shaft of his dick as I sucked it, causing multiple stimulation. That was double the pleasure and usually caused a trick to cum quick. I was a master at deep throating as well, but that wasn't what usually made a guy cum fast. So I concentrated and focused on the most sensitive part of the penis, the head. I sucked his dick, bobbing, while making half turns with my hands and mouth causing stimulating friction. I kept going faster, faster, faster! I felt his dick swell up in my mouth, an indicator that he was about to cum. I kept going, picking up speed and sucking at a steady pace.

"Uh! Uhh! Uhhh!" He said as he busted a fat load all through the condom. I sat up and pulled some wet wipes out of my handbag to clean up, and some gum for my breath. No sooner than I reached in my purse to retrieve the gum, I felt a hard blow as my head hit the side window. "Gimmie back my money, you filthy whore!" He reached into my bra and took out the $100.

"You won't be needing this where you're going!" I was still incoherent from the punch to the face. I felt a small stream of blood run down the side of my forehead. I was dazed and confused but knew if I didn't muster up the strength to fight back, I might not make it past today and live to see tomorrow. I started kicking, screaming and clawing for his eyes in the small car.

"Bitch, you wanna fight? I'll give you something to fight." He smacked the "shit" out of me like a seagull in flight.

"Get the fuck off me you bastard!" I screamed as I fought back as best I could. He climbed on top of me and began to strangle me.

"Ah! Ah! Ah! I can't…breathe! Ah!" I couldn't breathe. It felt like he was crushing my throat like garbage in a trash compactor. I knew I had ta act fast, but what could I do? I felt myself starting to pass out. I started grabbing for the door and accidentally knocked open the glove compartment. I looked over and saw a big ass knife about the size of a dagger. I tried grabbing at it, but couldn't quite reach it. It was only inches out my grasp. My eyes started to roll into the back of my head. My face was turning pale, tongue out gasping for air.

"Yeah whore, go to sleep." His hands around my neck felt like a vice grip. I knew it was now or never. With all my might and every ounce of energy I had left in my body, I stretched, reached and got ahold of the knife that was in the glove compartment. With one quick swift motion, I swung the knife and sliced him on the right cheek. The razor sharp knife split him open like a pig in a slaughter house. Blood poured from the wound like a leaking faucet. He still struggled to strangle me, adding more pressure. The adrenaline had him over-looking and bypassing the cut I put on his face. I came back across this time from left to right and sliced his other cheek.

"Ahhh! You fuckin bitch!" The knife cut so deep it penetrated his skin and went through his cheek. He felt that one. He let go of my throat for a split second to check his face and I reacted. I knew this would probably be my one and only chance to do something. I gripped the knife with two hands like Tarzan in the jungle and stabbed him in the right shoulder. I was aiming for his chest but missed. I pulled the knife out of his shoulder and stabbed again. This time hitting him in the chest, but just missing his heart. After that, I lost it, and started repeatedly stabbing him all throughout his upper body, until I knew he was dead.

"Take...that...Mutha...Fucka!" Blood splattered everywhere. **Shet! Shet! Shet!** The knife went. His limp body collapsed on me. For good measure, I stabbed him in the neck one last time like an inmate in prison. I didn't even bother removing the knife. I just left it there as I rolled his body up off of me. My entire body was covered in blood, his and mines, but mainly his. I hurried up and got out the car, ran down the alley in my blood drenched clothes, and flagged down the first passing car I saw.

"Help! Help! Help!" I said, waving my hands in the air as the approaching car lights came towards me. As luck would have it, it was a police car. The officer stopped in front of me as I jumped out in front of him to get his attention and stop his vehicle. He came to a screeching halt, got out and said,

"you alright, ma'am?"

"No, a man just tried ta kill me!" He removed his gun from his holster and surveyed the area.

"Where is he? Where's he at?"

"Down that alley in the car. He tried to strangle me to death and I got ahold of a knife that was in his glove compartment and killed him."

"Okay, ma'am, you're not under arrest but I'm a have to handcuff you and place you in the back of my patrol car until we sort all this out." Usually, I would have been upset or screamed about how I was the victim, but at this point, I felt like the back of the police car was the safest place for me to be.

"322 and Highland. I have a possible 187. I'm gonna need back up," the officer said into the CB on his left shoulder and approached the car in the alley with caution. Gun in hand.

"Police! If you can hear me, show your hands!" He circled around the vehicle and peered inside the window to get a closer look. The trick was slumped over with half of his body on the seat and the other half on the floor up against the door. The officer kept his gun drawn with one hand, and opened the door with the other. When he opened the door, the trick's body fell out the car, half inside and half on the pavement. The cop checked for a pulse and got nothing. He secured his gun back in his holster and called for more back up and paramedics. At the same time he was calling for back up, four more squad cars pulled up. Once confirmed that it was a homicide, they taped off the scene and took me downtown for questioning.

First, they took me to the National City Police Department before transferring me to Downtown Homicide Division. I gave my statement and told them exactly what happened. DNA proved that the man I killed was the infamous Dumpster Dive Killer. Evidence proved that I was a victim and that the killing was self-defense. Still being, they charged me with prostitution and misdemeanor trespassing for being behind the alley. I didn't give a shit, better that than murder. After that incident, I knew I needed a pimp. At least I felt like I needed one. No more renegading for me. I needed someone that would look out for me and keep me protected.

$$$$$

It's been six moths since Jackpot been out of prison. When he got out, he came home to nothing. He lost everything that he had worked so hard to accumulate. He lost it all. His money, cars, clothes, hoes, everything. All he had left was game and ambition. At first when he came home, he tried his hand at going straight and living the square life. After the suicide death of his bottom hoe Yuki, he felt a lot of guilt and no longer wanted anything to do with the game.

Funny thing about the game is, it always has a way of pulling you back in. The game had evolved by 2005. Hoes were still working the blade, but not as much as before. Now, top notch hoes worked the internet and escort services. There was a new breed of pimps as well. Old school pimps still wore flashy suits and Gators, but new school pimps looked like they were fresh out of high school. Wearing throw back jerseys and Air Force Ones.

Gang members jumped in the game and was banging on the tracks. Nigga's was killing other nigga's for knocking their hoe. Movies and DVD's were popping up everywhere exposing too much game, having the average square or lame nigga think he could pimp. Everywhere you looked, pimping was in your face. Even rappers like 50 Cent was screaming about how they were a P.I.M.P.

The shit was ridiculous and starting to give the game a black eye. The game was becoming a watered down version of what it used to be and Jackpot wanted no parts of it. He was disgusted by the sight of pimps in kindergarten color sneakers and track suits, pimping minors all in the name of pimping. In his eyes, this wasn't what the game was about, and since these sucka ass wannabee no real game having pimps jumped on the scene, the game had been breeding a new kind of hoe as well. Now bitches were talking slick at the mouth. Outta pocket with pimping and reckless eye balling. Why? Because they knew that their gang banging ass folks would shoot the first nigga that even thought about touching his hoe.

These new school pimps didn't play by old school rules, but I was an old school hoe that respected the game so I would never even consider paying one of these babe and ape wearing clowns. I needed an old school pimp with old school flava, but even more importantly, old school game. I ran into JP one day at a car audio place in Chula Vista called One Stop Auto. I was getting a CD changer installed in my car.

"Hello, how may I help you?" The man behind the counter said as I pulled up into the shop and got out of my BMW 335i.

"Yes, I would like to purchase a CD changer and get it installed."

"I'm sure we can help you with that. Was you looking for anything in particular?"

"No, as long as its good and top of the line."

"Well, we have a lot to choose from." He pointed to the display case that housed the changers and said, "This Sony is on sale for $200. It's a fine disc changer with a remote. We can install it in your glove box, under your seat, or trunk."

"That's cool, and how much for installation?"

"Installation is free if you buy the changer from here."

"Oh that's real cool. Okay, I want it installed in my trunk please."

"Not a problem." He walked over and took the Sony CD changer out the display case and walked around the counter behind the register. He rung up the charger. I paid him the $200 plus tax, as he gave me a receipt.

"This is a nice car you have here," he said as he grabbed some wires and popped the trunk.

"Thanks." He climbed in the trunk and started installing my changer.

"You know, you look kinda familiar. Do you have a brother or something?"

"Yeah but he died a long time ago."

"What's your name, if you don't mind me asking?"

"Not at all. They call me JP."

No! This can't be JP…JP, Jackpot the Pimp? "JP, would you happen to know someone named Sunshine?" The look on his face said it all. He sat up and looked at me as if tryna place my face and figure out where he might have known me from.

"Yeah, actually I do."

"Wow this is a small world, ain't it?"

"I don't know. Do I know you?"

"No, not quite, but I know you. I mean, at least I know of you."

"Really? And how is it you know of me?"

"Sunshine, she used to show me pictures and talk about you all the time."

"Is dat right? And wuts your relation to Sunshine?"

"She was my wife-n-law." JP looked at me shocked and said, "Well wuss the chances of that?"

"I know, huh? I'm sure you heard what happened to her, right?"

"Yeah I know. She didn't deserve that."

"No, she didn't. Thats what brung me down to Daygo. After F.A.B killed her, I left Oakland and came down here. I wanted to get away from everything and everybody, especially pimps. I was done with pimps after that. I haven't had one since."

"Yeah I been through my own trials and tribulations as well in the game. I kinda hung up my pimp stick."

"I see. If I wouldn't have seen it with my own eyes, I would've never believed that the famous Jackpot was working at a car audio place."

"Yeah my man owns it. I just needed a change, and money of course. After the death of Sunshine and the suicide of my bottom, I just lost all my ambition for the game."

"Your bottom committed suicide?"

"Yeah, while I was locked up. The news of me going to prison caused her to pass out and hit the back of her head on a coffee table. That put her in a coma and when she woke, she had lost control of half her body and was slightly brain damaged. That put her in a state of depression and caused her to commit suicide. I don't really like thinking about it. This is actually the first time I talked about since I been out."

"I'm sorry. I didn't mean to dig up bad memories."

"It's alright. Time heals all wounds and I'm barely starting to come around and deal with it, but I still blame myself. I don't know if that'll ever change." Now, I never met a pimp or even an ex pimp that actually cared about his hoes to the extent that JP did. You could see the hurt in his eyes when he talked about Sunshine or his bottom. Pimps like F.A.B wouldn't have given a fuck. JP looked like he actually had love for his hoes. This was a rare trait to find in a pimp. Most pimps used and abused their hoes till they were all used up. If more pimps cared about their hoes like JP displayed, I guarantee you they would have longer gevity and girls would stick around a lot longer.

We needed more pimps like JP and less like F.A.B in this world. JP laid back down in the trunk and continued installing my CD changer. I watched as I fantasized about what it would be like to hoe for JP or someone like him. Then I thought *shit, I never met anyone like him.* He was one of a kind. Just from the little I knew of him from our conversation, the way Sunshine talked and idolized him, and the way he talked and cared about his hoes.

I believe everything happens for a reason and it was meant for me to pull up into this audio shop today. I was in search for a pimp and here one was, and not just any pimp, but one I could actually see myself paying. Now if only I could get him to quit his job and see things that way as well. We continued making small talk while he installed my changer. I was low-key admiring everything about him. His looks, his style. When he spoke, he spoke with intelligence. If I had it my way and I usually did, this was gonna be my future folks. He finished up with my CD changer and closed the trunk, pulled a rag out of his back pocket and wiped his hands. Then said,

"All done."

"Thanks, and it was really nice talking to you."

"You, too."

"I was wondering if we could finish talking and getting to know one another in a more formal and sociable setting?"

"Yeah, that'll be cool. Take down my cellphone number." I pulled my cellphone out my purse and entered his name and contact info into it as he recited back to me.

"619…555…2732."

"Got it, and would you like mines?"

"Yeah but I don't have my cellphone on me so just call and when you do I'll store your number in my phone."

"Okay, I'll give you a call later on tonight."

"Alright pretty lady, I'll be looking forward to it." He smiled, shook my hand, and saw me off. That night, I called JP and we talked for hours. He had good conversation. I really enjoyed talking to him. We conversed into the wee hours of the next morning. I didn't want to hang up like a teenage girl talking to her high school boyfriend.

"Alright pretty lady. I need ta get some rest. I still have to get up in four hours and go to work."

"Okay."

"Wuss your plans for tomorrow?"

"Nothing at the moment. I have to pay a couple of bills in the afternoon, but other than that, I'm free."

"Would you like to go out and continue our conversation over dinner?"

"I'd love to."

"Okay, meet me at the shop around five when I get off."

"Okay, I'll be there at five."

"Alright, then it's a date. Now, let me get to bed before I don't wake up for work."

"Okay, go to sleep Boo. Sleep tight."

"You, too. Sweet dreams and I'll see you tomorrow." We hung up the phone and I don't know about him, but I crashed as soon as my head hit the pillow.

"You ready to go handsome?" I said as I entered the shop.

"Sure am. Just finishing up some last minute stuff before we go." He wrote something down in a notepad, closed the book, and placed it under the counter. "Shall we?" He said with his hand extended, smiling, looking handsome as ever.

"So where we going?" I asked as I unlocked the doors with my remote keychain and got inside the car.

"You hungry?"

"Starving."

"Good, I thought we could go to Anthony's in Seaport Village. You like seafood?"

"Love it. Let's go." I started the engine, put the car in drive, drove off and headed to Seaport Village. We talked for a few minutes on the way to the restaurant, then just sat back and enjoyed the comfortable silence of each other's company. I turned on the radio and CD changer and selected Disc One K-Ci and Jo Jo's Greatest Hits. We listened to the smooth grooves of one of R&B's finest duos for the remainder of the trip.

We arrived at Seaport Village and parked, got out, and walked over to Anthony's. We walked in, was seated, placed our order and talked while we waited for our food to arrive. We talked for about twenty minutes before our food arrived.

"It's kinda crazy that out of all the shops you could have taken your car to, you happened to take it to mines."

"I know. I was thinking the same thing last night. I really think that it was meant to be."

"Really?"

"Yeah, really. I didn't tell you this yesterday when we spoke on the phone, but I'm actually looking for some new folks. Someone that I know would be there for me 100% and I could see myself paying. I been in the game too long to just be paying anyone, or the first pimp that came along.

I don't want to end up with another F.A.B."

"Is dat right? Well, you know I'm retired. I don't have no real desire to get back in the life. I mean, don't get me wrong, I'd be lying if I told you I didn't miss it sometimes, and the pimpin's gonna always be in me because it's not on me. It's just, you gotta realize I been through a lot in this game and have come full circle. I don't know if you know this or not, well actually how could you, but I got laced and started my pimp career in that same shop you see me working at today. My mentor and good friend of mines own it. He's retired now as well, but was one of the coldest pimps ta ever play the game back in the 70's and early 80's. Anyhow, that's neither here nor there, the point I'm tryna make is, I gained a lot in the game, but lost more and don't know if I wanna go back that route. Especially now with the game being misplayed and saturated with these new school pimps who don't know the first thing about dressing and finessing. That have no conversation and look like they bought their wardrobe from the kiddie section of the Sears Department Store, or a circus clown's suitcase."

"That's why we need more bonafide pimps like yourself to keep that old school game alive."

"I don't know, Ma. I played the game the way it was supposed to be played and still got burned. I used to be a strong believer that, if you be true to the game, then the game a be true to you. Now, I don't believe that. Like I said, I lost a lot and somethings I can't get back. That's what hurts the most. I ain't tripping off the material shit because that's shit you can always get back, but I lost good people; my bottom, my mother, even my sister who I haven't seen since I went to prison. And to put the icing on the cake, all of this was behind a few jealous, non-loyal and scandalous bitches."

"Well, I would never do you dirty. I don't get down like that. I was taught snitches end up with stitches and found in ditches, and coming from Oakland where niggas really lived by that, I learned early on ta keep my mouth shut. I respect the "P" code. I'm an old school hoe looking for an old school pimp. I really think we would be good for each other."

I could tell he was thinking about it and taking my words into consideration. Shit, the game was hard to resist. It was like a tornado or vortex constantly sucking you back in. Especially someone of JP's caliber. He was one of the last of a dying breed. They just didn't make pimps like him anymore. The waiter came back with our food and condiments. We put our conversation on pause to eat and enjoy our food.

"Oh, I'm stuffed," I said as I took the last bite of my fish and set the fork down on my plate.

"Yeah, me, too. That was one of those unbutton the top button of your pants after you're done eating meals." We both laughed.

"Check please!" JP said as he summoned the waiter over to bring our bill. JP paid the tab and left a 20% tip for the waiter. He got up, placed his hand out for mines, and helped me up.

"Thank you," I said as he assisted me out my seat.

"You're welcome." The night was still young, the sky was clear, moon was out and the weather was great. Typical San Diego night.

"The moon looks beautiful. The way its lights shimmer off the water." I agreed.

"Let's take a walk on the shoreline," he said as he held my hand and lead the way before I even had a chance to deny or accept. It was fine though. I didn't mind. I was really feeling JP and enjoying his company and wasn't ready for the night to end anyway. We walked and picked up where we left off in the restaurant and finished our conversation.

"I really like you, JP, and would love to be with you. I wanna be the number one woman in your life that helps you accomplish all your dreams and goals and put you back on top. I'll prove to you in time that

I'm bottom material. I don't get jealous off other females, I would never snitch or try and cross you up Daddy. I just want to be with you."

I stopped walking, reached into my purse and faced JP so we were eye to eye. I took my hand out of my purse and handed him $5,000 cash and said, "I choose you, if you'll have me."

He took the money and looked down at it without counting it or saying a word. Then he looked up at me and stared into my eyes with a look on his face like he was contemplating my offer. He took a deep breath, slowly exhaled and said,

"Fuck it, Baby Girl. What I got ta lose? I accept."

I smiled from ear to ear, hugged him tight and told him, "I'm gonna make you proud and happy that you accepted me as your hoe. And I promise I'll never let you down or make you regret coming outta retirement, Daddy."

"Well, you can show me better than you can tell me so just continue to show and prove and everything a be smooth." He counted the money, folded it up, and put it in his pocket.

"So far, so good," he said, then gave me a nice kiss.

"And it's only gonna get better, Daddy."

$$$$$

3 Months Later…

All Star Weekend 2006 was in Vegas this year. This was gonna be as it always was, a star studded event, and where there's big stars, there's big tricking. Vegas was only a forty-five minute plane ride and a four to six hour car drive from Daygo. So to say I would be there heel and hoe'd out would be an understatement.

Since JP's release from prison and introduction back in the game, he'd been keeping a low profile. He wasn't as flashy and flamboyant as he used to be. He wasn't tryna expose his hand for the world to see and put himself out there. He was flying under the radar. Believe it or not, he even kept his job at One Stop Auto for the first couple of months, just on GP.

Every move he made now was well thought out and calculated. He didn't leave nothing to chance, not if he could help it. He didn't try and get at and knock every hoe he saw or ran into. He would always tell me "a pimp would accept any hoe, but a Mack accepts the right hoe." I respected him for that because I knew if and when he ever did bring another girl home, she would be top notch, non scandalous, down, dedicated, and fit into our family well.

"Okay Mya, look here Ma. I'm not going to All Star Weekend this year because it's not time for me to make my presence known. I'm still in stack mode and all Vegas got to offer for a Mack is knockin bitches and spendin loot. Which neither, am I interested in or concentrating on at the moment. It's a time and place for everything and this ain't the time and that's not the place for me to show the world who the real undisputed Mack of the Year is."

JP no longer considered himself a pimp. He saw himself as a Mack. A Master at Applying Correct Knowledge. He was pimping on a different playing field now. He still respected the game and played by all the rules, but now it was strictly bout the money to him. He could care less about the fame. He didn't walk around with a big old pimp cup with fake diamonds in it. He didn't wear flashy clown suits that weren't even worth the material it was sewn with. He didn't wear too much jewelry, but just enough to compliment his outfit. He was on some corporate pimping.

Don't get me wrong now, my Daddy was still fresh ta death. I had a lot of money saved up when I chose him three months back, so after we made it official, I gave him the rest of my money later on that evening back at my house. $68,000 on top of the $5,000 I gave him to begin with. Not only that, but I've made a thousand or better "every" night and haven't missed a beat since I been with him. So that's another ninety-thousand plus. Which we'll just round off to a hundred-thousand give or take a few dollars. So to all you non mathematical mutha fuckas, that's over $172,000. So money wasn't an issue.

My folks still looked and smelled like money when he stepped out, but now he looked like old money. Three, five and $10,000 Armani suits, Marc Jacob Italian leather shoes and silk ties. Benz Coupe with the factory rims still on them. Presidential Rolex with no diamonds in the bezel, 24KT VVS Princess Cut Diamond Pinky Ring, worth more than ten rings put together on the average pimp's fingers. JP would say like Jay-Z, "I'm on my grown man shit. No chrome on the wheels. I'm a baller for real."

The way he dressed and presented himself, he could function and make an impression in all circles and walks of life. Even white folks would treat him with respect when they were in his presence or saw him coming. He told me the night I chose up, that if he was gonna jump back in the game, then he was gonna play it on a whole different level. I knew I made the right choice choosing JP as my folks.

"You should be able to stack five racks or better each night while you're out there. Since you'll be in Vegas, shoot for ten. Stay where the action is. Follow the stars. Hit all the after parties and dress to perfection so that you can bypass standing and waiting in lines. Keep your eyes on the prize, aware and focused at all times."

"I will Daddy. You know your girl knows what to do. I won't disappoint you."

"I know, Ma. Just keeping you laced up like combat boots and on point like a #2 pencil at a final exam in high school. Watch out for the pimps out there because they're gonna be out in full stride, like a pack of wolves thirsty for meat. I know I don't have to tell you to stay in pocket, head down, blah blah blah and all that jazz. Just be careful, aware and watch out for the gorillas because they're gonna be in the mist."

"I understand, Daddy."

All Star Weekend was off the hook. Everybody who was anybody was there in attendance making their presence known, having a good time and spending cash. It was a hooker's paradise. Club Ice threw an after-party Sunday that had all the local ballas and hustlers in the building. Big Meech and BMF was making it rain all night like a spring day in Seattle.

I'd already made $15,000 in two days and still had one to go. My goal was to bring home at least twenty stacks. At the rate things was going, that shouldn't be a problem. I left the club early because I wasn't there to party and at the moment wasn't nobody talking about nothing that I wanted to hear, so I headed down to the MGM Grand where I met a movie producer named Chris.

"Seven! You win!" The crap dealer said as a tall, not too old, but not young, white man won again for the eighth time in a row as I stood next to him.

"You must be good luck, pretty lady," he said as he turned towards his left in my direction and spoke to me.

"Must be," I said and smiled.

"Ever since you walked up, I hit every point." He placed $500 on the line to hit and threw the dice.

"Seven!" The dealer said as he doubled up his chips. The man looked at me, smiled, then gave me two $100 chips.

"This is for my good luck charm."

"Thanks, but you ain't got lucky, yet."

"Is that so?"

"Absolutely." He smiled, then placed $1,000 on the table and said, "Blow on the dice for good luck." I blew on the dice. He threw them past the line and hit the back wall.

"Eleven! Winner!"

He smiled, turned to me and said, "Am I lucky now?"

"Not yet! From where I'm standing and the way I see it, your luck is just starting."

"Well, well." He stuck his hand out and said, "My name is Chris Patterson, but you can call me Chris."

I shook his hand and said, "My name is Mya, like the singer. Nice to meet you."

"Likewise." He picked up his winnings, placed them in his chip tray and said, "I was always a strong believer in quitting while you're ahead."

"True, but they also say, you should never leave a game while you're winning, until your winning streak is over."

"You know what? You're absolutely right." To my surprise, he put $5,000 on the pass line coming out and another $5,000 on the 12 ta 1 odds he would hit a hard ten I was shaking in my heels as he threw the dice and two ones hit the board.

"Craps!" The dealer said as he grabbed all his chips and scooped them up with his wooden stick.

"Well, easy come, easy go. Guess you can say my luck finally ran out."

"I'm so sorry."

"Oh don't worry your pretty little self, young lady. This is Vegas. That's what it's all about."

"But I'm the one who persuaded you to shoot again when you was ready to quit."

"Yeah, but you didn't make me put down ten grand as the bet."

"Well, I still feel guilty or somewhat responsible."

"Well, here. You can make it up to me by having a drink with me at the bar."

"Deal." We walked over to the lounge and sat down by the bar. I ordered a light drink because I knew better than to order anything heavy while working. That was a definite and absolute no, no. Under different circumstances, I wouldn't have drunk at all, but if a man can lose $10,000 at a crap table in one roll and not flinch or miss a beat, then he was a man I needed to know. We sat and made small talk. I gave it a few minutes before I asked, "So, what do you do for a living?"

"I'm a movie producer."

"Really?"

"Yep. You ever heard of Forrest Gump or Independence Day?"

"Yeah, of course," I said shocked, but holding back my enthusiasm.

"Well, I didn't make those." He laughed as I blushed and said,

"Okay, you got me. That was a good one." I playfully pushed him on the shoulder and smiled.

"No, but really, I have produced quite a few successful indy films. They mainly did well overseas. Most of them you probably never even heard of or knew existed."

"Well, obviously someone knows they exist if you can risk and lose $10,000 in one roll on the crap table."

"What can I say, I felt lucky."

"Well, good thing I'm still here, because you still have a chance to get lucky, and with me, it'll only cost you half of what you blew at the table." I knew that if a man could afford to lose ten stacks at a crap table, then he wouldn't think twice about spending half of that to sleep with a hot chick half his age.

"Wow, don't you think that's kinda steep?"

"Not at all. Good things are worth paying for and great things are priceless. So, looking at it that way, you're already coming out ahead."

"Really? I like your confidence and take charge attitude. Can you do that in the bedroom as well? Traditional sex doesn't get me off."

"Well, I'm not a traditional woman. Does that answer your question?"

"Very much so." He downed the rest of his drink, took my hand and said, "Shall we?"

"We shall." I left the remainder of my drink and stood up, fixed my Christian Dior dress and said, "lead the way."

We went back to his luxury suite on the top floor of the MGM Grand.

"I know that you say you're up for anything, but I truly wanna make sure before I pay you."

"That's fine as long as you know you gotta pay first before we do anything sexual."

"I know. I just wanna run down what I would like from you first, and if you're still interested, then we can get started."

He told me what he wanted to do and what he expected for his five grand, and as sick, twisted, disgusting and beyond freaky as it was, I wasn't about to turn down and walk away from five stacks. No real hoe about her money and worth her weight in gold would. He went into his bedroom and took five grand out of the hotel safe that was on the top shelf of his closet. He came back into the main living room where I was standing and patiently waiting for him, and handed me the money.

"Thank you." I put the money in my purse and said, "Shall we get started?" Time was money and I didn't plan on being there any longer than I had to. We walked over to the oversized jacuzzi tub that sat in the middle of the floor in the second living room of his hotel suite and removed our clothes. He got in the tub and laid flat on his back. The tub was big enough to fit eight full sized adults. More than enough room to do what he had in mind. I climbed into the tub and stood over him, squatted and pissed all over his face and body. He got an instant erection.

"Yeah, yeah! Piss in my mouth!" He opened his mouth wide like a hungry bird in a nest waiting to be fed by his momma. I aimed for his mouth but got him in the eyes. I laughed to myself as I watched him scurry and wipe the burning urine from his eyes. He laid back down in the piss filled tub and stroked himself while sucking the urine off his fingers. I kept my heels on to avoid coming in contact with my own piss.

"Shit on me baby. Shit in my mouth." Sick fuck! White people was always into some 'ole other shit. They couldn't just be regular freaks like everyone else. They had to take their freakiness to a whole nother level. I stood over his mouth like a toilet and squatted low like I was about to take a shit in the woods. I pushed out a log of a turd right into his mouth as the stench of my own shit and the act that was taking place before me made my stomach cringe.

He stroked himself like a mad man as he savored the taste of my shit in his mouth. I was disgusted. All I could do was concentrate on the five grand and the fact that this wouldn't last too much longer. Now it was time to go into phase two of our agreement. I got out of the bathtub and picked up my little bag of tricks which I always kept with me at all times. I was a professional hoe and a professional knows that tricks come in all different shapes and sizes with different fetishes to match. I had something in my bag to cater to 'em all. You name it, I had it. Chris washed my piss and shit off his face and cleaned up while I pulled out and put on my 10 inch dildo strap-on. Chris wanted to be dominated and I was the bitch to do it.

"Get the fuck on your knees and kiss my feet." He did as instructed.

"Now roll over." Just like an obedient lap dog, he rolled over. I began to walk across his chest with my six inch stiletto heels. The pain pleasured him. I proceeded to walk, then took a step on his groin area. He winced at the pain, but got aroused from the enjoyment. I couldn't understand how this type of pain could be enjoyable, but I wasn't there to understand. I was there to do a job. I got off his nuts and told 'em, "Now turn your ass around and get on all fours like the bitch you are!"

"Yes, mistress." He got on all fours and jacked his pale pink ass up in the air like a punk in prison. I pulled my mini leather paddle whip from the bag of tricks, and began to spank the fuck out of his ass until his butt cheeks turned red as an apple and sore as a muscle after an intense work out.

I walked around to the front of him and made him lubricate my dildo with his own spit by sucking it like a bitch. I could tell this wasn't his first time with a dick or dildo in his mouth by the way he sucked it. His head game could almost put me to shame. This dude was turning me off by the second. The shit a hoe had to do ta get money. I should write a book. I walked back around to his backside and spread his ass cheeks open. I could tell that his butt hole had been tampered with before. I really knew when my ten inch dildo just slid in with no problem like a master key to a car ignition.

"Oh yeah, fuck me mistress!" I fucked the shit out of his ass, literally, pun intended. The whole room smelled like ass and shit. I couldn't wait for the session to be over.

"Cum for me you piece of shit! Cum for your mistress!" He stroked himself as I fucked him in the ass. The harder I pounded, the faster he stroked.

"Oh, I'm bout ta cum!"

"Well, cum then you shit mouth freaky son of a bitch!"

"Yes, mistress!" He came and skeeted all over the place like a porn star in a XXX flick. I pulled my shit encrusted dildo out his ass, stood up and took it off.

"One more thing before I leave, go clean all this shit off my dildo and bring it back to me while I clean up." He got up with his limp dick hanging and did as I said. I went into the guest bathroom and took a quick birdbath and cleaned up. When I came out the bathroom, he was sitting in the living room with my dildo in his lap clean as a whistle. I put my dildo along with the rest of my toys away in my bag of tricks, fixed my dress, and got ready to leave.

"Thank you for a wonderful time and evening."

"The pleasure was all mines." I lied.

"You was well worth the five grand." I gave him my card and said,

"Anytime. Call whenever you;ll like to see me. I don't stay in Vegas, but I do travel. Just give me 24 hour notice, pay half the fee, my flight and it's a date."

He placed the card in his wallet that was sitting on the counter and said, "Will do gorgeous. You can count on it."

I smiled, shook his hand, said goodbye and was out. The night was still young, which meant there was more money to be made. And that's just what I did. Made more money! By Monday, I was back in Daygo. All Star Weekend went off without a hitch and was extremely profitable. All in all, I made $25,000, took care of and handled business like a boss bitch was supposed to. Needless to say, Daddy was pleased.

CHAPTER 10 THE CHRONICLES OF NAKEITA

March 21, 2004…

Today was my twenty-first birthday and I planned on doing it big. I was officially an adult, even though I've been out the house and on my own since I was eighteen. I was the daughter of a single mother and two half brothers. I never knew my father. My mother told me that she met him in 82 and they hit it off, right from the bat.

Six months later, she was pregnant with me. When she came home and told him the news, he wasn't happy and told her he wanted her to get an abortion. After she refused, he walked out on her. So needless to say, I never met my father.

My mother did her best to raise me and my two brothers as best she could, just as thousands of other single black women in America. My oldest brother died young when I was still little and he was a teenager. My mother didn't talk about it much but she did tell me it was due to gang violence. My other brother left the house when he was eighteen and started pimping. The last time I saw him was two years ago before he went to prison for pimping and pandering. Due to me growing up without a strong male presence or role model in the house, I started to rebel and act wild as I grew into a teenager.

My mother did her best to control me but was unsuccessful. I discovered the pleasure of sex at sixteen and unbeknownst to my mother and brother, was a full blown slut by the time I was seventeen. Ten months later, I met my folks, a pimp named Macknificent. He turned me from a slut to a whore. This too, my mother and brother didn't know. I was living a double life and kept the two worlds separate. On my eighteenth birthday, I moved out of my momma's house and in with Macknificent. He took care of me to the fullest and spoiled me like a newborn baby.

"Happy Birthday Baby Girl!" I was awakened by the sound of my Daddy's voice and him kissing me on the cheek. I smiled as I raised up, turning around and opened my eyes slowly.

"Hey Daddy."

"Good morning babe. Get up, get in the shower and get dressed. We have a long day ahead of us. I have something real nice planned for you." That was music to a bitch ears. I jumped up like a Jack in the Box in a pre-school class during recess.

"Okay, Daddy. Give me twenty minutes."

"Take your time." I hopped in the shower and got ready while Daddy sat back and watched TV smoking a blunt. Thirty minutes later, I was ready to go. This year, my birthday fell on a weekend, and every weekend Daddy pulled out his lowrider. Usually we'd go up to Mission Beach to floss and hit switches against other lowriders. Everybody came out to show off their rides on the weekend. Once it got dark, everybody with lowriders went to Fam-Mart, where it really went down. Some niggas took their shit so serious they were hopping for pink slips. Real shit. Daddy pulled his 81 Coupe Deville with the fifth wheel and Rolls Royce grill out the garage. I got in the car and sat down in the custom bucket seats and rolled down my window. He hit the switch to top it off and floss the chrome undercarriage. The candy apple paint job shined like wet Now & Laters in the sunlight. The triple gold Daytons matched the grill and, bumper. I loved this car, but not as much as my folks did. That was his baby. He built that car from the ground up, just like his hoes.

"Where we going Daddy?"

"It's a surprise. You'll see when we get there." We drove down the 805 Freeway going north towards Oceanside. Halfway to wherever we were going, he got off the freeway and took me shopping for a new outfit. We went to Saks & 5th Ave and spent $3,000. Then to the Gucci store and spent another $2,000 just on shoes. I went into one of the dressing rooms before I left Saks and put on my new fit. I was dressed down in my Donna Karan summer wear and matching sunglasses. I bought a couple of more outfits to wear in the evening and out to the club. In the Gucci store, I bought some cute sandals, a pair of slip ons, and some high heels with a matching purse. I was ready for whatever.

Daddy bought me another pair of sunglasses by Gucci incase I wanted to switch up. After shopping, we got back on the freeway and drove down to Oceanside by the beach, down the street from the Greyhound Bus Station. A pimp named Goldie from Daygo owned a luxury car lot off of Hill Street. Goldie was a good friend of Macknificent. They grew up and got in the game together back in the 90's. It was funny back then because Macknificent had a nice car, a few jewelry pieces and a little flash money. A nice set of tools to knock a hoe and jump in the game with. Goldie had none of thee above. But what he lacked in tools, he made up for in game.

So in the beginning, Macknificent would roll up and down the blade with Goldie riding shotgun, in hot pursuit of a new prostitute tryna knock their first hoe. One day, a hoe named Sin'namon, was on the blade working when Goldie spotted her from the passenger seat of Macknificent's Cadillac. Goldie had an all black pit bull he use to call Popeye for his love of fighting. Popeye was cool with people but hated dogs. He'd been in over a hundred and fifty dog fights, had over eighty-two kills and zero losses. Popeye was vicious. Goldie would have Popeye with him sitting in the back seat when him and Macknificent would hit the blade looking for hoes. So when Goldie spotted Sin'namon on the blade, he had Macknificent pull over to the curb and jumped out with Popeye. Sin'namon put her head down, turned around and high stepped it in the other direction.

"Bitch, stop or Im a let my dog go!" Sin'namon stopped dead in her tracks like a locomotive with no steam.

"Yeah, hoe. I knew that a get your attention. Hoe wuss up wit dis Daygo Mackin? Hit about face, choose up and let's get dis shit crackin. Pay a pimp his royalties so I can spoil thee. I mack tight when a hoe act right. Pay a 'P' so we can stack a 'G.'"

Something Goldie said must have caught Sin'namons attention because she turned around, looked him in the face and said, "Okay, so what now?"

And that was how Goldie knocked his first hoe. Since Macknificent had the car and all the tools, they decided to do something that had never been done in history. Share her. They called themselves "Twin Pimpin." Both of them were pimping and breaking the same bitch. They laugh about it now when they reminisce and talk about it, but that was how Goldie and my folks officially got in the game. After Sin'namon, another hoe chose up with Macknificent. Then another, and another! Then

Sin'namon brought two hoes home that wanted to be with Goldie. That's when they split the crew and pimped accordingly. From then on, Twin Pimpin was dead and Macknificent and Goldie, as individuals was born.

Years later, Goldie opened up an exotic car dealership with another Daygo pimp named 'Humpty.' They were part of a pimp clique named 'Scandalous' that was known for pulling bitches. You could spot one of Humpty's hoes a mile away because all of them was blasted with his name somewhere tattooed on their body in plain sight, walking, looking like a moving billboard. Daddy pulled into the car lot of his best friend Goldie, hit the third switch of his hydraulics, which laid the car down flat, and honked the horn.

Goldie walked out the building smiling, arms out like Jesus and said, "wuss up pimp? Long time no see!"

"Wut it do pimp juice?"

"Ah you know. Same old, same old." They gave each other a one arm hug and dap.

"How's business?"

"Good. You know these type of cars sell they self."

"Yeah dat."

"But wut can I do you for pimp? You looking for a new ride?"

"Somthing like dat. I'm looking for a Benz Coupe for my hoe. Today is her birthday and she been running hard for a pimp so Im a surprise and reward her with her own car."

"Right. Well, a hoe must be getting it in a real way for you to be dropping loot on a Benz, especially one that's on my lot."

"What, you don't know? I done checked over $500,000 out that pussy, pimp. The hoe's a go getter."

"Yea dat! Well, I got just the car for you pimp suit." Daddy turned towards me and his car, bent over and said, "Come here Keita," using his hands to motion me as he spoke. I got out the car and walked over to him, making sure I avoided all eye contact with Goldie, outta respect for my Folks.

"Yes, Daddy."

"Walk with us," Daddy said as Goldie led the way. He guided us over towards a 2003 convertible 500SL Benz Coupe, white on white with peanut butter insides and 22-inch Lexani rims on Yokahoma tires. It had my name screaming all over it.

"Happy Birthday Baby Girl!" Daddy said and opened the door to the Benz for me to get in. I couldn't believe it.

"Are you serious?"

"As a heart attack. Bitch, you been taking care of business like a real hoe pose to. I told you that if you stayed down, you'd come up. So all I'm doing now is honoring my word." Goldie handed me the keys and said, "Start it up and give it a test drive." I stuck the key in the ignition and brought my beautiful white kitty to life. I called it 'Kitty' because when I started the engine, it purred like one. "Oh my God! Thank you Daddy!" He closed the door and said,

"You're welcome. Now go ahead and test drive it while I handle the paperwork and pay for it."

"Okay," I said grinning from ear to ear like the Joker in Batman. I was all teeth and couldn't quit smiling. I was so happy that you could have told me today was Armageddon and was our last day on earth, and I would have still been smiling. I let the top down, backed up, drove off and took my new car for a spin. I drove up and down Hill Street by the beach, through the blade and back. I loved that car the moment I laid eyes on it. I pulled back into the lot, parked, got out and walked inside to the office where Daddy was paying for the car and handling the paperwork.

"So you like it Baby Girl?"

"I love it! Thank you Daddy!" I hugged and gave 'em a kiss on the cheek. Daddy finished up the paperwork and paid for my car. The car was $42,000. I couldn't believe he spent that much on me in one shot. A bitch nowadays was even lucky ta get a car from her folks, let alone a Benz. This made me wanna hoe harder for my folks. I no longer felt like I was fucking for pedicures and outfits. I felt like a boss bitch now. Like I was "that bitch." That one gesture motivated me ta wanna get any and everything for my Daddy or die trying.

If more pimps treated their hoes like this, most would stick around a lot longer, if not forever, but they don't. They sell their hoes dreams that never manifests itself. Then one day, the hoe smartens up, figures it out, and kicks rocks. Shit, a bitch can only get her hair and nails done but so many times. And as for outfits, after your closet is completely full with any and everything imaginable, and you have wall to wall shoes to match, a bitch can care less about shopping. At that point, a bitch needs more to motivate her to continue doing what she's doing on the level that she's been doing it. Pimps need to start investing in their hoes like us hoes invest in them. Would you keep pumping all your money into a stock that never generates any strong returns?

Alright then, then what makes you think a hoe wants to keep paying a pimp that never does anything financially significant for her, other than get her hair and nails done and a few outfits here and there from time to time? Pimps need to realize we count and keep track of every dollar we give them. Down to the last red cent. Even now, you think I don't know that I made my Daddy well over $500,000 since I been with him? Of course I do, but in the game, that's how it goes. So a hoe ain't gone trip. I'm only gone trip if I ain't reaping no rewards whatsoever, and the ends no longer justify the means. Take care of me and I'll take care of you, period!

Just like if I worked for a square's company. Of course he's making ten times the amount I'm making, even though I'm probably doing most, if not all the work. But employees don't care or worry about that as long as at the end of the week, they're getting paid what they deserve and earned. If a Boss promised you he'd pay you $500 a week to work for him, and then at the end of the week he handed you $100, would you keep working for his company? I think not, and if so, then you have the mentality of a dumb hoe. This was the best birthday of my life. I followed Daddy back to Daygo in my new car. He put his Lo-Lo up for the night and hopped in my car. He got in the passenger's seat, laid the seat back, like most niggas do, and said,

"Let's go out to eat. My treat, your choice."

"Sounds good to me. I'm starving, too." We drove downtown to the Spaghetti Factory, ate and chilled in the Gaslamp for a while sipping a few drinks. The perfect way to end my birthday. Well, almost perfect. What went down after we got home and went to bed was the perfect way to end my birthday. I had a full day and an exhausting night. We fucked for two hours straight. Daddy wore my pussy out like a nympho fucking thirteen guys in a porn flick. I came four times and passed out in a coma like sleep.

"Hello. May I speak to Keita?"

"Yes, this is her."

"Hi, this is Jim. We have a call for you set for Friday," my boss said on the other end of the phone. He owned an escort service called 'Exstasky.' It was basically an escort service in the sky. Jim was innovative. He was a millionaire and owned a G5 private jet. Straight luxury. The way it worked was a client would call and set up a flight to a specific destination and the type of girl or girls he would like to accompany him. Once the girl or girls and price was agreed upon, he would pay for the flight as well as the price of the girls he chose. For his money, he could get whatever he wanted, and once the plane was in the air, anything goes. The cool part about it was, vice couldn't bust you or do anything about it because for one, the state isn't about to pay the high cover charge for a private flight just to bust a hoe for a misdemeanor, and two, even if they did, once the plane was in the air and crossed state lines, the vice would be out of their jurisdiction, and no sex or sexual activities took place before the jet got up in the air. So there was a million dollar smart, secure and safe business. What I loved about it also was the fact that, "All" of the clients were rich and high paying tricks. If they could afford to charter a private flight on a G5 Jet, then you knew they could afford two or three thousand an hour to be accompanied by a girl, and that's exactly what it cost. I made $2,000 an hour and got half of the total at the end of the flight, so on average I'd make anywhere from $2,000 to $4,000 a flight.

"Okay, what time is the flight set for?"

"Its set for 12pm. His name is Doctor Madderson. George Madderson."

"Okay, got it." I jotted down the information, hung up the phone, and ended the call. 2004 was a good year. I was getting money, coming up, and on the rise.

$$$$$

"Bitch, sock it to a pimp!" Ah shit, here we go again, as always, a pimp tryna get at me. A hoe can't even get something to eat without a pimp tryna knock her. I just walked into the McDonald's not too far from the track in El Cajon City. I guess he spotted me walking in. It seems like pimps be having hoe-dar or some shit, a radar for hoes the way they can spot a bitch a mile away like a vulture high in the sky eyeing a body on the ground that's about to die. I stayed in pocket like a wallet, put my head down towards the ground, and tried to walk out.

"Yeah bitch, leave! Cause I'm the only big Mack in dis McDonald's worth talking about"

Rolex was a pimp from Daygo and a gang member from the notorious Skyline blood gang. In the hay day of the infamous rolling 80's, when niggas was seriously gang banging and killing each other everyday, he went by T-Roll. After going to the pen in the late 80's for a gang shooting and doing nine years, he came out on a whole different page. While doing time in Corcoran, a pimp named 'Dollar Bill' laced his boots to the game. When he came out, he was no longer T-Roll the gang banger, but Rolex the Pimp.

Although his heart would always be with the set, he was no longer with the bullshit. He put up his 9 glock for nine hoes that worked the block.

"Bitch, I know you hear me. Now turn around, listen and feel me. I got conversation if you got motivation." Rolex was a die hard pimp in every aspect of the word. Some of the hoes even went as far as to nickname him Bruce Willis because of the fact. He played by all the rules. One step outta pocket and the hoe was gonna get broke. I high stepped it out of McDonald's, got in my car and left. I couldn't get out of there fast enough. Pimps think that hoes like that shit, but believe it or not, most of us don't. All that slick talking, rhyming and speaking fast shit is garbage. That shit never made me wanna choose up or leave my folks. I have to admit though, it worked on some hoes, obviously. But I don't know how because to me it just sounded like a bunch of gibberish, and I know a lot of other hoes that feel the same way.

Still being, I respected the rules of the game. One thing about the game is you're gonna go through a lot of ups and downs like a roller coaster. For the past few years we were up. Today was the day our fabulous roller coaster of a life would descend and take a turn for the worst and bring us down. I came home to our three bedroom home in Mission Valley to find the door kicked in and busted off the hinges.

"Hello…Daddy…Are you here?" **Click Clack!** I heard the sound of the gun cocking behind me.

"Bitch, don't make a move or a sound, or I'm a blow your fucking head off!" I felt the nozzle of a gun barrel on the back of my head.

"Blood, a bitch just walked in. Bring me the duct tape," the voice behind me said as another guy with a ski mask on entered the room from the back holding a gun as well. He pulled a roll of duct tape out of his black hoodie and placed it on the coffee table to the side of me.

"Hold up, blood. Let's take the bitch to the back with her bitch ass nigga first, just incase someone else comes in she won't be the first thing they see." The voice behind me said. I was now shaking like a nigga in a crap game full of thugs getting caught with loaded dice.

"Please don't hurt me!"

"Shut up bitch," the deep dark voice with no compassion said behind me as he pushed my head forward with his gun signaling me towards the back bedroom where my folks was lying. Tied up, blind folded and duct taped.

"Blood, duct tape her up so we can finish robbing the house and get the fuck outta here Ru," the nigga behind me said, talking to his homie in a manner that signified they were Piru's. The one in front did as he was told and pulled a strip of duct tape off the roll and placed it over my mouth just as I was saying,

"Please don't hurt m…" That was all I got out as I was silenced by the sticky tape. He then spun me around by my shoulder, forced my arms around my back, and taped my hands so they couldn't move. I saw my folks on the floor squirming side to side, hog tied on the floor looking helpless. The masked gunmen then pushed me on the floor next to my folks and tied up my feet as well. I couldn't move even if I wanted to.

"Blood, where she say the safe was?"

"In the bedroom," I heard one say to the other then answer.

"Alright, you watch these two and I'm a check the room," the one that appeared to be the leader said and left to check for the safe.

Did I hear correct? I know he didn't just say where "she" say the safe was? Apparently this was a set up and the only person that could have set us up was me or one of my wife-n-laws, because we were the only "she's" that knew about the safe. My mind raced as to who could be the rat. My Daddy had four other hoes besides me, but only one had been acting up lately…Lisa!

Lisa was a white girl from Ohio that had went to the pen for drug trafficking, did three years, got released, then got turned out by a pimp she met at the bus station on her way home from the Pen. Rumor had it that she turned on her ex-folks and sent him to prison. It was never proven due to the fact that the pimp took a plea deal which meant she didn't have to go to trial to testify. Thus meaning, there was no paperwork in public record stating she snitched.

I never trusted her from the first time she stepped foot in our family. It was something in her eyes that I couldn't quite put my finger on, but it screamed scandalous. She hadn't even been in our family long before Daddy eventually picked up on her bullshit, too. She was apart of our family for about three months before Daddy fired her and let her go. That was mistake number one. Mistake number two was letting her know where he kept his money. I always felt like Lisa was the vindictive type and now I'm willing to bet my left tit I was right.

"Blood, I found the safe, but I'm a need help getting it open!"

"Nah Ru, this nigga right here is gonna open it for us," the gunman said, pointing his pistol at my Daddy as he talked. The other gunman walked back in the room and ripped the duct tape off my folks mouth.

"Ahhhh!"

"Shut up nigga! What's the combination to the safe?"

"If I tell you, you'll kill me."

"Blood, if you don't tell me, I'm a torture you, then I'm a kill you. You know what it feel like ta have your nuts squeezed with a pair of pliers until they bust? Keep fucking wit me and you're gonna find out!"

"Alright, alright! I'll tell you. Just please don't kill me afterwards."

"I'll think about it nigga. Now about that number?"

"32…16…28…"

"Good boy," he said, slightly smacking him on the face.

"Now, was that so hard?" He left the room and went to open the safe.

"Got it blood!" There was over $100,000 in the safe as well as $50,000 worth of custom jewelry. The gunmen came back in the room and said, "We got it, Ru. Smoke them mutha fuckas and let's get out of here."

The other nigga walked up, stood over us and said, "Lisa sends her regards." **Boc! Boc! Boc!…Boc!**

He put three rounds into Daddy's head and one into my back. I played dead and stood still. The heat of the moment mixed with fear and adrenalin had me overlooking and withstanding the pain.

"Let's get out of here, Ru." The nigga that fired the shots said as they ran out the house with a duffle bag full of loot. I played dead a little longer just incase they weren't done or came back. Daddy was completely motionless and silent. The bullets had killed him on impact. I was luckier. The bullet went straight through my back and out my front, just missing all my vital organs. Still being, if I didn't hurry up and find a way to free myself from the duct tape, I was gonna bleed to death. I fought, squirmed and struggled to get out of the duct tape, but couldn't. Now that my adrenalin was wearing down, I could feel the burning sensation of the gunpowder on my flesh. The pain was beginning to be unbearable. I began to feel weak. 30 seconds later, I passed out.

I awoke in a hospital bed with all kinds of tubes running in and out my body. *How did I get here?* I thought to myself. A nurse walked in with a clipboard to check my vitals and realized I was awoke.

"Hello and nice of you to join us," she said. "You're a very lucky lady."

"How…did…I get here?"

"Sshh! Try not to talk. You're still very weak. Apparently a neighbor of some sort heard gunshots from your house and saw two masked men run out the place, then called the Police. That phone call saved your life because if the Police and the Paramedics hadn't arrived when they did, you would have bled to death."

"How…how's…my husband?" She gave me a look of compassion and said,

"I'm sorry dear, but he didn't make it." A surge went through my body like a jolt of electricity through an extension cord. A lump formed in my throat and a cold feeling in my chest. Tears filled my eyes then ran down my face like water in the shower. I couldn't stop crying. I got so excited that my body began to go into shock. My heart monitor was off the charts.

"Mrs. you must calm down." The nurse got a syringe and stuck it into a bottle of clear fluid, drew 4 cc's and inserted it into one of the tubes that was connected to the IV that was stuck in my hand. I was instantly sedated and fell into a coma like sleep. When I awoke, two detective officers were by my bedside. They came to question me about the burglary and what took place at the house. I gave them my statement and told them everything I remembered, which wasn't very much good considering both men had on ski masks and I couldn't see their faces. The only clue that the Police had to go on was that both men were Bloods, possibly from Skyline or Little Africa Piru. Seeing how those were the only two Piru sets in Daygo, and both men said Piru often throughout the robbery. That and the fact that Lisa might have had something to do with setting it up, but that would be hard to prove without the would be gunmen to substantiate that.

All I could think about and remember was those last words before the nigga fired that pistol. **"Lisa sends her regards."** Those words would play over and over in the back of my mind like a broken record for days to come. I spent three weeks in the hospital then was released. The only thing on my mind when I came home was avenging Daddy's death. I was a down ass bitch to the end and had every intention on seeing this through. Lisa had to pay. If I ever found or saw the bitch again, she would surely die!

CHAPTER 11 THE CHRONICLES OF THE GAME

It been two years since my folks been back in the game and everything was going great. He was back on top and back to his usual pimping self. Jackpot was now four deep and all of us were down and dedicated. He chose his hoes wisely this time. I was with him for thirteen months before he brought my first wife-n-law home.

The same day he was discharged from parole for good behavior. He said he would die before going back to prison and had no intentions on dying anytime soon. So basically, both was out of the question. He had to stay ten toes down but ten steps ahead of the bullshit that came with the game. Somethings were unavoidable like potholes and broken concrete after an earthquake. And other things weren't. You just had to pick and choose and play your cards close to your chest while trying to make as minimal mistakes as possible, cause Jackpot already learned the hard way once, that mistakes can cost you dearly in this game. So this time around, he made sure that he had four equal hoes with the same common goals and no larceny in their hearts.

"Alright hoes, check this out. We bout ta bring in this summer in a real way," Daddy spoke to me and my wife-n-laws in the living room of our La Jolla eight bedroom house.

"Next week is the First Annual Players Picnic in Daygo, thrown by Pimpsy and Famous Players everywhere. It's gonna be a Pimp and Hoe star studded event and I'm sure I don't have to tell you, we will be in attendance."

We all smiled and got happy. It'd been awhile since we went to a Players Ball or Pimp and Hoe event. Actually, I haven't been to once since I been with JP. He always said it wasn't time ta show up and show out. He was more focused on stacking chips and building his empire. He said he would never make the same mistake twice and he only slipped once. So early on, he invested his money in a legal business to fall back on just incase he ever took a loss or fall.

He had a three year plan after which he was gonna retire, go legit and live the good life, without looking over his shoulder or hoping a bitch stayed down and didn't run off. He said whichever bitches was still in the picture when he was ready to call it quits, he would let choose if they wanted to retire as well and still be with him, helping run his business or businesses. If not, then they were free to leave and live their lives how they saw fit. Of course I was in it for the long haul.

Daddy's first investment was buying into his long time good friend Trust's One Stop Auto, Audio and Tint Shop. He bought 40% of the company so now he was part owner. His second investment was yet ta come. He planned to open a night club that catered to pimps and hoes. Of course anyone was allowed, but the theme and ambience would be game related. His last investment he wasn't sure of, but he said it had to be big.

The one that put him over the top. The one that made him a multi-millionaire.

$$$$$

It had been awhile since I been in Daygo. Ever since I snitched on Jackpot and had Macknificent set up. I didn't know they were gonna kill him though, but oh well. I couldn't cry over spilt milk. The deed and damage was done, so all I could do was take my cut of the money, leave Daygo and go into hiding. Now that the heat had cooled down, I was back to attend the Player's Picnic next week with my new folks Diamond, who I chose up with in Arizona while I was in hiding. He knows nothing of my past other than I was a hoe before he met me, and I was born and raised in Ohio. I felt like he was on a need ta know basis and he didn't need to know shit about my past. Period!

$$$$$

It's been six or seven months since the last time I spoken to Lez. I've been adjusting to prison life as best I could under the circumstances. One thing I knew for certain, Sweets wasn't gonna bow down to no bitch in here. When I first arrived, a big ass ugly bull dyke was in here punkin bitches and forcing them to sleep with her. Word on the yard was she had her sights on me. At first we were on different yards so it made it difficult for her to get close to me.

The only time we saw each other was when I had to go to R&R to pick up a package or special purchase, and that wasn't often. The only reason why she saw me then was because she worked in R&R. I wasn't stuntin da bitch either way because I was ready for wut ever. If the bitch thought she was gonna punk me, the hoe had me fucked up. It took six months for her to get transferred to my yard and that day was today. The word on the yard was that the bitch was coming to see me after late count. Yeah, okay. No problem bitch. You'll find out tonight that ain't shit sweet about me but my name.

$$$$$

It been two years since I chose Ka$hanova and got turned out to the game. I was now a vet at hoe'n. I jumped in the game full fledged and never looked back. I took to hoc'n like a fish to water to say the least. Now all throughout Daygo, Bambi was a household name. Daddy was now six deep, but only kept two of us in Daygo. We had our own pad and got ta spend time with Daddy every other day, unless he was outta town taking care of business or seeing one of his other hoes. I had wife-n-laws in Vegas, Texas, Atlanta, New York and Chicago, all of the major cities. Daddy was doing it big. He was the first pimp to buy a Rolls Royce Phantom and Bentley Coupe.

"Bambi."

"Yes Daddy?"

"I'm about to send for your wife-n-laws ta come down for the Player's Picnic next week. I want you to get on the phone and book a suite at the Marriott Downtown. Get the best room they have. Actually, make it two so I can have a back up room incase I knock some new work or wanna socialize with some of my pimp patna's after the picnic."

"Okay, Daddy." I got up out my bed and grabbed the phone off the side of the dresser as Daddy walked back out my room and closed the door behind him.

"Hello. Marriott. May I help you?"

"Yes, I would like to make a reservation."

$$$$$!

I'd just came back from San Fernando Valley shooting a porn flick for Vivid, and to film some new material to upload to my personal website. I got paid $1,500 a scene and $1,000 for anal. I was in three scenes and did anal twice so I made a total of $6,500. Not bad for a day's work. Plus, I filmed a shit load of material for my website, which I can stream and sell to tricks per download.

I arrived at my two bedroom country style apartment in Poway and noticed my folks, Get'It Escalade in the driveway. I got instantly excited and happy to see my folks. I didn't expect him to be here when I got home. He had his own house in Carlsbad and only came by mines on occasion. Most of the time I went over to "his" house when he wanted to see me. I placed my key in the lock, turned it to the right and opened the door. Daddy was sitting on my living room sofa smoking a blunt and watching football.

"Hey Daddy!"

"Hey Jennifer. How'd your trip go?" He said as he took another pull of the purple hazed filled blunt and blew out little smoke rings in the air.

"Good. I made $6,500." Dat's wuss up. Good job." I walked over, sat down next to him, kissed him on the cheek and gave him his money. "So, what brings you over to my house Daddy?"

"Juss chillin. Thought I'd be here when you came home ta greet my bitch."

"Ahh how sweet, but you ain't foolin me. You know like I know you came ta greet this money." We both laughed.

"Alright bitch you got me." He passed me the blunt and counted the money I gave him. I took a hit and said, "What, you don't trust me?"

"No offense Baby Girl, but…No!" I playfully pushed him on the shoulder and sucked my teeth.

"Nothing personal bitch. It's just business. Juusst business," he said sarcastically, dragging out the words as he folded up the $6,500 in a knot and put the money in his pocket.

"Damn Bitch! Puff! Puff! Pass! What you tryna do, take it all to the face?" I laughed as the chronic smoke filled my lungs and made me choke.

"Here Daddy." I passed him back the blunt.

"Oh yeah," *Puff! Puff! Puff!* "This weekend is the First Annual Player's Picnic and it's being held out here in Daygo," he said in between puffs of the blunt and smoke being blown out his mouth as he talked.

"Really?"

"Yea dat! So you already know we gotta go and represent."

"I know that's right."

"Yeah, it should be a moment to remember."

$$$$$

Since the shooting and death of my folks, Macknificent, I been renegading and respecting his honor by not choosing up with anybody else. It's been two years and I still yet to have run into Lisa. Word was she was hiding out in Arizona somewhere and had chosen up with a new pimp. She was spotted by another hoe named Tricksy on the track on Van Buren.

I took a couple of trips out there within the past couple of weeks hoping I'd run into her, but was to no avail. My mind and heart was set on making her pay and the price was death. An eye for an eye, and a tooth for a tooth. I recently purchased a Deuce Five just for the occasion when it went down. What goes around comes back around and karma's a bitch. So I know it's only a matter of time before I catch her slippin.

$$$$$

I knew the whole get down of what was finna take place because the prison grapevine moved swifter than a 747 Jet, with twin engine boosters running on rocket fuel. I went back to my cell early and got prepared. First, I got two cans of tuna out my locker and placed them in a sock. Then I put that sock in another sock and knotted it at the end so the cans were secure and couldn't move. I then poured Baby Oil and water all over the floor in front of my door. Now the trap was set. I grabbed a scrunchie off the top of my locker, took a look in the mirror and put my hair in a ponytail and bun, incase the bitch got ahold of it during the fight.

I was now ready for whatever. After nine o'clock count, it was going down. 9:15 the C.O walked, flashed her flashlight and counted the inmates as usual. After which I heard the cells pop open. Weekends were late night, which meant we were able to come out our cells and stay up till midnight, playing cards, writing letters or watching TV.

I stayed in my cell and waited for the six foot one, two hundred and fifty pound ambush. Like clockwork, she arrived right on time like I knew she would. Grinning a wicked smile like a rapist about to pounce on her prey and let loose. I picked up the sock with the cans and concealed it behind my back. Bertha walked into my cell, fist clenched, jaws tight, ready for battle. Little did she know she was finna lose the war. Two steps into my cell she slipped and busted her ass as her feet met with baby oil and water, causing her ta slip and slide all over the place. That's when I went in for the kill.

"Bitch, you want some of this?" **POW!** I swung the cans in a sock and came down with them on her head. **BOP! BOP! BOP!** I was swinging that shit like a pair of nun-chucks.

"Ahhh!"

"Don't start screaming now, bitch!" **WAP!** The sock met with the side of her head and face as blood splattered from the gash it caused and painted the cell. She was helpless, but I refused to stop. I had to teach the bitch a lesson and make an example out of her. I grabbed the sock with two hands and swung it with all my might towards her face, as the cans met with her mouth and knocked out five of her teeth. She was fighting for cover, but there was nowhere to cover to. I busted her in the face with the cans again and shut her left eye socket. By now she was in the corner balled up like a coward begging for me to stop. All the commotion that was coming from my cell must have alerted the guards because the alarm went off, signaling everyone to get down and stop moving.

Four C.O.'s came into my cell spraying pepper spray and swinging billy clubs to stop the fight and get me off of her. The pepper spray had my eyes burning and temporarily blinded. I dropped the sock and got down on the ground. The C.O.'s cuffed us up and took us to the hole. When Bertha got up and walked out, she looked like the elephant man or Rocky Dennis. The other female inmates was shocked when we walked out the cell and saw Bertha all fucked up like she just got jumped by the entire San Diego Chargers football squad, and me unscathed without so much as even a scratch on me. That got me my respect. From then on, I was the new H.B.I.C, Head Bitch In Charge.

I got charged with assault with a deadly weapon for the tunas in the sock. I didn't give a fuck though. What could they do to me? Gimme more time? I had life. Fuck them and their time. I wasn't taking shit from nobody, especially no bitches. I let it be known that if anyone else wanted it, they could get it too. Nobody took the challenge because it was obvious I was with the activity and wasn't afraid ta give a bitch the business. In here, it's about respect and respect is what I got.

$$$$$

"Welcome to the First Annual 2007 Player's Picnic. I'm your host, Pimpsy. Not the rapper, but the ice cold capper. I'd like ta thank all you macknificent pimps and fine hoes for coming out today to have a good time and represent this movement we call Pimpin-n-Ho'n, which we all know is the best thang going. So sit mack, relax and enjoy yourself players. Oh yeah, and bitches, hot wieners on the grill. And we all know, yawl know what to do wit those."

Everybody broke out in laughter as Pimpsy put the mic back in the mic stand and got off the stage. DJ Redlite was on the cuts. Redlite was a local DJ out of San Diego. This was the first event where pimps and hoes dressed down but still dressed up. Meaning, gone was the three piece suits, ties and long dresses. Today we showed up in short sets, flip flops, tank tops and sneakers. But even still, everything was name brand. Like take me and my folks for instance. We showed up in matching custom Burberry summer wear from head ta toe.

Get'It was looking so good hoes was trying their damnedest to stay in pocket and not look at my folks. I smiled when I caught a bitch sneaking and peeking and semi reckless eye balling from afar. When I say he was dressed from head ta toe, that's exactly what he was. From the sun visor to the sneakers. I had on a Burberry short set and sandals to match. Daddy went over to where all the Pimps was conjugating and said wuss up to some of his pimp patna's. I went to where the hoes was at. The grill.

"Hey Jennifer," a hoe named Tina that was cooking hotdogs said to me as I was approaching the grill.

"Hey girl. How you been?" I gave her a hug.

"Gettin money."

"I know that's right." I gave her a high five then said wuss up to some of the other hoes I knew and recognized.

"Hey Patty. Hey Latrice. Damn girl, you looking good in that skirt. Wuss up Amy?" Yeah everybody who was anybody in the game was out in full force, from the top pimps, to the baddest hoes. And I was one of them.

$$$$$

"Girl, ain't that that bitch Jennifer, your ex-folks Get'It bottom bitch?" I said to one of my wife-n-laws as we sat at a picnic table off to the side, enjoying the picnic and observing the scene.

"Yeah Bambi, that's her. I hear she be getting her money too. When I was wit Get'It, he was paid, stacking chips and making moves. I was cool with her too. The only thing I didn't like, and problem I had was, that he started paying more attention to her than me. I didn't feel equal no more. The shit got one sided and I wasn't gonna stick around and put up with that, especially when I was in the picture first."

"Yeah, I feel you girl. I wouldn't either."

"See, that's one of the biggest mistakes pimps make. Showing more favoritism to one hoe over the other. Acting like that bitch got a golden pussy or something. As long as we both got a mouth and pussy, she can't do nothing that I can't do. Even if the bitch look better, it ain't in the beauty but in the duty. As long as both bitches is producing and getting money, then they both should be treated equal. That was Get'It's flaw. He let his true feelings and lust dictate his pimping, and in a hoe's eyes, that's a game no, no. It's pimping suicide.

"If you noticed, that's why he ain't had another hoe since, because ain't no bitch finna stick around and deal with that shit."

"I hear ya. You know a lot of these cats ain't nothing but tricks in a pimps body."

"I know that's right."

"They talk all that pimp shit in front of their boys then get home and can't stay out the pussy."

"Girl, who you telling? A lot of these pimps is freakier than some of my tricks. Don't even get me started on some of the shit I done, heard and witnessed."

"Shit, I can imagine." Daddy walked over to where we were sitting and said, "Bambi, go to the car and bring me my weed out the glove box." He handed me the keys then sat down next to Wifey.

"Okay, Daddy. Be right back." I got up and walked towards the parking lot where Daddy's 2007 Platinum Range Rover was. As I walked to the parking lot, I passed by the extra long custom bbq grill where a lot of the hoes were at. I smiled and waved as I walked by. The ones that knew me smiled and waved back and the others just looked at me like I was crazy. Oh well, that's how females are, catty. Whether hoes or squares, that part of a female will never change. *Bitch probably just want something that I got and she don't. Hoe don't hate me cause you ain't me. Ain't my fault God made you that way.* I laughed to myself as I continued walking to the car to get my Daddy's weed.

$$$$$

"Girl, I hate that bitch! Look at her thinking she all that. That hoe wasn't shit before she got wit Ka$hanova."

"Tina, why you hating girl? You just don't like her because you feel like she took your spot after Ka$h fired you."

"No, I didn't get fired. I left. Get it right, Jennifer."

"Okay, whatever. Then, you 'left' after he said, get the fuck outta here and don't come back!"

"Girl, fuck you!" She said, and playfully pushed me on the shoulder.

"No, don't fuck me. Fuck them tricks. You're just mad because you know it's true." We both laughed.

"I ain't tripping off that nigga. I'm happy with the folks I have now."

"Em hmm, let you tell it."!

$$$$$

"Bambi," I called out as me and my folks Jackpot, pulled up in the parking lot to park with my wife-n-laws in tow, bringing up the rear.

"Hey Mya." She grabbed something out of her folks double R and closed the door.

"I'll holla at you in a minute, girl." I knew she wouldn't come up to the car and talk to me while my folks was in the car for obvious reasons.

"Okay." He parked his 745i and got out, brushed off his Louie short set, put on his matching glasses, and signaled for my wife-n-laws who was driving his 600 Benz to park right next to us. I got out the car next, walked over to Bambi and gave her a hug.

"How you been?" I said as we unlocked our embrace.

"Good, I just got back in town not too long ago from Hawaii. Girrrl, them Asian men be flying into town just to turn tricks. I made ten racks in a week like it was nothing. And on the blade out there, everything starts at $100. You can't get nothing for less than that."

"Girl, you know I know. My folks keep me movin and groovin. I been to Hawaii six times and every time I went, I made ten racks or better. Yeah, I love it out there. So, you're looking good. I see the game's been treating you well."

"Yeah a bitch can't complain. You're looking cute your damn self with all that Louie shit on tryna match your folks." We both giggled.

"I know that's right!"

"Bambi! Bitch hurry up with my shit," my folks yelled from across the park.

"Girl, let me go before my folks bust a nutty."

"Okay, I'll catch up wit you." Bambi high stepped it across the grass where her folks and wife-n-laws were, as we made our way to the picnic.

$$$$$

"Alright everybody, we got a special guest in the place," DJ Redlite said over the mic with music playing in the background.

"Everybody put your hands together for Suga Free the Pimp!"

We all started clapping as Suga Free took to the stage and grabbed the mic. 'Let Me Pimp or Let Me Die' blared through the speakers as Suga Free started rapping.

"Steppin in the place like whaaat! Jump on the stage and grab the mic like what!/ Nigga hair flying, all these hoes dying. Nigga I don't give a fuck cause Free ain't trying./Nigga, I ain't no trick. Fuck that bitch, nigga, all I want her to do is go make my chips/From El Cajon ta Hope Street in Pamona./A nigga got the prostitutes standing on the corner."

The crowd went nuts, especially when he said the part about El Cajon Blvd. Daddy rolled a blunt for me and my wife-n-laws and one for himself from the sack I brought him back from his glove box.

"Here you go Bambi. Yawl smoke that."

"Thank you Daddy." I lit the blunt and took a hit of the purp. Puffed it two times and passed it along to my wife-n-laws. We were smiling and groovin, enjoying the sounds of Suga Free, when I noticed an unfamiliar face across the way entering the picnic.

$$$$$

So this was the first event I attended in a long time. Actually, it was the first one since all that drama with Jackpot. I wasn't tripping on anybody recognizing me because I was sure most didn't even know I was the one that put him away. I heard Yuki killed herself and Green Eyes was missing in action, so other than JP, those were the only ones that knew I snitched on him. And as for JP, I heard he had retired from the game and was working at a car audio place. A couple of years ago I drove by the shop to check for myself and saw him working on somebody's car. I didn't stop though, because I didn't want him to see me.

I couldn't believe he went from pimping to audio boy, working a square job like the common folk. That was the last time I saw him, so with that and the fact that I was with Diamond, a pimp/gang member, I felt fairly safe. The picnic was packed. When we arrived, it was in full swing. Suga Free was just finishing up one of his songs. Most of the attention was on the stage. As I got closer, my heart nearly sunk to my stomach.

$$$$$

"Oh hell no! I know that ain't Lisa," I heard my folks say as I stopped dancing and looked over in the direction he was looking. I saw a white girl with long blonde curly hair in shock looking like a deer caught in the headlights.

"Daddy, you alright?"

"Yeah, I'm cool Mya."

$$$$$

"Oh my God! Say it ain't so! That can't be JP." My heart was racing a mile a minute. I could see the pain and anger in his eyes.

"Wuss wrong with you bitch? Why you just standing there?" Diamond asked me, noticing my hesitation to move. He looked in my eyes and followed my gaze ta see JP staring back at me with a menacing look like he wanted to kill me.

$$$$$

"Yeah I knew that bitch would show up here. I just had a feeling," I said to myself, standing behind a tree a few feet away from the picnic where I'd been all day. I was surprised ta see my brother when he had arrived after all these years. It looked like he was doing real good. I just wanted to run up to 'em and hug him and tell him how much I missed him, but I couldn't afford missing out on the opportunity of catching Lisa slippin. I knew if she arrived and saw me before I saw her, she would surely leave quicker than a tree in fall. That was a chance I could not afford to take. Now here she was, not even fifty feet away from me. The day I'd been waiting for, for two years.

$$$$$

"Bitch got the nerve ta show her face around here after putting me in prison for three years, costing me everything I worked so hard for." I could see the anger in Daddy's eyes. The rage that was building up inside of him with every glance he took of Lisa was rising and about to erupt like a volcano.

"Mya, get your wife-n-laws and go to the car."

"Daddy…"

"Bitch, I said go to the car! Now do as I said. NOW!" I never saw Daddy this upset in my life. I moved quickly and did as he said. As I was walking away to get my wifey's, he was walking towards Lisa.

$$$$$

"Bitch, who's this nigga walking up and looking at you like that? He your ex-folks or something?"

"Yeah ta say the least." I was shaking in my shoes. I knew there was no way this was gonna end good.

"Say, say pimp. Wut it do?" My folks said as JP walked up on me. He acted like he didn't hear Diamond say a word. He didn't even acknowledge his presence. That pissed Diamond off.

"Wuss up nigga? You don't hear me talking to you? Wut you running up on my bitch like dat for?"

"Because your bitch is a rat," he said while looking me dead in my face. Eyes locked to mines, still not looking away or acknowledging Diamond once.

"Look here playboy. I don't know what kinda history yawl had before, but she's my bitch now and you can't be running up on her like that."

"Look here pimp, no disrespect, but this here's bigger than you."

"Wut the fuck you talking bout?"

$$$$$

Wuss going on? Why are the two of them arguing? It looks like it has something to do with Lisa. Well, whatever it is, I can't let that get in the way of what I have to do. I pulled out my Deuce-Five and cocked it back. **CLICK! CLACK!**

$$$$$

"Dis bitch a rat! That's what I'm talking bout and I'm the cat that's gonna break her back!"

"Nigga, you better back up off my bitch. I don't give a fuck what she did in the past, because as of now, I'm a part of her present."

"Nigga, this faggot ass bitch put pimping in prison for three years! That's the kinda hoe you want?"

"Nigga I don't give a fuck about all that." I hid behind my folks for security and comfort. It felt good knowing he had my back. I felt a little safer now knowing that he wasn't gonna allow JP to do anything to me.

"Nigga, then yawl deserve each other. As well as the same fate. Rats run in packs!" JP took off on Diamond with a strong right. Diamond fell to the ground, but quickly regrouped, got up and regained his composure.

"Alright nigga, it's on now," Diamond said as he got his guard up, faked right, then hit JP with a hard left to his ribs.

$$$$$

Look at that bitch sitting there thinking shit's sweet. Everything was moving fast, but at the same time in slow motion like the Matrix. Lisa had her back to me, slipping, watching the fight. I crept from behind the tree, gun drawn, ready to make my move. "Oh my God! She got a gun!" Came from the crowd. It was now or never.

I turned around and for the second time today, my heart was in my stomach. *I thought she was dead,* I said to myself as I watched the crazed and upset looking Keita sprint towards me gun drawn, about to fire any second. My mind said run but my feet stayed put. I was frozen with fear.

$$$$$

"Nakeita!" I heard the voice of my brother call me as he saw me approaching and realized who I was.

"Oh my God, that can't be you!." I could see the excitement and happiness mixed with confusion in his face of seeing me again after all these years, but realizing what I was about to do once he noticed I had a gun drawn aiming at Lisa.

"Noooo!" was all he could get out before I let loose like a gang member in a shoot out. **POP! POP! POP!** The first two shots missed. The third hit Lisa in the shoulder.

"Ahhh!" She yelled out in pain as I took aim and fired again, hitting her in the stomach. **POP!**

"No Keita. Don't do this. She ain't worth it," I heard my brother say as he ran over towards me to try and disarm me and possibly stop me from ruining the rest of my life. Sirens were heard in the background as Lisa held her stomach crying and fell to her knees.

"Don't cry now, bitch! You wasn't crying when you had me and my folks set up. Me, shot and him killed!"

"I'm sorry. I'm sorry. I didn't know they were gonna kil…" was the last thing she got out. **POP! POP! POP! POP!** I emptied the clip in her worthless body and watched her pop lock it like a B Boy on 'So You Think You Can Dance.' Her lifeless body hit the ground, eyes still opened. JP ran over and hugged me to stop, by pinning my arms to my waist, but it was too late. The damage was done and the bitch was dead. JP took the gun out of my hand and said,

"Sis, what did you do?"

"FREEZE! Drop the weapon, put your hands up, and get on the ground." JP looked into my eyes, paying the cops that had just arrived behind me no mind and said,

"I can't let you go down for this. I can't let you go where I've been. You deserve better." The cops said, "Put down your weapon and get on the ground now!" I was speechless, and before I could get a word out, my brother said,

"I love you, sis," right before…"okay, yawl got me" and dropped the gun, fell on the ground, and took the charge. Tears ran down my face as I watched the Police cuff up my brother.

"I love you, too." It wasn't until that moment that I noticed the full extent of my actions. One of the bullets that I fired and missed had actually hit Diamond in the head, which killed him instantly on contact. Since my brother stepped up and said he did the shooting and was the one with the gun in his hand when the police arrived, they treated it like an open and shut case. Nobody snitched or said nothing out of respect for JP. He instantly put the word out that under no circumstances do anyone say or tell what really happened. His hoes was rightfully upset, but there was nothing they could do. The decision was made.

One never knows the cards that life a deal a person, or the path that a guide you to salvation. The ups and downs, twists and turns one must go through and face in life. The good die young and seem to never get a break, while the wicked ones prosper. No one ever said life was fair, a fact that proved itself everyday. The game is no different from everyday life. The strong will survive and the weak will perish. Contrary to belief, you don't always get back what you put in. Life is hard and the game is harder.

In the end, you gotta ask yourself...Was it all worth it?

-GAME OVER-

ABOUT THE AUTHOR

Caujuan Akim Mayo, also known on the streets as $ki.Bo and Ka$hanova, grew up hustling at a young age to make ends meet and help his single mother take care of his sister and 5 brothers. Early on, he had a way with words and women and found himself engulfed within, the Pimp and Hoe lifestyle and subculture. The same game that brought him up, eventually took him down and sent him to prison.

There, is where he found a knack and love for writing and penned his first novel, "Let Me Pimp Or Let Me Die." Upon his release from prison.

Caujuan changed his life around, formed Uprock Publications and released his novel, "Let Me Pimp Or Let Me Die." The book was an instant success and favorite amongst readers causing Caujuan to pen part 2. With 3 books under his belt to date, Caujuan is becoming an author to be reckoned with. Caujuan is currently working on his 4th novel. A fiction story loosely based on his life.

ALSO AVAILABLE

"Freeze mother fucker!" a cop spat, but the Skyline hardhead wasn't trying to hear it. He blindly reached on the floor for his gun as he slowly regained his eyesight. Jail wasn't an option for the young rida. He knew he had done too much to turn back. Fuck it, he was gonna hold court in the streets. As he placed his hand on the gun that laid dormant on the floor, that would be as close as he got to picking it up and letting off a shot…

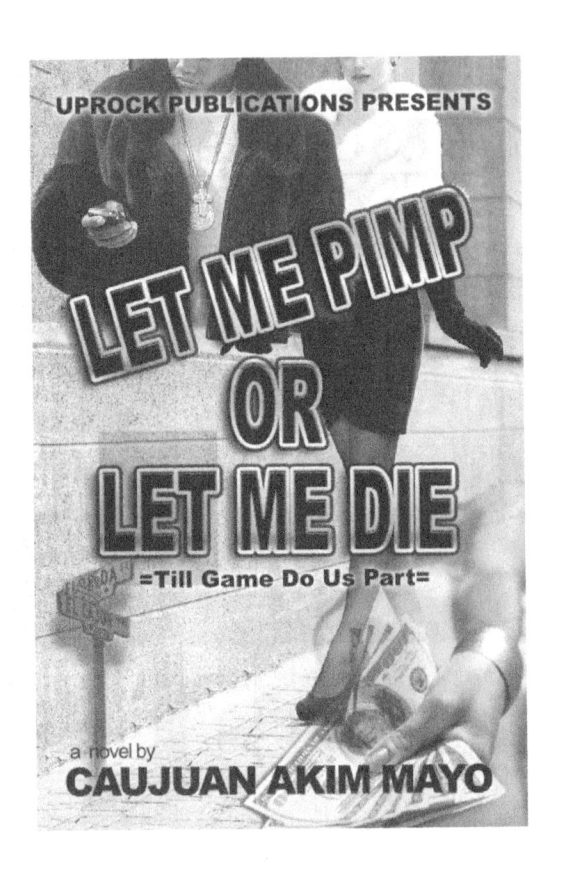

As JP was hanging up the phone Yuki was walking down the track towards him. *Perfect timing*, JP thought to himself. He called Yuki over and introduced her to her new wife-in-law. "Yuki, this is your new wifey Kathy, also known as Green Eyes. Green Eyes, this is Yuki. Welcome to the family." The girls smiled and got acquainted. "How much you got on you?" JP asked Yuki.

"I made $400 more daddy."

"Alright good job, excellent work. That brings your total to $2,000. Since the nights been so good to us all, we're gonna take it in early and get to know each other better." JP had the best night of his life. Between the 2 hoes he took in $3,150, bumped a new hoe, and was now 2 deep with no sleep. Life was good, and it was only gonna get better.

UPROCK PUBLICATIONS PRESENTS

FAMILY HONOR
The Seed
Timmy O'Neil Charity

"That's enough!" Silence filled the room, as two muscle bound gorillas moved away from the two men hanging by their shackled wrists. Both men wore handcuffs, as a steel chain was looped over the beam in the ceiling. They were stripped to the wrist, exposing their battered and bruised torsos, which matched their equally distorted faces.

The men were best friends. Having grown up together in the reform schools of Virginia, they solidified their brotherhood as they furthered their education on the mean, brutal streets of Richmond, aka Richtown. Neither man was afraid to die, because they knew they had fucked up. But the man carrying out their punishment, had did more than wreck havoc on their bodies. They had committed treason. And that caused him to lose their trust in them. "This is how you treat friends?"

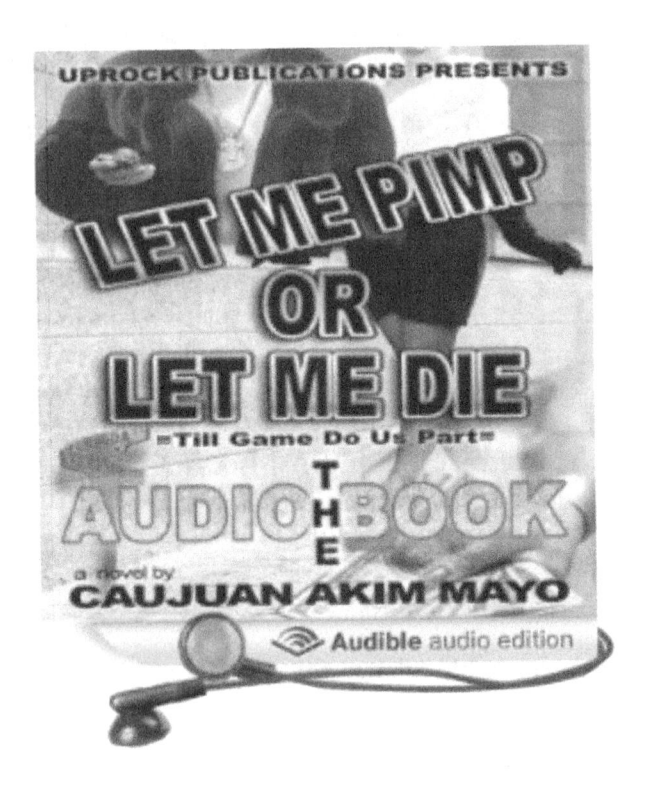

Don't have the time to read? Well, we have the solution. Pick up your audio version of "Let Me Pimp Or Let Me Die." The book by Caujuan Akim Mayo that started it all. Listen to this action pack audio book, loaded with special sound effects and cinematic music for dramatic effect, like no other audio book you've ever heard before. This is the audio book, that changed the game and set the bar.

AUTHOR CAUJUAN AKIM MAYO

- Website: www.uprockpublications.com
- Emails: caujuan@gmail.com
- Facebook: caujuan
- Facebook: uprockpublications
- Twitter: caujuan
- Twitter: uprockpub
- Contact: (619) 259-0298

Made in the USA
Las Vegas, NV
20 September 2023